Crestor

W9-BQT-656

I Ain't Perfect

11/13/07

I Ain't Perfect

Rená A. Finney

URBAN BOOKS

http://www.urbanbooks.net

This is a work of fiction. Any references or similarities to actual events, real people, living or dead, or to real locales are intended to give the novel a sense of reality. Any similarity in other names, characters, places, and incidents is entirely coincidental.

URBAN SOUL is published by

Urban Soul
10 Brennan Place
Deer Park, NY 11729

ISBN-13: 978-1-59983-021-6
ISBN-10: 1-59983-021-3

First Printing: October 2007

10 9 8 7 6 5 4 3 2 1

Printed in the United States of America

Prologue

I'd won. This exhilarating feeling was not the kind that comes from winning the Powerball lottery or calling Zoom 99 and being told that you're lucky caller number seven. No, it was a little more than that. This prize, the prize I was about to claim, would yield an even greater reward. A reward that would last a lifetime. In one hour, thirty minutes, and six seconds, I was going to become Mrs. Xavier Winston Phillips. In fact, I was about to become the wife of Rev. Xavier Winston Phillips.

Nervously, I touched the scalloped edge of the white chiffon veil, which was accentuated with pearls and attached to a tiara, complete with freshwater pearls and Swarovski crystals, made exclusively for yours truly, and realized that this was it. I was about to become a preacher's wife. This wasn't exactly what I had planned when I started dating Xavier in college five years ago. He was a far cry from being anybody's preacher. But even then he'd desired to be a chip off the old biological block, so I guess, it was just a matter of time.

At least I experienced his wild side before he fully converted and dedicated himself to the Lord for real.

Heck, he hadn't touched me in two years. Nothing more than a brush of his moist lips against my cheek or, if I was lucky, a hug. Not the kind of hug that two people in love exchange, but a holy hug, with his arms the only physical part of his body touching me. This display was always followed by an immediate departure on his part, the roaring engine and exhaust fumes of his car marking the conclusion of our evening. But as hard as the two-year adjustment was on me, it was no real concern since I had my share of excitement elsewhere.

What did he think would happen when he decided not to sleep in my bed until we exchanged vows? It only drove me to do what I had to do and get what I needed to get. Life is, sure enough, like a box of chocolates, and with each adventure, I never knew what I was going to get. Overall, though, I don't think I fared too bad. I had more than a few pinch hitters who provided sexual maintenance when my body craved a release. One poor guy swore he was in love with me and started coming around as regular as the mailman. It took me more than a hot minute to put an end to that madness. I even made regular visits with my sorority sisters to watch male exotic dancers. I figured if I wasn't getting any, I could at least enjoy some eye candy. The bottom line then was not to let anything interfere with what I shared with Xavier. And nothing did.

But I had needs that he just wasn't trying to understand. He had forgotten that it was his wild butt that turned me on. I knew next to nothing about the opposite sex, and I definitely didn't plan on giving up my virginity to anyone, until I met Xavier.

I can still recall the first time I saw him, at a Kappa fall fling. You would think he was the spokesperson for the fraternity the way he strutted around and grinned up in every girl's face. As much as I would have liked to deny it, I was as flattered as any other female in the room when he cornered me and swore he would be devastated if I didn't dance with him. After three straight dances, I was captivated by his good looks, easy smile, and quick sense of humor. His butterscotch complexion, piercing eyes, and dimpled chin didn't go unnoticed. Not to mention his six-foot-three-inch frame and sexy, thick body. All I wanted to do was grab hold of him and never let go.

That time, the beginning of us, seemed so long ago. And, after all this time, Xavier and I were still together and stronger than ever, despite his conversion and my secret indiscretions. It was all in the past, because today I would make a vow to love, honor, and, yes, even obey. I would put away my little black book for good.

Xavier was the love of my life, and I was going to be the first lady of New Horizons Ministries, in the beautiful city of brotherly love, Philadelphia. From this day forward, I would forever mentally erase my secrets and make our life together special.

I sat down in the ivory wingback chair and, smiling, watched my mother, godmother, and my best friend fret around me, making sure my elegant Vera Wang gown and all my accessories were in position, just waiting for me to step into them. The photographer had snapped so many photographs, my cheeks were already worn out, and this was just the beginning of the long-anticipated day, which I had dreamed of even as a small child playing dress up. I inhaled the sweet-smelling fragrance of orchids, Oriental lilies, and roses, and it awakened my sense of wedding bliss even more. I mentally tiptoed into my past and extracted the memory of the last time I'd cuddled against Xavier after passionately loving him beyond exhaustion. When the last spiritual love song serenaded us at the reception center, the limousine would whisk us away to the Presidential Suite of the Four Seasons Hotel, and I would dedicate myself to my new husband as if it were the first time all over again.

Trina, my best friend and hair stylist, directed me to change chairs so she could put the finishing touches on my hair. She stood over me, looking all glamorous herself, while she spinned me around from side-to-side and worked her magic. I glanced at my reflection in the nearby mirror and smiled. I actually liked the mirrored image of the person who looked back at me. The hairstyle Trina had whipped up for my big day was simple and yet elegant, with cascades of curls pulled on top of my head and a few curls spiraling down the nape of my neck.

"Monica, baby, you might want to start getting dressed," said my godmother, Zerenda, whom I had called Auntie Zee since I was old enough to talk. She stood next to the chair I'd been relaxing in since I'd begun the mental walk down my Xavier memory lane.

"Mom, are the boys here?" I asked. They had been teasing me for the past month, telling me that they were coming to the church late, and tipsy on top of that. They knew it wouldn't look right if the brothers of the bride showed up not only late, but smelling like they had just shared a forty before entering the church.

"Both Malcolm and Ted are with Xavier. Now go ahead and start getting ready," said Mom. She gave me a quick smile and waited to help Auntie Zee get me in my wedding attire.

Shirl Joyner was a strikingly beautiful lady. I never minded people telling me that I looked like her. In fact, I was flattered by it. She stood near my Auntie Zee in a mauve evening gown that made her look so elegant.

Mom had promised not to cry, but Trina and I had already caught her dabbing at the corner of her eyes at least twice.

"Okay, Auntie Zee. I guess I'm ready to put all this on and go marry my prince," I said as I shifted in the chair and stood up.

I tried to mentally still the butterflies that had suddenly begun fluttering around in my stomach. All eyes would be on me and Xavier. Some just wanted to witness the splendor that would be our wedding day, with little concern for our happily ever after, and a few sincere well-wishers actually believed that we loved each other enough to make our marriage work.

I just hope Xavier doesn't plan on me being the adoring and flawless first lady, I thought. *'Cause the truth of the matter is, I ain't perfect.*

Three years later

Chapter 1

New Horizons was packed to capacity. I glanced around leisurely and couldn't recall a time when the sanctuary had been overflowing with so many people. Since New Horizons was a "come one, come all" church, the pews included an array of races, which created a speckled congregation. The outreach ministry was one of the ministries that Xavier was so proud of. He was extremely proud of the fact that his congregation was multiethnic and grew with every service, embracing new members.

I wasn't surprised at the crowded pews or the conversation that flowed in the vestibule as the praise and worship team positioned itself to usher in the Holy Spirit. It was Easter Sunday, and since we'd opted to forgo the usual sunrise service, the regular, every Sunday parishioners, as well as their Easter weekend houseguests, were packed in the pews. The ushers were busying themselves with placing seats in the side aisles and along the back wall. The people who couldn't fit in the sanctuary were being directed to the education center to watch the service on the two 42-inch Toshiba plasma televisions positioned on the walls.

It seemed that everyone wanted to watch their babies and grandbabies recite their Easter pieces, which always ended up being jumbled together and incoherent, with the only recognizable words being "duck" and "egg." It didn't exactly tickle my fancy, but you would think that with the wide grins plastered on their faces, the kids were about to recite something straight from Shakespeare's *Hamlet*. But in line with my position at New Horizons, I, too, would smile and clap like it was amateur night at the Apollo. That was what everyone expected, and who was I to disappoint them? Especially since old Sadie Henson and nosey Hilda Timmons had had their eyes fixed on me from the moment I'd placed my feet, in Claudia Ciuti jeweled, satin sandals, in the sanctuary. You would have thought that they would have grown tired of watching my every move for the past three years and would have found someone else to eyeball, but they had become my personal overseers.

Walking in their direction on the way to my designated seat, I decided to pause and say good morning.

"Well, good morning, ladies. Don't you both look special." I could only say "special" because I had learned as a toddler never to lie. When I got older, I learned to tactfully stretch the truth and elude complete honesty. After all, my husband was a pastor, and I held the esteemed position of first lady.

Hilda Timmons spoke first. "Good morning, First Lady Phillips." Just the word "good" distorted her face, and she was having major problems allowing a smile to settle on her weathered, brownish tan lips. "You are looking your usual best. My, Pastor Phillips must have spent a lot of money on that suit."

I allowed myself to glance down at my attire. It was true that my husband spared no expense on my wardrobe, but what the bag of wind didn't know was that I was worth it and Xavier never complained. In fact, many of the outfits in my wardrobe had been picked out by him personally. He felt a first lady should always be appropriately dressed, and I had no problem agreeing with him.

I was especially fond of my new St. John suit, which was accented with pearls and beaded trim. The slim skirt, which hit slightly below my knee, was a perfect fit. I had chosen the clay-colored wonder of a suit because I refused to walk up the aisle in New Horizons wearing a jelly bean color and standing out like a bright, festive sign. I much preferred an understated, classy appearance that radiated my beauty, which had nothing to do with my wardrobe choice. I had conformed to the diva theory early on that clothes should not make the woman, but it should always be the other way around.

I have always been the type of person concerned about what people think of me. Despite their preconceived notions, I usually managed to overcome most of what they said and half of what they probably thought about Monica Joyner Phillips. But try as I might, I couldn't help wishing that they would take the time to get to know me. It was always someone with an assumption of who they thought I was, but everyone knows that assumptions can make . . . well, you know the saying.

Ever since I was a child, I'd been told that I was pretty. My daily trips to the mirror didn't confirm what everyone else said they saw. The only thing I noticed was a petite brown girl with a lopsided grin and dim eyes that looked sad most of the time. This was the exact opposite of all my girlfriends, who were high yellow, with perfect smiles and eyes that danced with a self-assured glee. They were what I thought I needed to be. I assumed that being blessed with a fairer complexion made you prettier, the envy of all the girls with darker complexions, and the desire of the cutest boys in school.

By the time I had been in high school a couple of years, I'd had a coming out of sorts. Not the typical Sweet Sixteen birthday celebration, marking a major milestone in a young girl's life, or a pumped-up, prim, and proper debutante ceremony, announcing a young woman's debut into society. It was an event for an audience of one, with a lighted mirror being the only item needed to complete the moment, reflecting the settled beauty that was me, an image that I had until then refused to believe.

At that precise instant, my self-esteem and confidence levels soared, and my ego overshadowed that of all the girls I hung out with and those that had already chosen not to like me. This, added with a little attention from the male species, acknowledging that what they saw, they liked, gave me the edge I needed to make my young adult life complete.

My skin was a radiant copper brown hue, and I had alluring facial features, from my arrow-shaped nose and my wide, exotic eyes to my petite lips. It all worked to my advantage. My hair wasn't the best grade, but I learned from my mother and later Trina, my best friend and one of the best hairstylists in Philly, how to maximize what I had. I never had to rely on the black girl's hair rescue kit, which included a goodie brush, pomade, black styling gel, and some yaka weave, available to match whatever your mommy and daddy gave you. No, that stuff just wasn't for me. I was especially fond of my shoulder-length hair, which was always well relaxed, well maintained, and sharp. So, I wasn't ever caught out there without my hair looking right—perish the thought.

I don't want to come off as conceited or stuck-up, but I was reared to be polished and sophisticated at all times. It was an inherited trait from the Butler women and a learned one from my auntie Zee, all of whom were known for putting their best forward. But this I always combined with keeping things real and simple. Xavier fell in love with me for who I was; that was enough then and it continued to be enough. I had no problem living in that big house in the suburbs of Philly, nor did I have a problem with the platinum Lexus 330 I drove or even the fine clothes I wore, but this was all image. At the end of the day and when all of that faded, I was still Monica.

The malicious treatment I received from many of the church members made me a little callous. They assumed from the onset that I was not the epitome of a first lady, and what bothered them even more was that I refused to kiss their butts. So, you can imagine, having another encore performance with the two lead church buzzards didn't faze me in the least bit.

"Shoes to match and, of course, you had to go out and get a matching purse. Pastor makes sure you come out looking good," said old Sadie, adding her two cents. "Lord, child, if you had a job, we'd have to build a new parsonage to hold your wardrobe. That's probably why we received a request for an increase in the pastor's personal budget, to keep you dressed in all these fineries."

"Well, don't worry about the job part. I have no intentions of seeking employment outside the community center." And besides, I didn't know how they could stand there and tell me I had no real job. I spent more than forty hours a week at the community center. Obviously, they somehow missed that part. "New Horizons and all its members, who have such special needs, keep me busy enough," I replied. I smiled smugly, hoping that they knew I was talking about them. "You ladies enjoy the service, and make sure you pick up one of the Easter treats I made especially for my special members. God bless you two real good."

With that I twisted my way to my seat, waving and smiling to those who acknowledged my entrance. I didn't mind waving and smiling, because those that waved were welcome faces for me each and every Sunday, unlike the two old biddies I'd just exchanged mock pleasantries with. I had told Xavier countless times that those two were going to catch me wrong one Sunday and get laid out, but, of course, I was reminded that I represented him and thus should grin and bear it.

Before long, the praise and worship team took their seats, and Xavier entered the sanctuary and stepped up to the podium. Shortly afterward, members of the congregation were looking at their neighbors and repeating after him. He looked good in his new purple and gold robe, which I had had custom-made for him. It had taken a little longer than usual for Royal Kingdom Robes to finish it up due to the large number of orders they'd received during a recent ministers' conference in Jersey. But with a little reminder of my past patronage and a couple of extra bills, it was delivered in time for Easter service. Now, as I sat fixated on my husband, what I went through to add this robe to his collection was well worth it. The robe fell over his well-built frame, giving him a regal stance befitting the man who pastored New Horizons and who was responsible for the membership growth in the five short years he had been standing at the helm.

The meager beginning of the ministry, which Xavier took over after the previous minister, who was well in his seventies, suddenly died of a heart attack, was still fresh in my mind. Rev. Steven Thomas was not only the pastor of the newly established nondenominational church in South Philadelphia, but he was a close friend of the Phillips family. My father-in-law, Bishop Winston Phillips, would recount stories of their times at Union Theological Seminary in Richmond, Virginia, and would declare how he respected Rev. Thomas because he was serious about the ministry, not to mention that he was known as a preachin' machine up until the day God called him home. While so many of the men in seminary were thinking of the fat paychecks and the prestige that came with being a well-known pastor on a fast-track plan to becoming bishop, and had high hopes and aspirations of sharing a platform with those that frequented TBN more often than most people frequent the neighborhood grocery store, Rev. Thomas was focused on winning souls. The relationship between the two older clergymen was sealed back then with a commitment to stand before people and proclaim the works of the Lord, with little concern for self-promotion. While my father-in-law was one of the most popular bishops in Philadelphia, he had no problem telling people he earned the title and was anything but an overnight bishop. Despite being retired, he still carried a big stick in the church circuit and in the city's political arena as well. His advice and religious views were sought after by many who held an office, whether they were black or white. Bishop Phillips was the equivalent of a black Jock Ewing, having as much authority in Philly as the older Ewing had in the drama series *Dallas* during the late 1970s. But, there was something about a legacy that my father-in-law held dear, and he was determined to see to it that Xavier honored it.

So, the legacy Rev. Thomas left, a ministry he did not see grow, was taken over by my husband. Xavier devoted tireless hours, much prayer, and great faith to the mission that would become the cornerstone of New Horizons. Now our congregation consisted of 3,200 members, a vast increase from three hundred that were already in the membership when Rev. Thomas passed. Because of the rapid growth, and with more coming through the doors each and every Sunday, wanting to be a part of this dynamic ministry, New Horizons had been featured in the *Philadelphia Inquirer* as one of the fastest-growing ministries in Philadelphia. It was no wonder Xavier was a great minister, a charismatic leader, and a devoted counselor, all the makings for a dynamic leader. If there was a male protégé for the Proverbs 31 woman, it would be Xavier.

Being a wonderful husband was just icing on the "got it going on" success cake. Except that wonderful bliss I experienced during the first two years of our marriage had taken a backseat to what he did and who he was. I kept reminding myself that it would get better, and I even threw myself into more projects than I had time for. All to support the man who shared my bed and who, undoubtedly since the day I said, "I do," had my devoted love and complete support. My spiritual life was completely devoted to the Lord, and I believed that all of this would make our relationship even more grounded and find us as much in love as we were in the early days. But something was changing, and I wanted to believe that it was just the ministry, that it was just his overloaded, busy schedule, but if I was to be completely honest, I was not sure anymore.

Pastor Phillips was nearing the close of his message, and people were standing and yelling all over the sanctuary. I'd been listening attentively, and although I knew Xavier was the real deal when it came to divinely called clergymen, I was always impressed, not to mention proud. As if by a divine holy ghost alarm, I, too, rose to my feet and began to wave my fan in the air and shout amen at every one of Xavier's pauses. Mr. Andres recognized the impending end of the sermon and began to echo the sermon's heights with musical notes. This cue was apparently just what Xavier needed to step away from the pulpit and charge to the front of the pews.

"When I think about the goodness of Jesus, I don't know about you, but my soul, don't nobody hear me, but my soul cries out, 'Hallelujah, hallelujah.' I thank God for saving me," cried Xavier. "Anybody here this morning thankful that the Lord saved you?" Positive responses resounded all over the sanctuary as Xavier swung left, then right, with sweat pouring from his brow. Brent, Xavier's armor bearer, walked swiftly behind him, attempting to wipe his forehead.

Someone behind me broke out in a shout, and I quickly turned around and noticed that people were beginning to shout in almost every pew. I felt the spirit move over me like an impending tide ready to take me under. This was such a familiar emotion and one that had been a part of spiritual life for some time now. Alongside this very familiar emotion was something I could not readily identify. For some reason, hot tears, which felt connected to something beyond my spiritual high, softly slipped from my closed eyelids. My heart felt so heavy, and a wave of sadness entered quickly and settled in before I had a chance to build up an emotional defense. I silently prayed, even before Xavier extended the altar call. I asked myself, without opening my mouth, *God, what in the world is going on with me?* I had no reason to be sad, not today and especially not here.

I turned my body slightly to the right to place my personalized fan on the seat. After I refocused my attention to the front, Xavier looked in my direction. I managed a smile and slightly tilted my head, glancing at him lovingly. Suddenly, I felt overwhelmed and quickly gripped the pew in front of me with both hands, hoping to steady the uneasy feeling deep inside myself. A puzzled look creased Xavier's brow, and unlike other times, I was unable to visually soothe any alarm that my action might have set off. Instead, I bowed my head and waited for him to begin praying for those who had gathered at the altar. I knew there were probably many who felt the need to answer the altar call and yet stood rooted in the pews for whatever reason, not wanting to go forward. This morning I shared their hesitation. At this moment I needed a balm to calm my spirit, and in my usual place at the end of the second pew, I earnestly prayed along with my pastor that this prayer would provide the balm that I needed.

As the service ended, Xavier made his way toward me as it had become a custom for us to walk to the vestibule hand in hand and exchange greetings and hugs with the members of and visitors to New Horizons.

"Hey, are you okay? You looked like you were about to fall over," Xavier quizzed, with a look of concern on his face.

"I'm good. I am just always blown away at how the anointing moves when you least expect it. I was completely caught up in the movement of God." What I said was the truth. I just conveniently left out the part about sensing that something was out of sync.

His eyes locked with mine for a brief moment before we neared the vestibule. "God is awesome like that. Always moving in an unexpected way," he said.

While the exchange at the end of the service was an extremely exhausting task for Xavier and pretty taxing for me as well, he continued to make his way to the back of the church Sunday after Sunday. Many of the members felt that they never got a chance to shake his hand, give encouraging words, or just complain. The latter was mostly why they felt this time was necessary. So, we stood sometimes for an hour and occasionally longer. It was not really me they wanted a piece of, but since I was standing beside their fearless leader, I got a spillover of love and respect every now and then.

We had been shaking hands and conversing with those exiting the sanctuary just as the sisters Hilda and Sadie, otherwise known as Doom and Gloom, peered my way. "Look, Pastor Phillips. Here come my two favorite parishioners," I said sarcastically, loud enough for them to hear.

Before they could coldly reply to my sweet-as-candy greeting, Xavier turned around and looked in their direction. "Good day, Sister Hilda and Sister Sadie. Don't you two look beautiful," said Xavier as he leaned over and hugged them both.

"Pastor, you sure preached us under the benches this morning," said Sister Sadie as she wiped her forehead with her dainty lace handkerchief, like she was still feeling the residue of the Holy Spirit on her brow. What she was probably feeling was the heat from the hot flashes she experienced from being two days older than dirt.

"Well, to God be the glory, Sister Sadie. He gets all

the praise," replied Xavier. He pointed upward and continued smiling. You would think that he enjoyed talking to Granny Grouch and her sidekick. God knows, it was a chore for me to even look at them.

"We told your wife how stunning she looks today," Broomhilda added, with a smile that made her mouth look like a dried-up prune. Gone was the nastiness. It seemed that she saved that for me. But when in Xavier's presence, both of them came across like Saint Theresa. "She's such a blessing to you, Pastor, and always the adoring first lady. We are blessed to have her."

That was enough. I had to attempt to expose them for the old farts I knew they were. "Yes, Pastor, they admired my new outfit and even complimented me on my new shoes and matching purse," I said. I turned my left foot so they could catch the glimmer of color from my jeweled sandal. "They are such sweet ladies and always concerned about our well-being, God love their hearts. They shared with me that they were planning to approve the increase in your personal expense budget at the meeting this Thursday." I moved in closer to Xavier, wrapped my arm around his, and smiled, showing all my pearly whites.

Sadie was the first to stutter. "Oh, well, hmmm, we looked over the budget review, and, well, Pastor, you know it's an adjustment based on some emergency expenses. The committee hadn't considered that you would need an increase in your personal expenses at this time. We, hmmm. Well."

"Oh, Sister Sadie, don't be so modest," I said. "You know, you and Sister Hilda are so good at getting the committee to see things your way. Besides, the church does so well because you have a gift for handling our financial affairs. I know I appreciate the extras, and I feel certain that Pastor Phillips does, too. Don't you, sweetheart?" Before Xavier could nod in agreement I continued to go overboard. "Don't be modest. Let the work you do speak for you and allow the Pastor to thank you for taking such good care of us." I watched carefully, making sure not to miss the appalled look on their faces. It was absolutely priceless. I knew we had never entertained a conversation about the budget, but I felt the little white lie was justified and served them right.

"Ladies, I do indeed thank you. It will be a tremendous help to me and to Monica," said Xavier. "You two are such a blessing. I don't know what I would do without parishioners like the both of you." The actual truth eluded Xavier, and I couldn't help but laugh on the inside. I made a mental note to tell him all about this later. He wouldn't appreciate my method of revenge on the two old crows, but, as I said, it served them right.

Sister Sadie opened her mouth and began to speak quickly. "Pastor, we don't—" Before she could finish, Sister Hilda interrupted, nudging her.

"We are glad to help out in any way we can, Pastor Phillips. Now you two go and enjoy the rest of your day. And have a blessed Easter Sunday." She reached for my hand and waited for me to extend it toward her. Instead of reaching my hand, I touched my lips and blew a kiss at her. She had to be upset and steaming under the collar, but she managed to add, "Take care, First Lady, and we will be in touch."

"I know you will. God bless you," I replied as I pivoted and headed toward the administrative wing of the church.

Chapter 2

I stirred the piping hot gravy and adjusted the burner to low so it could simmer without sticking to the pan. Wiping my hands on the end of my apron, I tried to mentally locate the gravy bowl that matched the rest of my Lenox Jewels Sapphire china. It was an exquisite set of royal blue–accented dinnerware. This was a special set given to Xavier and me as a gift from his parents on our last anniversary. They knew I loved to cook, and with all the company we had always that arrived right around dinnertime, some invited and some uninvited, Mrs. Phillips felt I could use another set fit for entertaining. I accepted the gift graciously because, one, it was one less expensive thing I had to purchase and, two, when Bishop Phillips gave a gift you embraced it for all it was worth. He was as tight with his money as he was with his compliments. But I learned to deal with him long ago. I let him think he was needed, that I couldn't possibly make a decision without his input, that nobody knew the word like he did, and, most importantly, that his one and only child was the spitting image of him.

I could easily agree that Xavier was the spitting

image of his father. It wasn't difficult to see why Xavier's mother probably ran to the altar, yelling, "I do" at the top of her lungs. He was a handsome man, even at sixty. The salt-and-pepper hair cut short and his always perfectly shaped mustache and beard made him appear seasoned and yet so distinguished. His heritage was so visible on his angular face, and he made a point of always mentioning that both he and his wife came from well-to-do families in Delaware. He also made a point of adding that they were descendants of Moors, a distinct name given to a multiracial people in the area of Cheswold, Delaware. The Moors had Black, Indian, and Irish roots, and some even had Spanish blood. This would, of course, account for their high yellow, almost white complexion.

The Phillips family heritage didn't impress me, and while I thought my husband was handsome, his heritage or complexion wasn't what sold me. I was swayed more by his personality and stirred by his body, which seemed to call my name in every known language. It was no wonder I was absolutely addicted to his love-making after the first couple of times, and once we exchanged vows, I made it a point to be in bed, revved up and ready to go when his boxers hit the floor. His love was just like that, and I clapped the happy, happy, joy, joy song with every upward stroke. Yes, I was saved, but I just had to keep it real. I didn't feel that being all uptight and righteous got me any closer to the pearly gates than me saying what was on my mind. If the good man upstairs knew I was thinking it, I might as well have expressed myself, even if it was just to myself.

The cordless phone signaled an incoming call with a loud, ear-piercing ring. "Hello," I said as I tilted the phone against my shoulder and reached for the gravy bowl I'd been searching high and low for.

"Hi there, Monica." My mother-in-law's soft voice came through the phone. "I was just giving you a ring before we walk out the door. The bishop wanted me to call to see if you needed us to bring anything."

"Oh, no, Mother Phillips. I'm finishing up, and Xavier should be back in a few minutes. He left something he needed back at the church." For the life of me, I couldn't understand why she always referred to her husband as the bishop. In the years that I'd known them, I'd never heard her call him anything else. I even asked Xavier once, and his reply was that occasionally she would call his father by his first name, but not often. It was a respect factor, he'd said. It didn't take me but a second to let him know that I would not be following the family custom. To me, he was Xavier, not only behind closed doors, but in front of family and friends. I did give him just due and respect at church and would refer to him as "Pastor." While his dad had been elevated to the position of bishop early in his career, I knew Xavier desired to hold the elite pastoral title. Regardless of his personal titles, present and future, I would continue to call him Xavier. But the personal exchange between my in-laws was too much for me. The man was definitely carried away by the prestige of being a pastor. Dag, I wondered if such strictness was mandatory in their bedroom. No, on second thought, I really didn't want to know.

"He should be there helping you out. That boy thinks you can do absolutely everything all by yourself." She sighed.

"It's okay. I really don't mind." I was doing such a

good job at juggling things around the house without the help of my husband, it was like second nature now.

My relationship with First Lady Cecilia Johnson-Phillips had always been special. She was such a breath of fresh, anointed air and was the sweetest woman I had ever met, with the exception of my mother. She never treated me indifferently or played twenty-one questions when it came to wanting to know something. Her approach was always direct and without a hidden agenda. I never really had to work hard at being the ideal daughter-in-law, because ours was a unique unity. I easily became the daughter that she'd never had, and the genuine love she felt for me shined through. I thought often of how difficult her life must have been throughout the years, always agreeing and always being the obedient wife, and yet she never complained. What a woman. I had come a long way in the first lady department, and yet I was still a work in progress. However, I didn't exactly want to be like Cecilia and completely lose my identity.

"Well, we should be there in a little while. See you then." Cecilia hung up the phone.

The minute I placed the cordless phone on the nearby counter, the doorbell rang. Glancing at the God Bless This Home wall clock, positioned in the center of the wall over the kitchen window, I couldn't believe that the past couple of hours had gone by so quickly and that Xavier had been gone for almost that long. Obviously, he must have gotten tied up on the phone or with one of the trustees or deacons, who were always in and out of the church.

Out of habit, I quickly scanned the living room to make sure nothing was out of place as I made my way to the bright and airy foyer. Swinging the front door open, I smiled gingerly as I greeted Xavier's best friend and his wife. "Hey, you two." I was excited to see my good friend Liz, but Patrick was far from my choice of company. I couldn't help but wonder what drama he would bring today. He wouldn't be Patrick if he didn't bring up something that was stuck on stupid or some point he felt Xavier needed to agree with. At the conclusion of most visits with him, Xavier and I would end our evening agreeing to disagree.

Patrick touched Liz's back slightly and guided her through the opened door. As if he read my thoughts, he smirked, "Monica, you look well. How is everything going?" He leaned over and kissed me on the cheek.

"Just fine, Patrick," I replied. "Xavier should be here in a few minutes. He went to the church to pick up some papers he forgot." I led the way to the living room and stood near the sofa, waiting for them to take their usual seats.

Before she sat down, Liz gave me a big hug. "Hey, girl. I'm sorry I didn't get a chance to return your call the other day," she said. "Pat wasn't feeling well all week, and I finally had to take him to the pediatrician." Liz and I had established a bond of friendship when we were both dating our spouses in college. We weren't the best of friends, but ours was an easy enough relationship, and through the years we had come to lean on each other as we dealt with first lady drama. We were cut from two entirely different cloths, and her dancing to whatever tune Patrick played got on my last black nerve. On many occasions, I had no problem telling her so. All and all, she was good people and one of the few women friends Xavier thought I ought to hang around with. But he knew choosing my friends wasn't something he wanted to do. So, for the most part, he gave me free rein to choose who kept me company in my inner circle, and in turn, I kept the circle to a size that I assumed he could deal with.

"Oh, I hope he's feeling better. I can't imagine him not jumping around, with his cute, overactive self," I said as I smiled at the photo of Pat on the fireplace mantel. He was an adorable little boy, with bright eyes and curly locks of brown hair all over his head. A mischievous smile was on his little face. When Patrick and Liz first asked Xavier and me to be godparents, I didn't want to accept. They were asking us to spend time and help to raise a child, when we hadn't been able to have a child of our own. By the time I saw Pat in the hospital's nursery, I dispelled my feelings as I held him and realized this was a chance to be part of a young life, even if it wasn't full time. No one could argue that we weren't the best godparents and we spoiled him rotten.

"That's when I knew he was sick for real. He wasn't going through the house, throwing things around and getting into one thing after another. Truth be told, I was one happy mommy when I gave him the first dose of cough medicine and he slept the entire afternoon. He only woke up long enough to eat a little soup, went back to sleep, and didn't get up till morning. Thank God for drugs." She started to laugh.

"Do you think he's going to be up to Disney on Ice? Xavier picked up the tickets weeks ago. We were planning on taking him for pizza afterwards and keeping him overnight. I believe we even picked up a DVD just for him." I tried to think of the title, but just couldn't. I had so much on my mind lately.

"Uncle Xavier called him last night to confirm the date for next weekend, and he cheered. If you had to roll him there on a stretcher, he wouldn't miss it." Liz chuckled.

"That boy knows he loves his Uncle Xavier and

Auntie Monnie," Patrick added. "You guys are good to Pat and we appreciate it so much. Monica, I know it's not easy."

He was attempting to be nice. "We love him and vowed to be good godparents," I said. "So, because God has not blessed us with one of our own, we two get to spend time with Pat whenever we want. I'd say we are getting a break." No one could really know how badly I wanted a child, but I had resolved to have a wait-and-see-what-God-has-in-store attitude. "Why don't you help me finish up in the kitchen," I said. "Bishop and Mother Phillips will be here in a little while. I just hope my husband decides to grace us with his presence before then." I looked at my watch, realizing that only ten minutes had passed since the last time I checked the time.

"I'm sure the man is taking care of some important business. You two don't have a clue what it takes to run a church," said Patrick. He barely looked up as he turned the pages of the business section of the *Philadelphia Inquirer*, which he had picked up off the mahogany coffee table.

"Of course, we don't, but I know you can tell us exactly what it takes," I interjected because I knew Liz wasn't going to say a thing. Just as I turned around to read him the riot act for elevating himself at the expense of not only his wife, but me, Xavier came through the back door.

"What's up, frat?" said Xavier. He bypassed me and Liz and walked over to the sofa to exchange a handshake and hug with Patrick, who now stood, stretching his slim six-foot-two-inch frame. He was so thin, a strong wind could easily have blown him away. What I wouldn't have given for a gust of wind to breeze through my living room and remove the excess baggage that stood there, receiving a warm welcome from my husband.

"Is that the only person you see, sweetie?" I asked, adding a little sugar on the end to make sure the bitterness I used with Patrick was all gone.

"Of course not. Hello, Liz," said Xavier as he hugged her. "And I saved the best for last." He gave me a quick kiss on the lips. "Sorry it took me so long, but the minute I walked in the church, Deacon Thomas cornered me."

"I was just telling the ladies how it goes," said Patrick. "Somebody always wants to bend our ear for just about any- and everything. As first ladies, they need to recognize that the church comes first."

"Oh, we do, Patrick honey," said Liz as she nestled snugly beside her husband.

I didn't ask her to speak for me. But since Xavier was home, I would play the gracious hostess and treat his friend almost civilly. It was a difficult job, only because Patrick made it that way. We had never been a member of each other's fan club. He didn't like me, because I had obviously ended Xavier's single days too early. He also felt that I was not the ideal woman for Xavier. I was too outspoken and too pretty. Patrick felt that understated beauty was better and caused fewer eyes to roam in the direction of the woman that would be the leading lady of the church.

I didn't like him, because he was not dedicated to anything, not to the church, his wife, or his son. Every woman, married or single, in the Philadelphia area that desired to have a taste of Rev. Patrick Garrett, Sr., had been given the opportunity and was often invited back for seconds and thirds. While his wife played the role of adoring mate to the hilt, she had to know about his roaming ways. Heck, everyone else did. I would gladly have accepted the job of town crier and yelled his indiscretions; however, my husband preferred that I mind my business and allow God to deal with Patrick. I had waited, but it didn't look like He would be dealing with him anytime soon.

"If you can tear yourself from Pastor Garrett, Liz, I could use your help placing dinner on the serving table," I said.

"Sure, Monica. I'm right behind you," replied Liz. Before she could move off the sofa, Patrick slapped her backside and chuckled.

"Watch that, Pastor. Don't tempt me to get our food to go," said Liz. "I'd love to drive right home and let you have your way with me." She sounded like a television advertisement for kinky phone sex.

"Hey now, Liz. Me and my baby don't need to hear that almost X-rated stuff," said Xavier. He pretended to be annoyed but winked at Patrick and leaned over to give him a high five.

"Man. I trained my woman right, and she knows how to treat Big Daddy," Patrick said, right before grabbing his crotch.

"Okay. You know what? I'm going into the kitchen and pretend that you aren't supporting this fool's madness," I said. I stomped out of the room, beyond disgusted. I couldn't believe that Patrick was grabbing his crotch for all of us to see.

"What do you want me to help you with, Monica?" asked Liz. She stood near the island, in the center of the kitchen.

"I can't believe you allow Patrick to treat you like that." There, I had said it. I knew I would regret it, since she told Patrick everything, and he in turn would say something to Xavier about me getting in their business.

She was getting ready to answer when I stopped her. "Don't worry about it, Liz. I shouldn't be saying anything. If you like it, then I love it."

* * *

With three pastors in the house, the dinner conversation was lively. Mother Phillips, Liz, and I spent most of it just listening and responding when we were asked to confirm that something had happened, was happening, or would happen. We ended up moving to the family room and having our dessert there. The red velvet cake was so delicious, and I enjoyed it as much as I did the compliments I received for the delicacy. The extra time it took to prepare the dessert last night, right before bed, had indeed been worth it.

"Sweetheart, you outdid yourself as usual. Everything was so delicious, and this cake is mouthwatering," said Mother Phillips. She leaned over and placed her empty dessert plate on the table and poured herself a cup of hot tea from the ivory bone and sapphire china teapot, which I'd placed on the table minutes before.

"Actually, it is Auntie Zee's recipe," I responded, not wanting to take complete credit. While I did put it all together and had perfected it over time, it was Auntie Zee's combination.

"Oh, how is she doing?" asked Mother Phillips. "I saw her at a fund-raiser a couple of weeks ago with Joe. I only got a chance to wave from a distance."

"She's fine," I said. "Keeping busy with this and that. In fact, she and Uncle Joe left yesterday to spend a couple of weeks at their vacation home in Florida." That reminded me, I needed to go over tomorrow morning and feed Zeek. I didn't know why Auntie Zee and Uncle Joe didn't take him to a pet spa. They knew I couldn't stand that white, long-haired cat. Every time I used that description, Auntie reminded me that Zeek was not an alley cat, but a pure white Persian cat. Like that made a difference. To me, he was just an ugly ball of fur that stank when it got wet. But having no children, they thought of that thing as their very own child. And in some twisted way, they thought that asking me to care for Zeek every time they left was going to bring us closer together. I just didn't see that happening.

"I can't imagine Joe taking a vacation away from his clients. That has to be the hardest-working attorney in Philly," replied Mother Phillips. She placed her teacup on the table.

"You know, he's probably down there working his BlackBerry overtime," I said. "You know, he just earned yet another award from the Philadelphia Council of Lawyers. They have dubbed him the best divorce litigation attorney in Philadelphia."

I was proud of my uncle. He wasn't raised with a silver spoon and had worked hard to earn that title and all the others that had been bestowed upon him. The big bucks he was pulling in were just the fruits of his hard work. And Auntie Zee was just as deserving. While working to put him through law school, she never complained. The minute he started making some real money, Joseph W. Payne arrived home and announced that she wasn't working another day. And since that announcement, she hadn't. That was also when he moved her from their first home to a five-bedroom, three-bathroom house in a gated community.

"Make sure you congratulate him for me," Mother Phillips added sincerely. While most people might not mean it, I knew she did.

Liz rubbed her stomach and leaned her head back against the cushion of the sofa. "It's time for me to have a black moment. You know what they say about us."

"Girl, I feel you," I said. "The guys haven't yelled in

a few minutes, and I'm ready to kick these shoes off and relax. Thank God for dishwashers. Everything is loaded and cleaned up with the exception of the dessert plates."

Mother Phillips spoke up. "You didn't have to do all that alone. We would have been glad to help out."

"You are my special guest today, Mother Phillips, and I will not have you lift a hand," I said. "And besides, you never allow me to help much when I come over to your place." I didn't consider myself company in my in-laws' home, and yet I was always treated like royalty.

"You've got me there, daughter," replied Mother Phillips. "I figured you need a break after waiting on Xavier. That boy has always been a handful. In fact, you girls need to take a little time away from these men and go to a spa, and I just might join you." With that, we all laughed. There was so much truth to the obvious need.

"What are you hens in here jawing about?" asked Bishop Phillips. He filled the room with his presence.

"Nothing, dear," said Mother Phillips. "Just enjoying the company of my daughter and Liz. Are you ready to go?" Mother Phillips stood up and ran her hands over the pleats of her black slacks.

"Yes. We better get home," replied Bishop Phillips. "I didn't get a chance to let Henry out before we left, and he's probably climbing up the wall by now. That dog thinks he's more human than animal. Monica honey, that was a great meal. You sure know how to please this old man." Bishop Phillips walked over to me and gave me a brief hug that was over almost before it began.

"Glad you enjoyed everything. I'll go get the cake I wrapped up for you," I said. I returned moments later and listened as our houseguests brought their conversations to a close for the evening. As if on cue, we all walked to the foyer methodically. I stood beside my husband as we said good night to his parents and to Liz and Patrick. He had decided it was time for them to leave as well. They had to travel an extra thirty minutes to pick up Pat from Liz's parents' house.

The minute the door closed, I grinned warmly at my husband, who stood at the window until the last car drove away. I watched his backside, oblivious to my own lust until my finger was tracing the outline of my lips.

At that moment it seemed we had changed emotional positions. Usually, it was Xavier who succumbed to his lustful yearning late in the evening, after entertaining and finally listening to the quiet echo of only each other in the room. Many times we never made it to our bedroom before the urge swept over us, and we ended up leaning against, lying across, and stretching out on whatever was close by.

"I'm going to go upstairs and do some reading before bed. Are you coming up now, or do you have a few other things to do down here?" asked Xavier as he walked around the table to pick up his large black Coach messenger bag.

"It depends. Can I interest you in delaying your reading long enough to give me a little quality time?" I moved toward him, pushed my ample breasts against his chest, wrapped my arms around his waist, reached under his shirt, and ran my fingertips along the lower portion of his back.

"I'd love that, but I really need to read these reports. With such a busy week in front of me, I don't know when I will have time to review them. Can I get a rain check?" Before I could answer or tempt him to change his mind, he kissed me lightly and slid away from me. He was already walking up the steps before I could answer.

Chapter 3

The early morning hum of the neighborhood waking up didn't help my mood. Around 5:00 a.m. I felt the bed sway as Xavier slipped out, trying not to disturb me. It didn't work, because if he knew nothing else, he should have known that I was a light sleeper. Creeping in on me in the early morning hours would never work, because I would be on him like a stalker in a night fright movie. And yet, an hour ago he'd fumbled around in the dark room without turning on any lights. I lay there and listened to him almost swear every time he bumped into something or ended up with two pieces of clothing that didn't match. Any other time, he would have kissed me on the cheek the minute his mind ordered his eyes to open and chatted with me nonstop until he was on his way out the door. But, obviously, this was another time, and no one had told me that my emotional device had stopped on out of sync.

I never understood when some of the women I counseled as first lady would say that they didn't know their husbands were cheating, unhappy, or that things had changed until it was too late. The psychological terminology for it was denial. I called it living with blinders on. I knew when we made love it was different, it lacked something that was so badly needed. Like those women, I had missed the tide changing, the threat of the incoming storm. I felt it was my job to put things back on track. No glue, no stitches, no gadget, just old fashioned love, attention and affection. That's what I'd do, I'd fix us.

I turned over on my back and stared at the vaulted ceiling, the skylights, and then at the slanted window in the loft area above our master bedroom suite. I tilted my head slightly to get a better view of the early morning sky. It held on to the remnants of darkness, with only a hint of light trying to cascade through the blanket of dark color. Already the day looked gloomy, but that could very well have been the leftover hurt I felt from being turned down by my own husband last night.

Normally, I could bounce back, but it was happening so much lately, it was getting harder and harder to overcome the negative vibes he threw my way or the constant excuses I received right around bedtime. You would think it was the witching hour and I was one of the lead witches, equipped with a broom, spells, and warts.

Angrily kicking the comforter off my body, I sprung to my feet just hard enough for them to hit the floor with a soft thump. I mumbled, "Why me, Lord?" It was a loaded question that I was sure would plague me for the remainder of the day. With no real desire to dwell on the matter, I decided on an assertive approach. I didn't want to let the situation get to me.

I slipped my feet into my Dearfoam slippers, which were next to the bed, and slid my way to our bathroom. Turning on the light, I blinked a couple of times until my eyes adjusted to the brightness. The large room was decorated in ivory, burgundy, and gold. I had taken great care to make sure that the bathroom held a hint of warmth and was an inviting addition to our master suite. A large floral arrangement sat on the corner of the bathroom counter, enlivening the room with an array of vibrant colors that matched everything perfectly. While washing my face with cleanser and toweling it off with a fluffy white hand towel, I replayed Xavier's turning me down over and over again in my mind. I needed to turn it off, but I just couldn't.

Just as I slipped my black silk gown over my head and dropped it to the floor, I noticed a piece of paper on my toiletry shelf. The note confirmed Xavier's early departure. I read it quickly:

> *Monica, I'm hitting the gym at the community center early so I can start my day. I'll shower and change there. Drop my laundry off at the cleaners, and RSVP for the charity function at the hospital. Nora has my schedule if you need me for anything. Talk with you later, and I love you.*

That was it. His schedule was becoming so busy, he hardly had time for anything. His usual workout time was late afternoon, so this change convinced me that Xavier needed to revisit his commitments and make time for me. At least he'd said he loved me, and for today that would be enough for me to go on.

Rushing through my morning ritual and dressing in a simple Donna Karan black wrap dress, I slipped my black, sheer panty hose–covered feet in a pair of black BCBG slingbacks. I put on a pair of pearl-accented hoops and hooked my three-string pearl necklace around my neck. After pulling my hair back and placing it in a holder, I twirled it around and held the twist knot I had created in place with a few bobby pins. A little Bobbi Brown face coverage, mascara, and bronze lip color highlighted with lip shiner, and I was ready to hit the door in time to beat the morning rush-hour traffic.

My cell phone went off at the minute I positioned myself in the driver's seat. Without looking, I assumed it was Xavier and clicked the button on my steering wheel to access the blue tooth device. "Hey, sweetheart," I said.

"Sweetheart? Lady Phillips, it's me, Nita. I was just calling to tell you that I'm out of school today at eleven, and I'll come in early to help out at the center." Her words ran together. I swear, I didn't think that girl ever took a breath when she talked.

"Okay, Nita. That's fine. Mrs. Epps will be there this morning, so it shouldn't be too hectic. Oh, don't you have a test this morning?" I leaned up to look in the mirror to check my reflection before backing out of the driveway.

"Yes, I sure do. But thanks to you, I'm ready. I mean, I studied all the material we went over and did exactly what you told me and quizzed myself several times. I just hope I'm ready. I mean if they go with the last chapters, I'm going to have to think real hard, because I studied that section last and sort of crammed it in."

"Nita, breathe and slow down. You will do fine. Just take your time. Now, go ahead and get to school. I'll see you later." I had to smile. She had been such a lifesaver for me. Her mother, Ms. Vincent, was the choir director and had insisted that Nita help me out at the community center after school. I was hesitant at first, thinking that she was a little on the quiet side and nerdy. I definitely didn't have time to help her blossom into a butterfly.

After a lot of persuasion and a couple of pleas in between the sheets from Xavier, I gave in. I couldn't have been more wrong about Nita Vincent. It only took a couple of days for her to warm up, and after that she was my shadow around the center, always talking nonstop. It was like a flash from my past since she didn't think she was pretty and needed reassurance that she was in fact a jewel. Now she pranced around like she was a true princess. I initially wanted to label her as one of my giving-back projects; in my heart I was emotionally attached with no desire to let go.

"New Horizons Community Center. This is Monica Phillips." I had no idea where Mrs. Epps had run off to. With her nosy butt, she was probably across the street, at the church, trying to catch the gossip over there so she could bring it back over here and spread it all before lunchtime.

"Mrs. Phillips. How are you this morning?" Deacon Thomas said breathlessly.

"Good morning, Deacon Thomas. What can I do for you?" I could tell his raspy, asthmatic voice anywhere.

"I wanted to see if you would be available around eleven thirty to meet with Mr. Jackson and some others from the tourism office." He paused, and when I didn't reply quickly, he continued. "You know, they are interested in including the church in a new advertisement project that will begin this summer. Pastor Phillips thinks it's a wonderful opportunity for New Horizons."

I sipped from the Styrofoam Starbucks cup and savored the taste of the caramel latte with extra caramel.

"Actually, my schedule is full this morning. Why didn't someone mention this to me last week?" I flipped through my planner and saw no notes about the meeting. As I listened to him catch his breath, I grabbed my cell phone, thinking I may have put a note there. After clicking a few buttons, the electronic calendar feature came up empty as well.

"I thought Pastor Phillips mentioned it. You were there at the fund-raiser a couple of weeks ago, if I recall correctly."

"Yes, I recall being at the fund-raiser, but I don't recall Pastor Phillips telling me anything about a meeting to discuss the advertising venture." I tilted my chair and looked at the ceiling and counted to ten. I was a little sick of the church administration thinking that I was privy to all the goings-on at the church. Contrary to what most of them thought, I often received information on a need-to-know basis. Obviously, my husband didn't think I needed to know about this meeting.

"Well, when Mr. Jackson called, he asked if you were going to be there, since he is working on a couple of other projects he was interested in getting your views on. Everyone in the city knows you are the mastermind behind the man when it comes to the business affairs of the church and the community center. You think you can reschedule your meetings?"

"Don't try to flatter me, Deacon. It's not that easy to reschedule all of the appointments I have for today to come over to the church just to sit in on a meeting." I pushed my chair back and uncrossed my legs. I couldn't believe that they thought I could just adjust what I had going on over here to go over there.

I went on. "Deacon Thomas, if Pastor Phillips had mentioned it to me, I would have adjusted everything. But I can't change my schedule at the last minute. I'm working on the mentoring program. The prospective mentors are important people in the city, and I don't think they would take it lightly if First Lady Phillips was not here to greet them upon their arrival. I don't think that would look too good for New Horizons, or Pastor Phillips, for that matter."

"First Lady Phillips, I understand what you are saying." Deacon Thomas coughed several times before continuing. "I'll try to hold them off as long as I can, but if you can get here, that would be nice."

"I'll let you know if something changes. Have a good morning, Deacon Thomas." I hung up the phone and reached for my cup of latte. Darn, while I was messing around with Deacon Thomas, my coffee had gotten cold.

"One more sacrifice for the good of the church," I said out loud. I looked over my calendar and decided to reschedule both my morning appointments. That should do since my only other appointment was in the afternoon.

I walked into the church a half hour later and went directly to the conference room. I leaned my ear against the door and could hear voices. I took a deep breath, tapped lightly, and opened the door.

Xavier was the first to look up. He was positioned at the head of the table with two other gentlemen I didn't know. I recognized Mr. Jackson, and of course Deacon Thomas was sitting in his usual chair to the right of Xavier. He had Xavier's best interests at heart and was there whenever Xavier needed him and even when he didn't. The two were fond of each other. The other deacons were a little jealous of the relationship he shared with Xavier. He involved them all, but they had to understand that he needed to rely on at least one that would be his confidante. My vote would always be Deacon Thomas. He was devoted, compassionate and the one who knew the location of the best restaurants in Philadelphia, New Jersey. New York, and Delaware.

"Please come in, First Lady Phillips." Xavier stood up and pointed to the chair next to Deacon Thomas. "I knew you had a lot going on over at the community center, but I'm glad you could make it and assist us here. You remember Mr. Jackson?" He extended a hand in my direction.

"Yes, I do." I reached to shake his hand as he stood with a smile on his face. "It's very good to see you again. I was told you have some projects that New Horizons might be able to be a part of."

"Well, Monica." He paused, glanced in Xavier's direction and then looked at me. "I'm sorry, can I call you Monica?" Mr. Jackson asked.

"No one else does, at least not while I'm conducting business. So, if you don't mind, let's stick with First Lady Phillips." I smiled and put on all the charm I had. If Xavier wanted me to handle this deal, then I would. But, it would be in my usual professional, direct, and no-nonsense manner.

He looked in Xavier's direction again and witnessed the smile that endorsed my way of handling our church business. "You are a bad woman." He leaned back and laughed. "It's going to be a delight working with you." He paused. "So, let's get down to business, First Lady Phillips."

By the end of the meeting we were included in four new projects that were sure to benefit the community center.

"I think you are a bad woman." Xavier laughed as he opened his office door and allowed me to walk in first.

"Did you see the look on Mr. Jackson's face when I quoted his year end report off the top of my head?" I smiled smugly. "He had to be impressed." I walked around the desk and sat in Xavier's taupe executive chair, which enveloped my body. He retrieved two bottles of cranberry-grape juice from the mini refrigerator in the corner of the room. "It's been a while since I read that report. I'm surprised I remembered the figures."

"Doesn't matter—he was impressed and so was I." He placed one bottle on the edge of the desk and opened the other and handed it to me. "For my wife."

"Thank you, my husband. I believe you owe me dinner, a massage, foot rub, or something." I took a long sip of the chilled juice and looked up at him sitting on the edge of his desk.

"How about I pick up Thai or Chinese and we can watch a movie. But it will have to be late. I've got a trustee meeting."

I tried not to look disappointed. I didn't want to say, "forget it," but I wanted so much more than a quick, late dinner and a movie. If history repeated itself, he would forget to pick up the food and would more than likely fall asleep before scene one of the movie. "Tell you what. To make sure you don't forget to pick up the food, give me a call when the meeting is over and I'll order Thai and have it delivered."

"You know me too well and yet, you still love me." He drank the remainder of the juice in one swallow and rose to his feet.

I waited, anticipating a kiss or some other show of love. When none came, I spoke up. "You may want to remember that." Closing the distance between us, I stood on tiptoes and kissed him on the cheek right before I walked out.

Chapter 4

Looking at my watch, I noticed I had only been in the office for an hour, and yet I was beyond exhausted. The marathon shopping spree with both my mother and mother-in-law had taken a toll on me. Saks opened its doors at 8 A.M. for a preferred-customer sale and, like a few other loyal customers, we whisked through their doors to take advantage of the savings. I had no intention of shopping. I was merely along to act as fashion consultant. It was still hard to believe that despite my fashion savvy, they concluded their spree with only a few perfume samples and silk ties for the men in their lives. I had to select one for Xavier if only to follow suit. I tapped my pen a few times trying to focus on my to-do list. Turning around in my chair, I reached for the plastic Saks bag on my credenza and slipped the pure silk printed fabric from the white tissue paper. I admired the tie and mentally viewed Xavier's closet for the ideal suit that the tie would complement.

Nita came bouncing through my door, which was slightly ajar. "First Lady Phillips, would you like me to pick up some lunch for you? It's almost one o'clock, and your next meeting starts at two," Nita said.

"That would be great. I have been trying to concentrate on all this paperwork for the grant. I'm starved." I stood and rotated my head in a circular motion to loosen the tightness that gripped my neck muscles. "What do you have a taste for?"

"How about cheesesteaks from Pat's? We haven't been there in a while." She talked while she checked her My Space account and bounced to the beat that came through the computer speakers. Her hair was up in a banana clip, and she was wearing her signature tight jeans and T-shirt. On her feet, she wore a pair of white Air Force Ones. Despite my tips as her fashion advisor, she would not give up her jeans and T-shirts. It didn't really matter what she wore, because she was a pretty girl and could pull off almost anything.

"What are you listening to?" I said. I often censored her music listening to ensure that it was tasteful and befitting a young lady, especially the young lady that had become the special assistant to the first lady of New Horizons. While her mother preached fire and brimstone and dared her to listen to anything but gospel, I was a little more lenient. As long as the songs were tasteful, didn't include any illicit lyrics, and didn't cause the female hormones to rage out of control, I didn't have a problem with them.

"Heather Headley. She's pretty cool, and before you quiz me, her music has a positive message. Here. Why don't you listen to it for yourself while I go pick up lunch? I'll be out and back before you know it." She busied herself with removing the CD from the CD drive of the computer and walked past me swiftly. Nita placed her slender body in my cognac brown executive swivel chair and clicked the mouse to open my CD drive. After a minute or so, sultry music flowed from the desk speakers and filled the room with deep, rhythmical notes, which the blues-sounding songstress sang above.

Nita smiled up at me and snapped her fingers. "Don't answer right now. Just listen to it while I'm gone, and tell me what you think when I get back. And, First Lady Phillips, don't go trying to hijack it so you can romance the pastor. I can't have you throwing it on him and interrupting his direct line to the man upstairs." She laughed uncontrollably.

"Get out of my office. Your fast butt shouldn't even be thinking about me throwing anything." I couldn't help but laugh along with her. "Go get my lunch before I starve, and make sure you get me an AriZona Green Tea." I reached in my Dooney & Bourke satchel and pulled a fifty-dollar bill from the side pocket and handed it to her. "Go on, big spender."

She held the fifty-dollar bill up to the light and turned it over and over as if she was determining if it was real.

"Girl, go order my food, and get out of here," I insisted. I playfully hit her butt with a nearby file folder and walked to the file cabinet in the corner. I wouldn't dare tell her that I had listened to Heather Headley after seeing her on *The Tyra Banks Show* and that I didn't find her music offensive.

My body was aching all over. I couldn't figure out what I had done to cause these aches. I knew what it wasn't. I just had to figure out what it was. I allowed my back to relax against the back cushion of the navy blue contemporary sofa and closed my eyes for a moment. Maybe if I took a quick nap, the aching would subside, and I could continue with my day. Dealing with my consuming thoughts of Xavier would require more than a quick nap. Opening my eyes, I reached for my reading glasses on the side table and began to glance through the file I had been holding. I carefully reviewed the new grant we were working on to acquire land and begin construction on a transition house.

A knock on my door caught me off guard. Up to this point, the events of my morning were hurried and rushed. Don't get me wrong, I was glad to help Mom and Mother Phillips out, but short of that, I didn't feel moved to bounce happily around the office.

"Hello. I'm looking for Monica Phillips," said a male voice. A gentleman peeked around my office door, which was slightly open. When all of him had stepped into the office, I realized at once that he was a fine specimen, tall, dark, and handsome. I knew that was such a cliché, but it was the God's honest truth.

I slowly removed my Fendi glasses and stood up casually. "I am Monica Phillips. And you are?" I stared at him, puzzled. My next appointment was at 2:00, and with a slight turn of my wrist, to see my watch, I saw it was only a little after one. I doubted very seriously if there was anyone in the city that would be that eager to mentor the children in our community.

"I'm Bryce Sinclair." He paused and waited for a response. When none came, he cleared his throat and continued. "You were supposed to meet with Jeffrey Donaldson from the 76ers business operations office."

Again, he paused and looked at me with one eyebrow raised. "The Philadelphia 76ers, the basketball team," he added.

"I'm familiar with the 76ers. I watch them play all the time, Mr. Sinclair. What I don't know is why Mr. Donaldson sent you when we have been discussing the program here at New Horizons Community Center and talked about how he was interested in volunteering as a mentor for our young men who are currently a part of the Kings Vision."

"Sorry, I'm not Mr. Donaldson. But he seemed to believe that I have a lot to offer these young men." This man, who had just introduced himself, and whom I didn't know from Adam, stood in the middle of my office and gave me a look of defiance that said he was somebody. I just didn't know who this somebody was.

I had put up a front all day and thought it time to revamp my attitude long enough to seem agreeable. "Well, Mr. Sinclair, since you're here, why don't you tell me a little about yourself."

I was a little affected by this unknown person, and I couldn't exactly come to grips with the fact that the one thing that stood out was how very good he looked. Yes, I was irritated that Mr. Donaldson hadn't taken the program seriously enough to at least inform me that he was sending someone else in his place. But if he had to send a substitute, I had to admit, if only to myself, this Bryce person was easy on the eyes.

I pointed him toward one of the plush navy and metallic gold Leighsford chairs, which complemented my navy Alli sofa. The spacious office reflected my taste and style perfectly. I'd been blown away when Xavier unveiled its contents to me a year ago. I had been delayed in getting started on the office decorating project after coming down with the flu. The community center was my brainchild, and I had spent every waking moment planning and decorating. I'd saved my office for last and had been more than upset when my physician advised me to stay in bed for a week. I knew the official opening wouldn't happen with me confined to the bed and hanging my head over the toilet. To my surprise, Xavier completed my to-do list and designed an office for me that reflected who I was and what I liked. I recalled thinking how deep our love must be if this man would add a unique splash of my identity, sprinkle it with class, and arrange everything stylishly to create the Monica Phillips suite.

"Mr. Sinclair, if you would take a seat, we can get started, and then you can be on your way," I said. He moved toward the chair, without taking his eyes off me. Maybe it was due to his professionalism, but it was making me nervous.

"Ms. Phillips, I haven't been in the area long, but I've heard wonderful things about the center and the church as well. It seems that what you guys are offering is just what South Philly needs." He sat across from me, seemingly at ease. His attire was casual, but yet it gave him an attractive appearance that couldn't be missed.

"Thank you so much for the compliment. We've worked very hard, and our pastor is such a visionary. It's not difficult to catch his excitement and go forth to make things happen. Are you from Philadelphia?" I turned slightly in my chair to mute the computer speakers.

"Actually, I'm not. I relocated here from North Carolina." His polished speech told me that Mr. Sinclair was obviously well educated. Maybe he worked in the public relations arena.

"Oh, I see. Since Mr. Donaldson sent you, I'm assuming you work in the 76ers' corporate office. How long have you been there?" I slid my chair back a little to open my desk drawer. Retrieving a black Cross ballpoint pen, I closed the drawer cautiously and began to write on the small legal pad in front of me.

He chuckled and then covered his mouth to shield his outburst of laughter. "I thought you said you were familiar with the 76ers?"

I was disturbed that he was laughing when I hadn't found anything funny. "Yes, I am, and the problem with that is?"

"I've only been their starting shooting guard all season. You obviously haven't caught a game lately." His outburst of laughter revealed cheeks that held a deep set of dimples. I also noticed that his teeth were terribly straight, and unless he'd been obsessed with dental hygiene from the time he had two front teeth, they could only be the result of years of braces.

"I have, but I guess I just missed you. Your name wasn't one I stored in my memory bank. Forgive me for not being that familiar with the team roster," I replied bluntly. "Now, could we conclude this meeting by you telling me why you are interested in mentoring with the Kings Vision program?" My cool attitude and bluntness didn't seem to rattle him, and his eyes continued to focus on me. He would not break eye contact and seemed to be amused at how jittery I was as I flipped from page to page and moved around in my chair.

"Why don't I have Donaldson send over my portfolio and some other pertinent details about me? You were not prepared to meet with me, and I feel that I have you at a major disadvantage." He smiled that full Colgate smile again and stood up slowly, towering over my desk.

I tilted my head back a little to take in all of him. "Well, that would give me a chance to review everything. My number one concern is whether what you have to offer will benefit the kids. I hope you understand that." I really didn't care whether or not he understood. I had already made up my mind that Bryce Sinclair was not going to be hanging around the community center in any capacity. And, for the record, the next time Xavier watched a 76ers game, I would do more than pass by the television en route to doing something that was actually interesting.

"Until I hear from you, Ms. Phillips, take care." He reached out his hand and swallowed my small left hand. As he grabbed it, I felt a slight jolt of electricity shoot through my hand.

I snatched my hand away quickly and cleared my throat to mask the disturbance, which might have been visible. "I'm sure you can find your way out. You have a good day, Mr. Sinclair. And please tell Mr. Donaldson that I will be contacting him."

I watched him depart and reached for my satchel to get a tissue to wipe my moist forehead. I couldn't understand what had just happened. Why in the heck was I sweating like a slave caught in the thick of the Georgia woods, attempting to get away. And why had he referred to me as Ms. Phillips? Didn't he know that I was leading lady Monica Phillips? I assumed that he knew that the pastor was none other than Xavier Phillips. The last names matched. What was he thinking? Then I glanced down at my left hand, which was still vibrating from the handshake, and remembered that I hadn't picked up my rings from Barsky Diamonds. In addition, my nameplate had only my simple married name, not my full hyphenated married name, which was usually a sign that a woman was married. I grabbed my cell phone, frantically hit a button to speed dial the number, and waited for someone to pick up. I needed to retrieve my 2.5-carat jewelry perfection so there would be no mistaking that I was indeed a married woman.

The minute I confirmed that my ring was ready, Nita came in, carrying a ton of bags. "I picked up our lunch and a couple of snacks for later," she said as she set the plastic bags on the nearby table and began to take everything out. "Oh, First Lady Phillips, guess who was in the parking lot?"

Before I could answer, she fired away. "Bryce Sinclair, one of the new players for the 76ers. He is sooo fine in person. I could only sit in my car while he got in his Mercedes sports car. Who was he here to see? I can't believe I saw him in the flesh. Wait till I tell my friends."

"He was here to meet with me," I said. I could understand her being consumed with his appearance. He was fine. I moved to the table and reached for a fry. It was hot, and I blew it a couple of times before placing it in my mouth. I usually tried to limit my intake of fast food, but the salty taste of the french fries was worth it, and the cheesesteak was going to be the indulgence I needed to pacify my mood.

"Get out! I can't believe he was actually in your office. I should have been here. Is he coming back again?" Nita walked over and got right in my face, obviously not wanting to miss a word I uttered regarding Sinclair.

"I don't believe so. Now go ahead and eat your lunch. I have a couple of projects for you to complete before we leave." I took a seat at the table, opened the tea, took a big sip, and tried to ignore Nita's visual hint that she wanted to stay put and question me about my recent visitor.

I giggled as I watched Nita hunch her shoulders, grab her part of our lunchtime bounty, and go out the door and down the hallway. I'm sure she had already mentally picked out an outfit for Bryce Sinclair's return visit to New Horizons Community Center. Not wanting to think of him a minute longer, I walked over to my desk, picked up the phone, and dialed Xavier's direct line. The sound of his rich, deep voice was matrimonial music to my ears. "Hey, handsome. How is your day going?"

"Busy," he stated in a matter-of-fact voice.

"What do you say we go out to dinner tonight? I was thinking we could leave straight from here around six, drop my car off at home, and go to Sullivan's. We haven't been there in a while."

"I can't. The community ministers' monthly meeting is tonight at six. You know how those folk go on and on. I probably won't be home until after ten. Why don't you grab something to eat from around the corner and sit in on the couples' Bible study? I'm curious to know how it is going and just haven't had a chance to check it out yet. It would be good for one of us to show our support for this new group."

"The operative word there, Xavier, is 'couples.' Wouldn't it be better if we planned a time when we could go together? You know, as a couple." I was getting irritated and wished I hadn't called at all.

"You may have a point. But I'm sure there is something else going on over here that you may want to check out." I could hear him flipping papers, as if our conversation wasn't of the utmost importance, and to add insult to injury, he kept talking to himself under his breath.

"I'll see what else is going on. If nothing else is happening, I'll drop by the couples' Bible study and check it out for you. How many wifey brownie points will that earn me?" I rocked back in my chair and closed my eyes to get a visual of the man that was my world. I could have been insulted at Xavier for planning my evening, but I knew he couldn't be everywhere at the same time, so I often had to be his clone. It made me feel good that he trusted me to be his eyes, ears and the second face of the ministry. While he was acting out of character, I knew he had spread himself too thin. I'd just do more to lighten his load and in no time things would be back to normal.

"Major brownie points. Monica, I'll have to finish this conversation later; Patrick is blowing my cell phone up."

Before I could respond, he had disconnected our call. I felt uneasy and my stomach did a flip. "God, I should have had a salad. Those fried onions have turned my stomach upside down," I whispered to no one. It was much more than an upset stomach. This intense, troublesome feeling had lasted for the past two months and it had to go. I had no intention of making it a trinity offering.

Chapter 5

"So, tell me hubby, how was your day?" I asked as I brushed my hair back, held it loosely in my right hand, and placed the elastic band I had been holding around it. My regular routine of wrapping my hair and putting a satin scarf on was not going to work for the image I wanted to create for Xavier tonight. Although I often coordinated my silk scarves with my nighttime attire, I wanted him to be free to run his fingers through my freshly relaxed, silky tresses.

Weeks had gone by since I'd had dinner with Auntie Zee and Trina. Adding their theory to that of my parents, what they came up with was a very busy, overwhelmed, and stressed Xavier. I was inclined to believe them because they always dished up a helping of advice with love, consideration, and concern. It was also easier to believe that this was the case, and that I wasn't dealing with a cheating husband or one that just wasn't in love with me anymore.

The one thing that I had admitted, the morning I had breakfast with my parents, was that my husband hadn't been the same in months. That was such a hard pill to swallow. It was easier to believe that it was an overnight change, but the bitter truth was that a chain of actions had brought Xavier and me to our current state. It stung. More than that, it hurt, and all I had been doing was pretending that things were the way they'd always been. I hadn't bothered to ask him what was going on or to suggest that there was a problem. Like so many other sweet, submissive wives of pastors, I had become a member of the "don't ask, don't tell" society. Who would have thought that I, Monica Phillips, would play by someone else's rules and deny that the music had changed, and that I was too naïve to find out why.

I did one more mirror check to ensure that I looked delectable from every angle in my hot pink satin flyaway baby doll nightie with matching panties. The only thing holding the nightie together over my ample breasts was a satin ribbon bow. I moved gracefully toward the bed, noticing that Xavier's eyes were no longer on the book he was holding, but on me. He had positioned himself in the burgundy wing chair, which accentuated the regal hues of burgundy, gold, and ivory throughout our spacious bedroom suite. The sitting area where Xavier relaxed was surrounded by glass on both the east and west sides, and overhead were skylights. His muscular body was slumped slightly in the chair, and he wore only a pair of striped navy and green lounging pants and a white, sleeveless, ribbed T-shirt that didn't completely conceal his hairy chest and strained against the rippled muscles of his shoulder.

A hint of warm vanilla sugar hung in the air and followed me across the room. It was my preferred nighttime fragrance because it wasn't heavy or overpowering. Regular visits to Bath & Body Works kept me well supplied, and every now and then, I would add a couple of other fragrances, not wanting my aroma to be too predictable. Of course, my daytime stuff was more upscale and pricy, and I spent much too much on most of it, but it wasn't often, so I felt justified.

I waited for an answer. "Baby, did you hear me? I was asking how your day was."

"Oh, I'm sorry, Monica. My mind was miles away." He rose to his feet and placed the book he was reading on the nearby accent table.

"I wasn't expecting you to say your mind was miles away. What I saw was that your eyes were on me, and I figured that your mind was here as well." I turned my back on him and pulled the duvet back and then the matching sheet.

"I was looking at you. It's just that I was thinking about all the things that I have to complete before the end of the month," he said.

"So, looking at me reminds you of your workload. I don't exactly get that, but, hey, whatever." I sat on the bed and waited for him to join me.

"Monica, I'm sorry." He walked toward me and sat beside me and took my hand. "I've been running around lately like a chicken with its head cut off, and it seems the more I run, the more stuff I have to get done."

If he was fishing for some sympathy, it wasn't going to be easy to get. Not after the way he had been treating me. "Oh." That was the only thing I could say, the only thing I wanted to say.

"I've been difficult, and you haven't said a word." Xavier squeezed my hand and pulled it to him slightly. "It'll get better. Just hang in there with me."

I could only look at him. It seemed that the words he really wanted to say had trailed off in another direction and left these few to make sense of the last six months.

How could they? This black man must have bumped his head while he was in the spirit, because it just wasn't enough.

Without saying another word, he began to kiss me. At first, I felt no heat, no rise in my body temperature, and then suddenly, I felt something stir deep down in the pit of my stomach. Not in the area of choice, but at least something stirred. Xavier pulled the satin bow of my baby doll nightie, and it fell open, revealing my breasts. He stopped kissing me long enough to look down at them, as if he were seeing them for the first time. He reached for them with both hands and massaged them a little rougher than I was used to. Licking his lips, he kissed me deeper than before, and I listened as his breathing became heavy, with a panting I hadn't heard in forever. The next thing I knew, Xavier was removing what was left of my sexy lingerie and turning me over. He removed his T-shirt and then his lounging pants. Mere seconds passed before he pulled me to a kneeling position and moved in behind me. I gulped in a big breath, surprised at the way he was handling me. My usual sweet, passionate lover was totally out of sexual character with this art of seduction. I wasn't sure if I should complain.

It was over almost before it began. Xavier hardly had enough energy to move away from my kneeling body, collapsing the minute I crawled to his side of the bed and pulled the sheet over my moist body. I wanted to shower and allow the hot, steamy water to awaken me from my present state of mind, but Xavier threw his arm over my back and whispered, "I love you, Monica. You should know I love you."

What timing. His discernment must have kicked in, because I was wondering if there was a fiber or a remnant of something that resembled love. That was a crazy thought, though. I knew that Xavier loved me, and I'd been acting insane by questioning his feelings. "I love you, Xavier." With that, I closed my eyes and allowed the ache between my legs to join company with the unknown ache I felt deep inside.

I sipped the chilled grape juice from the crystal flute and flipped through the pages of last month's *Cosmopolitan* magazine while I waited for my full-body aromatherapy massage with Suzy. I wore the spa's customary gold-monogrammed fluffy white cotton robe, with only my undies underneath and a pair of white slippers on my feet. This was a much-needed treat. The first thing I'd done when I rolled out of bed, and noticed that it was after ten o'clock, was call Suzy at home and make an emergency appointment. It was good to have not only the spa number but her home number on speed dial. Times like these required that my muscles be massaged, my nerves stimulated, and my tension knots rubbed, until I felt myself on the edge of an orgasm. Normally, I would have felt guilty about spending money on something that Xavier would consider unnecessary, but he couldn't deny that there was some therapeutic benefit to going periodically. I would use my credit card and worry about explaining the impromptu visit when the billing statement arrived in the mail next month. If I timed it just right, I could intercept the bill and make the payment before Xavier had a chance to go through all of the bills. The fact that I was disciplined enough to pay it before it was due and give him one less statement to look over meant I would avoid a lecture about spending without his approval.

Suzy came bouncing into the waiting area and spoke her hard-to-understand, broken English. She was from Sweden and was loving the heck out of being in the United States. She had even caught jungle fever and was the live-in bunny of one of the guys who owned the Jamaican restaurant around the corner from the church. Once the door was closed behind us in the dimly lit room, which smelled of eucalyptus, lavender, and sandalwood, we exchanged pleasantries.

My massage therapist left the room long enough for me to remove the robe and slippers and slip under the sheet, with my face against the specially designed pillow, which allowed me to see the floor. I waited a few minutes for her to reunite with me in the room.

"Come on over here, Ms. Thang, and let me get your body feeling nice, yeah?" Suzy pulled the sheet down slightly and began to work her magic. I lay there patiently and prepared myself to take an hour-long out-of-body tour to someplace where I could be completely me.

When I walked out of the spa, I was free of stress and had, as the Jamaicans would say, "no worries, mon." I felt like I was walking on cloud nine. I hummed a tune as I exited the day spa and decided to forego the community center and head back home. Reaffirming my decision to stay on this side of town, I reached in my purse and pulled out my pocket planner. I went to the May tab and flipped to today's date. There it was in ink. The missionary meeting was being held in the community center boardroom at 1:30 p.m. The president and vice president were none other than my good friends, sisters Sadie and Hilda. I would have wagered all the money in my wallet that they would drop by my office, park their brooms in the hallway, and bombard me with their unwanted presence. I saw no need to waste the residue of pleasure from my good massage on the likes of those two ingrates.

With that quick conclusion, I put my key in the ignition, pulled the gearshift into drive, maneuvered out of the day spa parking lot, and waited until some kind motorist allowed me to pull in front and merge with the midday traffic. Yes, home would serve as a wonderful afternoon reprieve. Maybe I would have enough time to surprise Xavier with a roast, complete with all the fixings.

Chapter 6

I rushed through the lobby, toward the women's rest-room, speaking and nodding my head without slowing down for any real conversation. I could have easily jour-neyed back through the administrative wing of the church, but I didn't want to encounter Pastor Garrett and Xavier. Pastor Garrett was going to be the guest speaker for the morning service. Every now and then, Xavier invited someone in to speak. It gave him a break and allowed the congregation to hear a fresh and new voice. Pastor Garrett was flirtatiously fresh, but he wasn't new to the church. He spent more time at New Horizons than he did at his church up the street, which had a membership of two hundred people, maybe. What had started out as a large congregation had dwindled to nothing by the time he'd bedded half the women in the church and seduced the other half, either verbally or with his eyes. Pastor Garrett was a piece of work; that was for darn sure. But, for some reason, when Xavier consulted with the deacons to see who they wanted as a guest speaker, the unanimous vote was: other pastors, 0; Pastor Garrett, 12. I knew why. Birds of a feather always,

always flock together. New Horizons had its share of
bow wows, and as sad as it was to say, most of them sat
in the deacons' stand, all pimped out. Let me tell you,
they sat there like their stuff didn't stink, sporting Stacy
Adams from head to toe, their gold teeth sparkling, their
diamond signet pinky rings catching every eye, and
their lips dripping lust with every mack line they put
down. Who could overlook the senior deacons, who
always stood in the vestibule, plastic tag pinned in
place, identifying their post in bold white letters. And
there they stood, patting their pockets every time a
young tenderonie slowed in their path. This was their
signature move to let the ladies know that they had a
little bank and plenty of Viagra on standby.

Just as I was about to push the restroom door open,
someone called out my name. "Ms. Phillips."

Can I just get to the bathroom? I asked myself silently.
I didn't dare speak out loud for fear of offending the
person who obviously needed my immediate attention.
All I wanted was to change my overpriced off-black
panty hose, which had a major run from the thigh, past
my knee, and all the way down to my ankle. You would
think at ten dollars a pair, they wouldn't run so easily. I
had every intention of driving downtown to Josie's Boutique tomorrow and getting my money back. That lying
heifer had assured me they would not only look good on
my copper brown, well-defined legs, but that I could
stretch them every which way and still have them cling
flawlessly to my legs. I had been hustled, bamboozled,
deceived, and hoodwinked, and she could just forget
about me returning to her little, cluttered hole-in-the-
wall establishment to buy a pair of edible underwear
with angel's wings right in the middle of the tunnel of
love. I would get over the bad purchase, but not before I

informed Mrs. Epps to forewarn everyone she knew. She would put the news on her crier list and go forth and do what she did best, spread the news.

Thank God, I was always prepared for wardrobe emergencies and had sent Nita to the small corner of the church that had been dubbed my quiet place. It wasn't much, but I guess, I should have been grateful. I was sure there were many first ladies that didn't have their own offices or areas of rest to take a reprieve from the hectic stuff that sometimes occurred around the church. The minute Nita turned the corner, I grabbed the stockings and was on my way before someone spied my below-the-knee disaster. A quick look had let me know that it was worse above the knee, but thankfully, my skirt fell slightly below my knee. My intention was to change the panty hose and make it back to my seat before Xavier entered the sanctuary with Samson's partner, Patrick.

"Ms. Phillips. It's great to see you again." Bryce Sinclair stood in front of me, with a sharp black suit that I was sure came from one of the top designers. He had accented it with a sea foam green, French cuff shirt and contrasting tie in green and burgundy, with small squares of brown. I never knew those colors could look so good together, but the tie stood out, and I couldn't take my eyes off of it or him.

"Mr. Sinclair, what an unexpected pleasure." I smiled smugly. His presence was unexpected; however, the word *pleasure* was pushing the envelope just a little.

"I'm sure you are thrilled to see me. Did you forget all about contacting me regarding the mentoring program? I enclosed my number with the portfolio I sent over." He tapped his forehead with his fingertip. "Somehow I must have missed your call." He played well at the game of sarcasm, and here I'd thought I was the master of it. I was not usually competitive, but with him, I wanted to give as well as I got.

"I keep up with and stay on top of things that are important to me or that serve to better the community center. Let's review the facts. You had your package delivered via courier; it's been a couple of weeks, and you haven't received a call or a request to come in to discuss a plan. I would say that brings you back to 'I'll be in touch.' Good-bye, Mr. Sinclair. If you are planning to stay for the service, I hope you are blessed by the message."

Just as I was getting ready to turn and enter the restroom, he touched my elbow lightly. "I hate to tell you this, but you have a serious run in your panty hose." His eyes followed mine down to my lower leg, where the run disappeared into my shoe.

"Aren't you quite the observer? I was on my way to change them when you interrupted me. But thank you for alerting me of my fashion mishap." He stood there grinning at me, and I felt like I should give him a treat for being so observant. "You may want to go on in and get a good seat. The sanctuary tends to fill up pretty quickly."

This time I dared not reach to open the restroom door. Instead, I stood at the door and watched the usher hand him a program, a tithing envelope, and a fan. Equipped with the church necessities, he glanced toward me one last time and went through the opened door, toward the sanctuary.

Him again, I thought. I really hadn't planned on seeing him again. To ensure that a chance meeting wouldn't occur, I had called Mr. Donaldson, and after giving him a piece of my mind, I'd told him that Mr. Sinclair didn't seem to be what we were looking for.

Yakking on and on, I'd told him that a basketball player wouldn't really enhance the program, since the kids would be too caught up with who he was and what he did, instead of learning the qualities that we felt were important to our program. After that, I prayed that Donaldson wouldn't share our conversation with anyone, for fear that it would get back to my husband. And now, today, of all days, in stepped Mr. Sinclair, who could very well tell Xavier that I had turned him down flat. Oh well. I wasn't going to worry about it now. There were more pressing things for me to worry about, like changing my panty hose and taking my seat before the service began. I didn't mind making an entrance, but today I was more concerned with keeping Bryce Sinclair in sight at all times. He would not get a chance to get close to Xavier, if I had to run interference all morning.

The minute I took my seat, one of the ushers handed me a note. I opened the small slip of white paper and read the contents once and then once more to confirm what was written. I turned to the usher and asked, with one eyebrow raised, "Who sent me this note?"

"The new lady in the choir. I believe her name is Leslye." She looked toward the back of the church, where the choir members were assembling to take their stroll up to the choir stand.

"Give this note right back and tell her that her first lady says to be about the business of singing God's praises." I handed the note back, glanced over my shoulder, and caught Leslye's eye. She was all teeth until she noticed that my look was stern, with no hint of a smile. I couldn't believe she was asking me to give her phone number to Bryce Sinclair. Obviously, she'd seen me talking with him in the vestibule and wanted to put her bid in early. The nerve of that hot heifer. If she was that bold, Bryce Sinclair's appearance here was sure to affect the other single women, too. *Wait a minute*, I thought. As good as he looked and as rich as I was sure he was, every woman in the church, married, engaged, or single, would be looking his way. Heck, he was so fine, he could make a lesbian change her mind.

After Xavier had served the benediction, I didn't wait for him to come to me but quickened my steps to meet him at the altar.

"Monica. This is a switch. I usually have to make my way over to you." Xavier chuckled and reached for my free hand.

"I thought I would try something different today. Maybe if we get to the back sooner, you can hit the shower and leave at a decent time." I hoped my facial expression matched the story I was telling. I did, of course, want to get home at a decent time, but I also needed to keep Bryce away from my husband.

My neck was sore from whipping it first one way, then another. So far I hadn't seen him. Maybe he had already left the sanctuary. The minute the thought entered and rested in my head, Deacon Thomas, with his short-of-breath self, walked toward us, with Bryce at his side. Deacon Thomas was laughing, with his hand on his oversized belly, like he was Santa Claus. "Reverend Phillips, I want you to meet the newest addition to the 76ers. I just know you saw him sitting over there near the back, all tall and athletic-looking," said Deacon Thomas.

Xavier held out his left hand to Bryce. "Hello. I'm Pastor Xavier Phillips. It's so nice to have you join us. Did you enjoy your worship experience?"

Bryce flashed a big smile and shook Xavier's hand. "I did indeed. I was hoping to hear you preach, but I received the message, nevertheless. I'll just have to come back another Sunday to get a good word from the pastor of New Horizons." He looked in my direction when mentioning that he would be back again. I wanted to interrupt them and say, "Absolutely, positively not."

"Of course, you are welcome anytime," said Xavier. "I'm sorry. Allow me to introduce the first lady of New Horizons, Monica Phillips." Xavier moved slightly so that I could move forward and extend a greeting to Bryce, but I stood in place and watched his shocked expression.

"Oh. Well, I met your wife a couple of weeks ago," said Bryce. He continued to look at me with a perplexed look on his face. I even noticed a frown of sorts and looked at both Deacon Thomas and Xavier. Neither of them seemed privy to what I saw.

"Yes, Pastor Phillips. I had the pleasure of meeting Bryce Sinclair at the community center a little while ago," I said. "I believe Mr. Donaldson sent him over. Obviously, there was some mix-up. Mr. Sinclair is much too busy to be interested in mentoring the boys in the Kings Vision Program." I stumbled over my words, trying to put a story together quickly. "There is probably another area that would be better suited. You know, those boys would be all up on Mr. Sinclair, and not for the right reasons."

"To the contrary, Monica, I think Bryce would be just fine." Xavier turned to Bryce and said, "Can I call you Bryce?"

"Sure," Bryce answered.

Xaiver went on. "Bryce is exactly what the boys need to inspire them to reach for greater things. He would bring a presence to the center that is sorely needed. We are doing good things there, and Bryce can bring more boys out and turn some young lives around." Xavier smiled broadly.

"Thanks so much for that vote of confidence," replied Bryce. "I mentioned to your wife that I am sure I can offer the young men a little insight and assist them in some positive ways. I'd even be willing to fund a couple of projects if you'd accept my assistance."

Before Xavier could speak, Deacon Thomas interjected, "Pastor Phillips, please allow me to mention that one of the trustees slipped me a note informing me that Brother Sinclair here made a sizable donation this morning and earmarked it for the community center." Deacon Thomas leaned back and rubbed his belly again. "Hallelujah anyhow!"

"What a blessing that is, Bryce. Well, I tell you, call Monica this week, at your convenience, of course, and arrange a time when you can come down. I'll personally sit in on the meeting, and we can get the ball rolling," Xavier stated, without even giving me a sideward glance.

"That would be great, Pastor Phillips," said Bryce. "I'll be going now. I have an early dinner engagement. It was nice meeting you, Pastor Phillips and Deacon Thomas." He extended his hand and ended up being embraced by both men as if they had known each other for a lifetime. "And you, First Lady Phillips. It was nice meeting you again, and I look forward to working with you." He reached for my hand, and only because all six eyes were on me, I obliged. The same familiar sensation shot through my arm and into my shoulder blade. I had to grin and endure it or risk alerting them that this man I had met only days before was getting under my skin and not in a bad way. I sent myself a mental reminder that I was the first lady and should not—I repeat, should not—be aroused by anyone other than my husband.

That's what I told myself as I shook hands and smiled as church members filed out of church. It's what I told myself when I told Xavier I needed a few minutes of private time and made my way to the prayer room. Closing the door behind me, I kneeled at the altar—draped with purple—and sighed. I needed a divine intervention and I needed my husband in the worst way.

Chapter 7

Overcast skies hung densely in the air as I pulled away from the church. The paved roadways still held pockets of water from the overnight rain. It had been a long day, and I was more than anxious to get home. Flipping down the sun visor, I opened the lighted mirror to catch a quick glimpse of myself. I had taken great care in my morning ritual of getting ready, and now my mirrored image wore the affairs of the day like a heavy cloak that provided a shield but did nothing to ease the wear my body felt. We had had less than an hour between services since the early morning manna worship experience went over.

Rev. Garrett wooed the congregation, and no one saw through his well-delivered sermon and glimpsed his real identity, a designer suit–wearing gigolo preacher. It didn't take much for our crew. They'd shout, holla, and speak in tongue at any semblance of good Jesus. I thought the floorboards would come up, people were shouting so hard. A couple of ladies across the aisle from me appeared to be getting their praise on in a different way. One would shout for a minute, then tap the other to pick up where she had left off. I watched in surprise as they kept it going for more than ten minutes. I wondered if the spirit was really upon them, but who was to say. All I knew was that I had spotted that phony Rev. Patrick Garrett a mile away years ago, and I wasn't about to sweat out my upswept do or scrape the heels of my beige Vera Wang pumps by physically endorsing the church hype he had created.

Without warning the event from the morning service crept up on me. I blinked as if I were a genie trying to make it go away. Seeing Bryce again had unnerved me, and the handshake had caught me by surprise yet again. What was it about him that made me jump like a Mexican jumping bean every time he came around? It just wasn't normal, and for the past five years, everything about my life had been normal and predictable.

Just as I was turning into our well-manicured and landscaped estate entrance, my stomach began doing mini flips. I did a quick U-turn and headed toward Trina's house. Hitting the dial button, I waited for Xavier to pick up.

"Hey, honey, I've got to swing by Trina's to pick up something." I had been listening to my DeWayne Woods CD ever since I'd left the church, and I reached to turn the volume down so I could hear his response.

"Well, you need to hurry it up. I invited deacons Thomas and Harvey and their wives for dinner. We need to start planning the summer retreat, and I was thinking we could brainstorm and get some ideas together." I heard a horn blow in the background, and Xavier mumbled, "Thank you, Jesus." Usually, I would have asked, but I assumed that God had spared his life yet again. "Where was I? Oh yeah, did you make dessert? You know they will be expecting one of your homemade desserts, especially Deacon Thomas."

"Yes, I made a German chocolate cake." He knew I always made dessert on Sunday, so why ask the question? I tapped my manicured french tip fingernail methodically against the steering wheel and mentally took hold of my sanity. "I will have to figure out something for dinner. I stuffed some pork chops, but I know we don't have enough for six people."

I counted down from ten and listened while he went on and on about preparation and always being ready for the unexpected. I interrupted his lecture, which I usually never did, saying, "Xavier, I'll see you at the house."

I clicked the device off and felt like screaming. Having a second thought, I hit another button, turning it off altogether. Knowing Xavier, he would call me several more times to ask me to do one more thing. I was six minutes from calling him as a stranger, and God knows, he was getting on my last African American nerve.

I steered my truck to the curb, put my foot on the brake, and hastily put the gearshift in park. With the engine still running, I leaned my head back and covered my face with both hands. How was I supposed to stretch my dinner menu to include his posse in this short span of time? I was so upset and hurt at the same time. Xavier was always impulsive, but this was a little much. Angry tears rolled down my cheeks, and I inhaled and exhaled a few short times and attempted to pull myself together. I could not let this get me down. I didn't understand it, but I was determined to keep my head.

I turned the phone back on and hit Trina up on speed dial. "Hey girl, whatcha doing?"

"Nothing. I thought you were coming by," Trina stated.

"I was, but Xavier invited a bunch of people over, and I've got to do some major additions to pull dinner off." I forced myself to sound positive about my dinner guests. "But I'll be over tomorrow to pick up the vase. I can't believe you found it."

"Well, believe it. I searched every shop in New York until I located it. I can't wait until you lay eyes on it. It looks better in person. I must say, you have excellent taste."

"I surround myself with beautiful and nice things, and that includes you." I tried to smile because I knew she was smiling on the other end.

"Okay. Well, do you need me to do something? I'd be glad to come over and help you. I don't have anything planned until later this evening." Trina was such a good friend, always willing to help me with anything and everything.

"Nah, girl, you just have a good evening, and I'll see you tomorrow. Kiss, kiss." I ended the call and again clicked the phone completely off.

"Wait a minute, Monica. Why are you letting Xavier control everything? Actually, when I think about it, he's changing and altering things, basically calling all the shots. You've just been going along with the program." I could hear her suck air through her teeth. "This just isn't you."

"I can't talk about it right now, Trina. We can talk about it later. I already feel bad enough."

"You need to put his big butt in check," Trina mouthed off. That was why I didn't share everything with her; she knew no boundaries when it came to voicing her opinion.

"Well, that butt belongs to me and I'll deal with him."
I ended the call and again clicked the phone completely
off. Trina had just joined Xavier on the list of unwanted
callers for the day.

Reaching into the console, I pulled out a tissue and
quickly wiped it across my cheeks, then tucked a strand of
hair, which was hanging loose across my eye, behind my
ear. Not wanting to waste any more time, I shifted the truck
back into drive and set out in the direction of Warmdaddy's,
mentally pulling together the dishes I'd need to make our
Sunday dinner complete. A quick call to them would have
everything hot, packaged, and ready to go.

I'd think of a way to open up to Xavier in hopes that
he would assuage all my doubts. We needed to work to
get things back on track. There had to be a solution, and
I'm sure that Xavier wanted to find it as much as I did.
I believed that. I had to believe that.

Chapter 8

I crawled around on hands and knees, crammed into the display case. I moved around, trying to put up the display. We were displaying the talents of the kids in the cultural arts program. There were many who were talented and didn't realize their potential. No one had bothered to tell them that they could be somebody and go someplace. That was where the community center came in. We had taken it upon ourselves to bridge the gap and do what many parents either couldn't or wouldn't do.

My back was to the display opening when Nita interrupted my flow. It had taken a while to get started, but now I was moving around in the small, closed area, glad that I was almost finished. "First Lady Phillips. You have a visitor." Her usual high-pitched voice seemed to be dancing with excitement. I assumed she was getting ready to laugh at my awkward position.

"Who is it, Nita?" I asked, irritated because I couldn't get the double-sided tape off my fingers, and now I was pulling to try to get my hand untaped from the floor of the display case.

"First Lady Phillips, Mr. Bryce Sinclair needs to speak with you." She started giggling and jumping up and down.

"What? Where?" I backed up a little too far and hit my butt against the glass door. "Darn. Girl, help me get out of here." I had gotten myself stuck in the case, and all of a sudden, I felt claustrophobic.

"Allow me," said Bryce as he moved the nearby chair closer to the front of the display case and guided my feet until they hit the seat of the chair. "Okay. Now stand up slowly, and I will steady your legs so you don't lose your footing."

Once I was safely standing on the chair, I felt foolish for having needed assistance to get out of the jam I'd been in. "Thanks. I appreciate your assistance," I said.

I know it wasn't a romantic gesture, but it rendered me weak, and when my feet finally hit the floor, they were wobbly. There had to be something wicked about this man. At his slightest touch, my body reacted as if it suddenly had a will to do what he desired it to do. *Somebody in his tree must throw bones for a hobby and play with hair and pieces of clothing to cast spells*, I thought. I didn't partake in any practice, but I knew that witchcraft was real, if for no other reason than the Bible saying so.

"Are you okay?" asked Bryce. "That was a tight area to work in. You probably need to take a few minutes and get yourself together before you start to walk." Bryce stood in front of me, with a concerned look on his face.

"I'll be just fine," I said. I noticed that Nita had not left my side, and instead of offering me support and ensuring that I was okay, she stared at Bryce without blinking. If it wasn't for her chest rising and falling noticeably, I wouldn't have been sure she was breathing. "Nita, sweetheart, are you okay?"

"Yep, I think I'm okay." She held her hand over her heart and swallowed hard. "I know who you are." She pointed at Bryce with one shaky finger.

"You do?" he said and smiled. "Well, I'm glad that you recognize me. I was in Ms., excuse me, Mrs. Phillips's office a while ago, and she didn't have a clue who I am. So I'm flattered that you recognize me."

"I sure do. My friends aren't going to believe that I was close enough to smell your cologne," replied Nita. "Oh, my God. Nobody is going to believe that you talked to me." She was still holding her hand over her heart.

"Well, young lady, you will probably be seeing a lot of me around here," said Bryce. "I'm going to help out with the Kings Vision program. So, you might want to tell me your name."

"Nita. You can just call me Nita. Or if you don't like Nita, you can call me whatever you like. You know what I mean. Well, you probably don't know, but I'm just hoping you do."

"Nita, girl, stop going on and on. Go over to the church, and get the rest of the prints from Mrs. Epps," I said. "I thought she would have been back by now, but obviously, there is some juicy gossip over there she is trying to get."

"No problem," said Nita. She continued to stand in the same position and didn't budge one muscle to move.

"Nita?" I said. I raised an eyebrow, hoping she would catch the hint and allow herself to come out of the trance.

"Oh, I gotcha," she finally said. She blinked a few times and laughed nervously. "It was nice meeting you,

Mr. Sinclair. If you're still here when I return, do you think I could get your autograph? And maybe take a photo with you? Or do you think you could ride around the corner in my car so my friends can see us together? Or better yet, I could ride in your car, with the window down."

"Nita!" I cried. I was too done with this girl. She was acting like she had fallen and bumped her head and got it stuck on stupid.

"I'm gone," she said as she turned around and bumped into the chair, almost falling over. Bryce reached out quickly and caught her before she tumbled to the floor in a heap.

"Oh my God. He touched me. First Lady Phillips, he touched me," whispered Nita. She ran out the door, saying it over and over again. I guess I would have acted the same way if I had had the opportunity to meet someone up close and personal who just happened to be a well-known athlete I admired.

It had been a couple of weeks since he'd showed up at the church. And that long since Xavier and I had had a heart-to-heart conversation. Although it had been one-sided, I felt a lot better. Most of what he'd said went in one ear and out the other, because I was emotionally blinded by being put off, but what I hadn't heard lately, and wasn't totally convinced about, was his love for me. So once he said those words, nothing else really mattered. As long as Xavier still loved me, I felt that all the other stuff could be weathered like a storm.

"I'm sorry I haven't had a chance to come by until now," said Bryce. He was dressed in a 76ers T-shirt, matching shorts and some type of midcut white Nikes. A gold tone watch fit snugly on his wrist and looked very similar to a Rolex. In fact, a closer inspection told me that the diamond accented watch was definitely a Rolex. I wasn't surprised in the least bit. That was how many of the big-name athletes got down. They spent more money on their wardrobe and jewelry than third-world countries spent to feed their hungry.

"I wasn't exactly sitting around waiting for a call." God, how I had prayed that he would change his mind. I had even fasted one afternoon to plead with God for a little favor in this situation. And here he was. My direct line must have a flaw, and I was going to sit down and make sure things were in order 'cause my reception wasn't as clear as it usually was.

My leather mules made a clicking noise across the tiled lobby of the community center. The floor was buffed to perfection, and you could see it glistened like water in a pool. The ladies that cleaned the building and the church were a one-of-a-kind group. And no one ever heard a complaint about their work. I was always pleased, and because I was someone that they liked, they would often leave homemade goodies on my desk or other small tokens. Everyone knew I was into antiques and collectibles, so whenever they saw something that they thought I would like, it ended up on my desk—and from there, in my house, where I would proudly display it on a shelf.

Bryce followed me to my office, walking slightly behind me and responding only with a nod. I hoped he wasn't looking at my back asset, because I would have been too upset. Wait a minute. Maybe I would have been a little upset and a whole lot flattered.

Once I walked into my office, I turned around and extended a hand toward one of the chairs that sat opposite my desk chair. "Now, Mr. Sinclair, why are you here again today?"

"Why didn't you tell me you were married?" He looked straight at me, like he had just posed a question about the weather or had asked what time it was.

"What?" I snapped. This man was a piece of work. Why should I have told him anything? The first time he showed up at my office, he didn't ask my marital status, and I didn't go around broadcasting it. I didn't have to. Everyone in the Philadelphia, New Jersey, New York, and Delaware church circuits knew that I was the wife of Pastor Xavier Phillips. And in this area, our faces were plastered on billboards, on flyers posted on barber and beauty shop walls, and at several local fast-food eateries. Xavier wore me like a person wears their favorite piece of jewelry they want everyone to notice.

"I walked into your office that day, and I didn't see a ring, your name wasn't hyphenated, and on top of that, you were listening to Heather Headley. Now, correct me if I'm wrong, 'cause my traveling prevents me from making it to church on a regular basis, but I don't think Heather is the first ladies' anthem these days." He leaned back in the chair and waited for my reply.

"I'm only going to tell you what I'm about to tell you because after today I want us to keep our personal lives personal. Now, according to Pastor Phillips, I have to work with you. The business part of me can handle that, but for the record, I'm not all that impressed. Everyone else seems to be falling all over you because you are a hotshot ballplayer with a little bank, and that's all fine, dandy, and swell, but at the end of the day, you are just a man, and a very vain one at that. You put one leg at a time in your pants just like everyone else, and because you are that species, I'm sure you don't even put the toilet seat down after you piss. Am I warm, or do you want me to keep striking?"

I stood near the side of my desk, with my hands on my hips, hoping I was close enough to get my point across and not so close that he could read through my verbal attack and see that I was a little impressed as well. I turned and took a position of safety behind my desk, just in case my legs decided to show signs of nervousness.

Bryce held his hand up in the air and examined his manicured nails. "So, how often do you take off your rings? I thought that wedding rings were physical symbols of love bestowed upon two beings."

"Look, I'm not going to spend my morning explaining anything to you. If I choose to take my rings off for whatever reason, it doesn't make me any less married. And my listening pleasure doesn't affect my spirituality. I'm free to embrace what I like as long as it doesn't degrade or hinder my spiritual being." I leaned forward in my chair and rested my hands on my desk, with my left hand on top. "You, like so many, have a stereotyped opinion about church folk, and as many of them are, you are wrong in your assumption."

"Oh, well, it seems I will be learning a lot from you, Mrs. Phillips. I'm going to really enjoy mentoring the boys, but I believe there will be a lot of other benefits. By the way, that is a very nice ring. If you had had that on the other day, there would have been no way I would have missed it." He continued to focus on my hand.

"I'm glad you like Xavier's selection of jewelry. I'll be sure to tell him that you complimented his taste. Back to our business." I paused long enough to let him know that we were switching gears, and as far as I was concerned, I wouldn't be switching back. "We have great plans for the Kings Vision Program. Our plan is for it to be much more than just a mentoring program, and our hope is that it will evolve into several developmental arenas."

"Well, Mrs. Phillips, I'm sure your ideas are great ones. But I met with Pastor Phillips and Deacon Thomas last week over lunch, and they have asked me to spearhead the program entirely. They mentioned that you would be a consultant and would be available to assist me in carrying out the plans I have for this new venture." His arrogant look remained intact.

"What? Pastor Phillips didn't mention that to me. Could you excuse me while I make a quick call?" Before he could respond, I was already out the door.

I ducked into the conference room and closed the door behind me just in case I had to raise my voice to the angry black woman level, which is the only level that demanded 100 percent attention. "Xavier, this is Monica."

"Monica, sweetheart, I think I know your voice by now." He started laughing. Ever since we had had a heart-to-heart a couple of weeks ago, things had improved some. They weren't back to the bliss I was used to, but I could see that he was really trying. He'd shared so much that night as we sat in the cedar wood swing on our large, spacious porch, holding hands. And as quickly as he opened up, he sealed himself off from me the very next day in some place that I didn't have access to. A man could become so driven that any threat to his not achieving his vision can submerge him in doubt, which can cause things to tumble into a catastrophic zone.

"Is there anything you forgot to tell me about Bryce Sinclair?" I pulled a chair out from the conference room table and plopped down. I crossed my legs and fumbled with the cuff of my white slacks.

"Oh, did he call you? I was meaning to talk to you about it." Xavier's voice didn't have its usual direct and assertive edge.

"Well, obviously not soon enough. Bryce is sitting in my office and just told me that he will be spearheading the Kings Vision Program. The same program that I have been developing since its inception. Imagine the irony in that, Xavier." I stood and began to pace the floor as far as the phone cord would allow. I couldn't believe Xavier would undercut me like this. His part in the daily running of the community center had always been minimal, and never, not even once, had he made a decision without consulting me, without seeking my approval.

"Please, Monica, let me explain. We thought it would be a good business move. Bryce has a lot to offer New Horizons, and we just wanted to position ourselves for any assistance he wants to extend to us."

"What you mean is, you are pimping the Kings Vision Program." I couldn't believe what I was hearing. This had to be more Deacon Thomas than Xavier. The Xavier I knew would never put money before the best interests of our programs. That was not to say Bryce couldn't contribute positively, but who was to say that his vision was in line with our vision? I would wager that Rev. Garrett had endorsed this decision. He was always one to be looking for a fat cow.

"I'm not pimping anything, Monica. This is in the best interest of the program, and I've looked over Bryce's portfolio and talked to a lot of people, and he is impressive. He has experience in mentoring and has done a lot of volunteer ventures with kids." He cleared his throat and continued. "Unlike many that don't give back, he is one of the brothers that has given back. He has put his money where his mouth is, and I really think he can help us out a lot."

"You are the pastor, and the ultimate say lies with you, so fine. I'll cooperate if that is what you want."

"Monica, listen. I know what is best for the church and the community center. You just need to relax and trust that Bryce's presence will be good for everyone."

"Fine. I'll talk to you later." I placed the phone back in the cradle and circled the conference room table to clear my head. They had their eyes on Bryce's money. I just couldn't believe Xavier was ringleader. Just when I had thought things were better, here came another twist. I would be spending a lot of time with Bryce. I wasn't about to let him go forth without my input.

Xavier had put me in the line of fire, and unless he did a 360, I would be an easy target.

Chapter 9

Xavier was running around our bedroom like he was the one getting ready to leave for a conference. I had my stuff together, and my Louis Vuitton luggage was packed with an array of outfits suitable for all of the occasions that would come up during my weeklong stay at the First Ladies Conference in Hampton.

"Xavier, stop and breathe," I said. I wanted to burst out laughing, but I knew that would only push him further to the edge, and he was already dangerously close. "I have everything I need. Everything coordinates. I've got plenty of bath gel and perfumes, so I will not only look good, but will smell good, too."

"You don't understand how important this event is."

"It's not all that you are making it out to be." I walked around him to get my lens case, which I'd left on the bathroom counter. "You are acting like this is my first conference."

"You didn't go to half the stuff they had last year. The sole purpose of the conference is for you wives to get together and network for us husbands. Most of the big-name pastors consult with their wives about who to invite to speak at their church conferences and other big events." He stood in front of the bathroom door, going on and on. "I need to get my name out there. You know how important this is for me, so please act like it."

I rolled my eyes and counted to ten as I walked past him. "I know that this is important to you. I'm just not the kind to grin and pretend. You have a name already. Bishops and pastors call you from all over the place to come and speak, to serve on a panel, or to motivate, so why are you tripping?" I felt like a preschooler. Every time I turned around, I was counting up and down to ten.

"Monica, just be mindful of the reason why you are there. That is all I'm asking."

"Okay, Xavier." I walked down the steps as I did a mental check. I knew I had everything, but now that Xavier was on my heels and ranting and raving, I was beginning to second-guess my extraordinary organiza-tion skills.

I flipped open my cell and hit the speed-dial button for Liz. I waited for her to answer as I got a juice glass from the cabinet, opened the refrigerator, and poured myself a glass of juice.

She answered, sounding like she was still asleep. "Hello."

"Liz, are you up yet?" I turned and was starting to sip my juice when I noticed that Xavier was standing on the other side of the breakfast nook, looking at the clock on the wall. I frowned at him.

"Yeah, I just finished packing. I'll be ready when you get here." She sounded like she had just muffled a yawn. "Why do you sound like you've been up for hours?"

"Because I have. Pastor Drill Sergeant Phillips got me up at four and has been on my back since then. If I hadn't drawn the line, I think he would have gotten in the shower and scrubbed me down just so I could get finished quicker." I started to laugh as I watched him point at the clock.

"I'll see you when you get here. You haven't had breakfast, have you?" Liz asked, but she probably already knew the answer.

"Girl, you know I don't have time for that. We can grab something on the road. If I were to act like I wanted to fry an egg in this house, Xavier would explode. I'll be there"—I glanced at the clock—"at quarter after six."

Xavier stood at the door as I was walking out. He had already loaded all my things in the truck. "Monica, remember why you are there. And all the names I mentioned to you."

"Xavier, I feel like you want me to go on display, a walking, talking billboard for you and for New Horizons." I turned to face him, expecting him to tell me I was wrong.

"That's exactly what you are. Don't leave that convention center without attending every function this time."

Finally in my vehicle and on my way to Liz's, I breathed a heavy sigh, leaned back and tried to relax. I couldn't believe how hyper Xavier was about this conference. Then again, I could. He was absolutely right. The conference really wasn't for us; it was a tool used for networking, and networking only. Those ladies were most concerned about the size of your congregation, how much money your husband was being paid, if he was in a PhD program, what size house you lived in, and what kind of car you parked in the conference center parking lot.

I didn't consider myself a round-the-way girl and I could be bourgeois, but I wasn't going to turn it on to appease anyone. Not even my husband. I wanted him to do well, which to him meant walking a tightrope and dealing with church propaganda. Xavier had changed so much. It seemed he was driven solely by popularity, which he conveniently labeled success in his ministry. He no longer gave credit where credit was due. Each well-delivered sermon was captured on CD and a DVD and placed in the hands of our parishioners for a price. This was done every Sunday, with a verbal encouragement to go out and let folks know about the good sermons they were receiving at New Horizons. There was no mention of sharing the gospel for the gospel's sake and reaching through the message. The stated focus was more about the messenger.

I had met with Bryce a few times since he informed me that he was taking the lead on the Kings Vision Program project. I still wasn't pleased to work with him, but it was for the community center, so I could get past how and why Xavier appointed him. This was just another reminder that things were out of sync and order needed to be reestablished, not only in our marriage, but in the affairs of the community center as well.

I remembered the signed documents on the edge of my desk that Bryce would need before I returned. I had stored his number in my cell just in case I should ever need to reach him. I clicked the numbers to reach him and thought I would just leave a message since it was still early and he was probably not awake. This last minute task would free me up to enjoy the conference as much as I could, considering I didn't really want to go.

"Hello." A groggy voice answered after the second ring.

"Bryce, this is First Lady Phillips. I'm sorry to be

calling so early and waking you up. I was hoping to get your answering machine."

"Good morning to you too. Sorry I picked up and denied you the opportunity to leave me a message." Even early in the morning there was a smart edge to his response.

"I'm sorry. Let me start again. Good morning. I'm on my way out of town for a conference, but the documents you needed me to sign are signed and on my desk. I left a message for Mrs. Epps, so if you give her a call she'll have them ready for you to pick up."

"Okay. Thanks. I didn't know you were going out of town."

"Yes." I wanted to ask what business it was of his, but I didn't even bother.

We stopped at Denny's to have breakfast when we got to Delaware. I had already received two calls from Xavier, telling me that we should simply stop at a convenience store and get some coffee and doughnuts and keep it moving. Conference check-in wasn't until 3:00, and according to my watch, the digital clock in the Lexus, and confirmation from Liz's watch, we were going to make it to Hampton by 1:00 p.m. I didn't know if two hours early was good enough for Xavier, but it was good enough for me.

We were seated in a booth near the front of the restaurant and handed two signature laminated Denny's menus.

The aroma of bacon, sausage, and coffee filled my nostrils; and my stomach growled as the smell reminded me I needed to eat. I perused the pages and tried to decide which entrée would appease my hunger and thoroughly satisfy my palate. I knew I had to have some coffee, the stronger the better. Coffee was an indulgence

I had to limit, because caffeine really did a job on me. But, as I thought about the drive ahead and glanced over the menu at my riding partner, I reasoned that I'd have to drink a couple of cups and suffer the consequences. For balance's sake, I'd have some orange juice and pray the small good would outweigh the bad.

"Can I get you ladies something to drink? If you've looked over the menu I can take your order now too." The server had returned with pen posed over the pad. She was an older lady who seemed tired, and her voice lacked the exuberant touch that should have been a pre-requisite for the job. But I reminded myself that I was at Denny's and not some five-star restaurant. Don't get me wrong, I'll eat a Denny's meal any day of the week, but if I had to work there my voice would have probably sounded very similar to our waitress.

I looked at Liz and she nodded to let me know that she was ready to order. "Well, I'll have coffee and a small orange juice. And let's see how about an Ultimate Omelette with hash browns and a blueberry muffin with extra butter." I closed the menu and smiled a smile of pure joy. In a few minutes I would be indulging in my first meal of the day, and I was much too excited. It didn't take much to excite me these days: a good meal, a little shopping, a good movie, complete with buttered popcorn. When I returned home I was going to sat down and contemplate life before I became a member of the bored, predictable, and restless.

Liz added her order. As soon as the server walked away she began to talk a mile a minute. It was all about Patrick and being the wife of a pastor. I had come to adore her, but she was as irritating as all get out.

"I wish I had ordered some meat." Liz dug in her purse and came up with a bottle of pills. I was curious to know what she was taking, but I didn't want to get in her business. We were friends, but if she had wanted me to know what ailed her, she would have told me.

"Why didn't you?" The server brought our drinks and placed them on the table. She placed an empty coffee cup in front of me and poured from the white carafe. I inhaled as the liquid flowed into the cup.

"Patrick would have a fit. He's been getting on me lately about losing a little weight. He suggested that I lay off meat for a while. So, I've been trying."

"Do you think you need to go on a diet? I mean, you are always so health-conscious, and I don't know how you find time to exercise with all the things you do."

"I have to exercise just to keep up with Pat. But, honestly, I don't want to go on a diet. I'm sort of happy with my weight."

She was a far cry from overweight. And although I didn't know her exact weight, and she volunteered the information now that the subject of weight came up, I'd guess that she weighed about 120 pounds. She'd been the same size for as long as I'd known her. Even during pregnancy she didn't gain a lot of weight. Patrick was just talking out of his butt as usual. But, I wouldn't be saying that part out loud. "Well then, you do what you think is best for you. But, if you're asking me what I think—" I waited for a word or a cue to go on.

"You know I care about what you think. I wouldn't have brought it up if I didn't." She opened the bottle, took one pill, placed it in her mouth and drank some of the apple juice.

"I don't think you are overweight at all or even close to overweight. You've been that size forever even when you started dating Patrick. If he liked it then, he should like it now. Case closed and don't fret." There I went, putting my ten cents in. Xavier was going to read me the riot act when I got back to Philly. I'd have Liz singing "I'm Every Woman" by the time we hit the bridge tunnel

"Let me ask you a question, Liz." I pushed the remains of my omelette around on my plate, wishing there was more. "Do you think Patrick has changed much over the years?"

"Where did that come from?" She glared at me with a puzzled look.

"I was just wondering. I mean, it's just a question between us. Nothing you need to write a 200-word essay on." Raising my coffee to my lips, I waited for her to respond.

"Well the truth? Yes, he has changed a lot." Liz put her fork down and reached for the napkin in her lap to wipe her mouth. "I know you don't like him very much, Monica, and I guess if he wasn't my significant other I probably wouldn't like him either. But he is still the man I dated and fell in love with.

"I'm not as naïve as a lot of people think and I don't reside on a planet where the handwriting is on the wall and I'm too dense to see it. But, the truth of the matter is, I'm still in love with the man I married; he just happens to be one in the same. Changed and yet somehow he's that same guy that went out of his way to win my affection back in the day." She looked around Denny's as if Patrick was going to pop out from around a corner and knock her upside the head for talking about him to the enemy. "I guess, Monica, what I'm saying is I've learned to take the bitter with the sweet and make the best of both."

What could I say to that? I didn't know that Liz could be that deep. Her words were profound and full of wisdom. She looked like she understood completely what she expressed, and yet she placed it on a shelf with all the other heavy stuff she couldn't identify or make sense of anyway. "Liz, that was such a mouthful. One time I thought that all my worries and concerns could be overcome by the love I feel for Xavier, but it all gets so overwhelming. I'm still doing my best to overcome; I just feel more and more like I'm doing it alone."

Once we had finished our breakfast and had another cup of coffee, it was time to get back on the road. I pulled out my credit card, paid for both our meals, and left a generous tip. Hopefully it would be enough to put a temporary smile on the server's face. She didn't wear a name tag. She came to the table a few times and yet I don't remember her telling us her name. Oh, well, it didn't matter. She'd done an okay job and the tip should show her that we appreciated the service without a smile.

Back in the Lexus, I pulled my sunglasses off the dashboard and put them on. I readjusted the mirror and put on my seatbelt. "Alright Liz, let's get to Hampton. You know they can't start until we get there." My husband thought so and I thought maybe I should endorse his thinking across the miles.

"I'm with you. I don't want to miss a thing." Following suit she put her sunglasses on and rested her head against the headrest.

"Don't you dare go to sleep!" I pulled onto the road and cut an eye at her.

"Girl, I'm not going to sleep. You just drive." She smiled.

I had barely been driving an hour when her responses were getting slower and slower. "Liz, did you bring pens? I know Patrick ordered some the same time Xavier did. Xavier made sure our box was packed." No answer came. I looked over and her head was hanging to the side. I couldn't believe the chick fell asleep. It was no big deal. I was used to driving for hours alone. I turned up the Sirius radio and sang backup for every song I knew.

The first two days of the conference weren't that bad. I went to every event per my husband's mandate and actually enjoyed the sessions. It seemed that the event planners were a little more aware this year of our need to focus on ways for us, as women, to create our own worth. One particular session was entitled "All about You." I listened and took notes, hoping to share what I gained with Liz. Once she scanned the session topics and saw that one, she immediately told me she didn't think she could get anything out of it. I guessed not. Liz didn't want anyone to tell her that there was a "you" in her.

Now, I had come to the event that I dreaded the most, the social exchange. This was an event that occurred right after dinner, with the purpose of exchanging introductions and brief husband/ministry bios. In short, it was the Preacher Wives' Who's Who. I was equipped with a mental roster of who I needed to spy on, hobnob with, and befriend so that our quick fake friendship could serve to link our husbands together. Xavier so wanted to partner with the elite, well positioned, and influential. He had already arrived and was already a member of the grandest entourage, and he didn't even know it.

Liz and I were seated with two pastors' wives who had churches in Richmond. Not just churches, but the two largest churches in the city. After we introduced ourselves to each other, I smiled to myself. I couldn't do that again if I tried. I had ended up sitting with the top two wives on my hit list. I mentally threw the list away and put on my game face, all in the name of love and support.

"I've heard of your husband before," said First Lady Watson as she pushed her mixed green salad around and looked at it like the ingredients used to make it weren't to her liking. She had such a regal appearance and was absolutely stunning. The photos I had seen of her didn't do her justice.

"Well, New Horizons has grown tremendously in the five years since he took over. And, with the addition of the community center, I'm not surprised," I said. I sipped from my water glass goblet and forced myself to continue. "That is such a beautiful suit you have on. Is that St. John?"

"It sure is. You recognize the style. I'm very impressed," replied First Lady Watson. She eyed my suit, which was St. John as well. And I knew she knew it by the way her eyes had been fixed on it from the time I sat down. "You know, tomorrow is our free day, with nothing to do until the farewell conference address. Would you like to join me for a little shopping? Nothing spectacular. I was just going to drive up to either the MacArthur Center or Lynnhaven Mall. We can see what styles the other half is wearing so we know what not to duplicate."

"That would be great," I said. I smiled and acted like she had just made my day.

"Oh, dear, I forgot that I didn't drive up. I came with a friend from Charlottesville, and she detests shopping. The Internet is her best friend." She paused, as if she was devising a plan. "I guess I could ask to use her car."

"That won't be necessary. I drove my Lexus," I

answered, being sure she eyed my confident persona at the mention of my ride.

"Oh, then, we are on." She touched my arm as if to confirm my introduction into the first ladies' club. "And you can bring your friend, if you like. A girl's day out, it's going to be fun." Up until then she had barely said a word to Liz. I guess when they accept you, they open the door a little to include a member of your company.

I returned her overly expressed smile. "I look forward to shopping with you." With that said, we turned our attention to the worship leader who stepped to the podium to introduce the guest messenger. A shopping outing with First Lady Watson was sure to be interesting.

Glad I hadn't shared a room with Liz, I looked around at my things scattered across the other double bed in my room. I had wanted a room with a king-size bed, but they didn't have any available. But it had worked out for the week and served the purpose of rest at the end of a long, tiring day. I began the process of packing everything up so that I could be out by checkout time. I was more than ready to go back to Philly.

Overall, the week hadn't been a total waste: I had captured the big fish. First Lady Watson and I had hit it off. After we'd toured all the malls in the area that we had time for, we'd eaten lunch at the Cheesecake Factory. Liz had decided not to join us, because obviously Patrick had sent her in another direction. We'd gone from first lady to a first name basis by the time we left the first store. When the time we got back to the hotel, she was laughing at my quick wit and humor, finding "me" refreshing yet refined, and as classy as the next first lady.

I sat down on the bed and pulled the business card out of my purse. There it was, Xavier's key to kingdom. Bishop Watson's personal business card, complete with office, fax, home, and cell phone numbers. Flipping it over, I eyed the handwritten note from First Lady Brenda Watson. It included the dates of their summit conference, one of the biggest conferences in this area. The biggest names in Virginia, North Carolina, South Carolina, Delaware, and Maryland would grace the platform. The word *fifteenth* was circled, with the word *confirmed* beside it. That was the date that Xavier would be the special guest speaker. And it just happened to be the very last day of the conference. Anybody in the church circuit knew that the last day of any conference was considered "bringing down the house" day. I tucked the card back in my purse and smiled, more for my husband than for myself. Xavier had arrived in his circle of choice. I wondered what further changes that would bring and more importantly, how it would affect our marriage.

Chapter 10

Shopping was therapeutic, and every woman I knew would suggest it for whatever was ailing you. The sound of registers ringing up purchases, hangers gliding along clothes racks, price tags showing reductions, and the hustle and bustle of people getting their shop on were to me the epitome of relaxation.

I returned from the conference feeling pretty good about what I had accomplished. Xavier all but kissed my toes when I pulled in the garage. I had already told him about my shopping trip and the invite. As he needed to see it in person, he asked for the business card before I could get in the door. Once I handed it over, he ran in the house and didn't stop until he was behind the closed door of his study. I stood in the kitchen with all my luggage and packages still in my trunk and no one to assist me. That was two weeks and a "just because" bouquet of flowers ago. He said it to show appreciation for the connection I had made.

Xavier had worked out all the details with Bishop Watson and was excited he would be the keynote messenger for one of the biggest conferences on the east coast. He gave me instructions to make weekly calls to First Lady Brenda Watson. That part wasn't hard; we had been keeping in contact through e-mails and late night calls. She was a power-hitter for the preacher wives' circle, but under all that churchly persona, she was a good person tired of the games that church folk played.

As I walked through the doors of the King of Prussia Mall, my spirits suddenly lifted, and I hummed as I scanned the food court area for Trina and my mom. The day's plan had involved just a twosome, but both of Trina's afternoon appointments had called in to cancel. So, at the last minute, Trina decided to take part in my mother and daughter afternoon. Mom didn't mind at all since Trina had hooked her up earlier that day with a wash, rinse, and a fresh set of curls. It would also give Mom another person's fashion opinion when she tried on outfit after outfit.

Trina was an only child. She'd never known her father, and her mother passed a couple of years ago. Although she had aunts and uncles, we were as much a part of her family as they were. The relationship she shared with my parents showed that bloodline was not always necessary to seal a bond. I was fine with their relationship because Trina was much more than just a friend. It didn't bother my brothers, Ted and Malcolm, either, who were always sending their women over to the shop to get a slamming hairdo at their expense, only to swing by the shop later and beg Trina for the family discount. Out of love she obliged and would call and tell me how crazy in love and thrown off my brothers' latest flavors of the month were.

My mom was the first to spot me, waving me over to the Fruit Sensation stand. I removed the print scarf I'd chosen to accent my brown blazer, plain white button-down shirt, and simple pair of Gap jeans. My usual heels were replaced with a pair of brown crocodile leather loafers. My hair hung freely, with a coordinating wide headband.

"Hey, girls. Mom, your hair looks so cute," I said. I touched it lightly while she turned from side to side, with a wide grin on her face. She was a youthful-looking seventy-five, and her small, slender frame hadn't changed much over the years. Her skin glowed, and her bright eyes sparkled. My mother took great pride in the way she looked and ate the right food groups and didn't indulge in anything that wasn't good for her. The proof of years of disciplined eating and regular exercise was visible in her appearance, and her unending energy attested to her ritual.

"Hey, girl, we thought you'd never get here. I know I'm slow, but you got me beat today," said Trina. She hugged me and leaned her drink toward my mouth so I could take a sip.

"Yum. That's good. What did you put together to make this concoction?" I asked and savored the sweet and tropical taste that remained on my palate.

"It's a blend of mango, papaya, pineapple, and strawberry, with a splash of coconut," Trina answered, while looking intently at the cup like she was visually confirming what she had asked for.

"Well, I'm here, so let the shopping begin," I said. I led the way to the first store, which just so happened to be Victoria's Secret. I needed to purchase some lingerie since I had decided not to go back to Josie's Boutique. I was toying with the idea of rethinking that plan because as upset as I was about the panty hose, those thongs with the angel's wings would probably get some extra attention from Xavier. I could see him now, looking down at me, and the minute his eyes caught sight of the flimsy fabric barely covering my secret place, he would grin that boyish, shy, yet devilish smile and finish the deed of removing it.

That was what my baby would do, and I would enjoy every moment of it. That was the way it was supposed to be. Despite how I had been living, that was the kind of woman I was, plain and simple. And there was no use denying it. I'd pick up a couple of things from Vicky's special line, but I would give Josie another chance. I had a new plan, and the way I saw things today, the better equipped I was, the easier the task would be.

This had better be good. Right in the middle of my shopping spree, Xavier rang my phone to no end. I ignored the first two messages and even fought my inner gut feeling to listen to the voice-mail messages he left, but when he rang for the third time, I knew that it had to be important. As insensitive as he was sometimes, he would never begrudge me my quality time with my mother. Now, if he thought it was just me and Trina, he wouldn't blink an eye before calling to put an end to our day of gossiping and complaining, which was all he thought Trina did. Xavier felt that her occupation had become a hazard and believed that her daily listening and exchange of information, some fact and some fiction, had carried over into her personal life.

When I didn't answer his third call on the second ring, the call ended. A minute or two later, my mother's cell phone went off, vibrating inside of her purse. When she finally removed the phone from her large Coach hobo bag, she glanced down through her bifocal glasses and handed the phone to me. "It's my son-in-law," she said. "Go ahead and talk with him. Obviously it's important. I'm going to take this dress back. I don't think it's right for me." With that, she turned, with Trina on her heels, telling her how great the dress looked on her.

"Hello," I said. I spoke loudly over the noise in the store. "Hello," I said again after looking to be sure that the phone was getting a reception.

"Monica. Why didn't you answer your phone?" Xavier's voice came loudly through the phone.

"Xavier, what is so urgent that you've been using Cingular, Verizon, and Alltel to try to reach me?" Right before Trina had walked away with Mom, she'd showed me her phone, which also showed a missed call from my husband. Her phone was on mute because once she focused on one thing, she was not the kind of person to be interrupted. "What do you need?"

"You! Why didn't you answer your phone? I don't know why I provide one for you if you don't even care enough to answer it." He was getting ready to lecture, and I wasn't up for that.

"Xavier, could you just tell me what it is you need? I will do my best to oblige you." I fought to keep my happy-go-lucky mood.

"Could you please meet me at my parents' house in an hour?" Xavier allowed the words to spill from his mouth, and yet they held no hint of what the conversation was going to be about.

"For what? Is something wrong with your parents? I just talked with your mother this morning, and everything was fine at that time. In fact, we were planning to work in her garden tomorrow afternoon." I walked out of the store and over to the marble bench strategically positioned not far from an enclosed fountain.

"They are both fine. I just have an announcement, and I want to share it with the three of you together.

So, if you leave the mall now, considering traffic, you can make it around the same time that I'll be there," he said flatly.

I didn't like it when he asked me to do something, suggested what it would take for me to accommodate him, and assumed that I would make the adjustment no matter what. "Okay, Xavier. Let me say good-bye to Mom and Trina, and I'll be on my way."

"Thanks, babe. I appreciate it. See you in a little while." He ended the call just like that. But why shouldn't he? I was ending my afternoon outing and meeting him, which for today was what he wanted.

Saying good-bye to my mom and Trina only took a couple of minutes. As was her custom, Mom slipped a gift in my bag. Probably something I saw and, for one reason or another, didn't get. She always knew when my life was slightly unbalanced. Mom never said a word, but her quiet and reassuring demeanor said she knew and was available should I need her. I wished that I could open up to her, but like everyone else, she expected me to survive through whatever and saw my world as a fairy tale. Who was I to disappoint?

Before I changed my mind, I began to navigate my way through the packs of people gathered around in front of specialty stores and stands, carrying everything from earrings and designer bags to incense and fragrances. Once I was outside the mall, I immediately wanted to retreat as a light rain fell from the sky. I took a minute and put my smaller bags in my large shopping bag, repositioned my purse strap on my arm, and tied the scarf I was wearing over my head, hoping it would keep my hair from frizzing up.

After settling into my vehicle, I was off to go see what

was so pressing that my husband would call a meeting with not only me, but my in-laws as well.

I pulled into their cul-de-sac a couple of minutes after five. Parking behind Xavier's slick black Mercedes CLK, I inhaled deeply. *Don't let this news, whatever it may be, set you off*, I thought. There was an uneasy feeling that loomed within me, and I couldn't shake it. It hadn't been there when I left the house, or while I was shopping. A process of elimination told me that it had come over me the exact moment I received the phone call from Xavier. Before I could get to the door, Xavier opened it and closed the distance between us.

"There is my wonderful, sweet wife." He grabbed me in a bear hug and lifted me up off the ground.

"Okay, what did you do? Is there a mistress inside, and is she having your baby?" I was only half joking.

"Stop tripping. The only people inside are the ones that live here. Now come on inside so I can share my news." I allowed him to take my hand and lead me into the foyer of his parents' home, which was a large two-story, four-bedroom, two-bath Cape Cod. While the house had some age, the Phillipses maintained it well. Always having a flair for decorating, Mother Phillips was adamant about changing window treatments often and rearranging furniture on a whim. Everything in the house was regal and befitting an older couple with little concern for keeping up with fashion, and more concerned with being surrounded by rich and expensive pieces. All the rugs in nearly every room were covered with plastic runners, and every piece of furniture had been Scotchguarded. The best part of visiting Xavier's parents was the pool area out back, which was more of a small sanctuary. The gardens surrounding the pool were just breathtaking, and I could sit out back for hours, just taking in the scenery and enjoying the sounds of the birds that took the time to stop by and grace the yard with their melodic chirps and beauty.

Xavier's parents were seated in the family room. Mother Phillips was nestled in her beige wing chair, knitting a pale green and white afghan. Bishop Phillips was reclined in his brown suede easy chair, watching the evening news on the television, which covered a portion of the wall facing him. The 42-inch plasma on the wall was the only item in the room that was actually contemporary. It was a gift from Xavier and me. They'd fussed at first, but it took no time at all for them to get used to it. Especially Bishop Phillips, who watched news channel after news channel, and every boxing event, and scanned every channel in search of documentaries.

"Hey, Bishop," I said as I hugged and kissed his cheek first. "Hello, Mother Phillips." I touched her shoulder and walked around her chair and took a seat on the sofa across from the chairs they were seated in.

"You're looking mighty casual, Monica. You weren't at any church function dressed like that, were you?" asked Bishop Phillips as he looked at my outfit with a look of disdain.

"No, of course not, Bishop. I just happened to be doing a little shopping with my mother and my friend Trina. I didn't have a chance to go home and change," I answered and looked in Xavier's direction, hoping he would sense my need to leave immediately and get on with things. He stood beside the sofa, with his hands in his pockets.

"Mom, Dad, Monica. I wanted you all together so I could share some important news," said Xavier. He paused and gingerly glanced toward the plasma television.

His dad watched his eyes and reached for the remote and hit the mute button. "Carry on."

"Well, I've been thinking about this a while, and I've done some research, so please don't think I'm making this decision suddenly," said Xavier. He paused and took a seat beside me on the sofa. "I have decided to serve as overseer for a church in Wilmington, Delaware."

Before I could open my mouth, his dad was on the edge of his seat. "Oversee a church? And who, pray tell, is going to be the preacher for this church?" he asked. "That's a big step you are talking about. You will be responsible for everything that goes on there, good and bad."

"Well, I've thought about all that, Dad," said Xavier. He stood back up and walked to position himself in front of the white marble fireplace. "Reverend Garrett is going to be preaching there, and it's a failing church that we are buying together, and since we are making the investment together, he decided to pastor it, and I will oversee it. Patrick will be resigning from his current church at the end of the term.

I waited for Bishop Phillips to say something else. He looked at his son as if he was asking to get a pet dog or hamster. When no one said anything, I had to speak up. "Xavier, why didn't you talk to me about this? Shouldn't this have been a decision we talked about together?"

Xavier didn't answer and looked around, first toward his dad and then his mom. Neither one said a word in his defense, nor did they speak up to agree with what they knew I was probably thinking, that my normally sane husband had lost his mind.

No one had to say anything. The silence in the room was loud enough for me to want to leave and find a place where my thoughts could release themselves and explode. I picked up my purse, said good-bye, and was out the door in search of sanity.

Chapter 11

Weeks had passed since Xavier had dropped the bomb on me and his parents. His mother and I had talked about his sudden decision, and while neither of us wanted to come right out and say it, we both assumed that Xavier was merely a puppet being played by no-good Rev. Garrett. It seemed I wasn't the only one who could read through this man, Mother Phillips wasn't overly fond of him and had been telling Bishop Phillips for years that he was no good for Xavier. Now she went so far as to say that the chicken had come home to roost. After Bishop Phillips asked her to decipher the adage, she basically said that the shit was about to hit the fan. And unless someone stepped in, it was going to be all over my husband.

As upset as I was with him, I wasn't about to let that happen. He wasn't making it easy for me, though; every time I attempted to talk to him about his decision, he would abruptly change the subject. I would have to do something for Xavier and for the well-being of New Horizons. Good sense wasn't even in the same boat with Xavier these days, and I was going to do my best to

rescue him from the grips of the devil's playmate. I
didn't want to admit it, since I had been the one to make
it happen, but ever since he'd preached to a filled-to-
capacity audience at the summit conference, he'd felt
that overseeing another church would make him look
better. He went so far as to tell me that most bishops had
more than one church, so in essence, in addition to
working with the enemy, he was seeking to change his
title to bishop.

"Monica, do you need me to stay with you until you
finish the last report? It's only 3, but I was going to go
on home." Mrs. Epps' voice pulled me out of my dazed
thoughts.

"No, go on home. I shouldn't be too far behind you."
I rubbed my temple in an attempt to soothe the headache away.

"I've been meaning to ask you if you could give my
daughter Sandy's number to that ball player. What's his
name, Sinclair something?" She stood looking in the air
as if his name was going to mysteriously show up in air.

"His name is Bryce Sinclair." I removed my glasses
and looked at her.

"She's been watching him every time he comes up in
the church. And since she's not going back to that no-
count man she married, that young man might be the
one to help her get her life together." She took a seat and
waited for me to reply.

"Her and almost every other woman in New Horizons. I can't tell you how many calls, e-mails, faxes and
drop-ins I have received from members wanting me to
hook them up with Bryce." My voice surprised me with
an edge I couldn't understand. My face felt like it was
one fire. "I'm going to tell you like I told all the others,
I'm not playing matchmaker." I leaned forward. "Now

if Bryce is interested in your daughter or any other lady in church, he's a grown man and can make the connection on his own."

"Well, I don't see no harm with helping things along." She maneuvered her body out of the chair slowly. "The next time I see him, I'll just have a little talk with him and allow the good Lord to do the rest."

"You do that. I'm pretty much done for the day, so you can go on home." I couldn't believe Mrs. Epps. Her daughter was a nice enough girl, but she was nothing to write home about. And that trail of four kids, all with different daddies, wasn't exactly an attractive package. She had some nerve. Bryce would not be remotely interested. But who was I to speak for him?

Just as Mrs. Epps was turning to leave me to finish the last report, Xavier came into the office. "Mrs. Epps, how is everything going?"

"Just fine, Pastor Phillips. It's so good to see you. I've been meaning to tell you that I appreciate you praying for my grandson Toby. He is home from the hospital and is getting along just fine."

"Well, thank God for that. You be sure to tell him that if he needs anything, anything at all, to let me know. I'll try to get by to see him sometime this week." Xavier spoke in a concerned manner.

Some would think that it was a put on. I would beg to differ; the one thing that moved my husband to compassion was his congregation. We both walked Mrs. Epps to the door and turned to face each other. "Well, what brings you all the way across the street?" I asked.

"I was coming over to tell you that I'm going to catch a game with a couple of the deacons. We're joining a couple of the executives and Bryce on a private plane to Salt Lake

City." He leaned his back against the etched glass door. "Bryce was kind enough to ask us to go along."

"Oh, I see." I looked directly at him, hoping he would realize that he had made plans with me. "That sounds like a lot of fun. You wouldn't by chance have an extra ticket for your wife?"

"Monica, that wasn't exactly what the deacons and I had in mind. We were planning to spend a little time after the game rubbing elbows with some of the big dogs." He still showed no sign of remembering anything about our conversation this morning.

Finally, I had to say something. "Xavier, did you forget anything?"

"Monica, what could I have forgotten?" He pushed away from the door as if I had suddenly irritated him. "Oh, wait a minute. I was supposed to take you to dinner."

"That's right. We were supposed to go out to eat."

I tried to remain calm, but I just couldn't. "Xavier, it's not even about dinner. We can eat together anytime. What bothers me more is that you dropped the news of opening a church with Patrick more than two weeks ago, and the buzz is all around me regarding the planning, and yet you haven't said more than two words to me about it." I crossed my arms over my chest as it heaved up and down, and patted my right foot.

"I told you and my parents that I would be moving forward with our plan. So, the buzz should have come as no surprise to you. I know he isn't your favorite person, but this is a business decision, and I've prayed about it, and since I have, you need to trust that God isn't going to lead me astray."

"I'm not worrying about God leading you astray, but

Patrick Garrett may lead you someplace you really don't want to go."

He looked as if I had slapped him. He knew that when I didn't agree with something, I could be very defensive of my opinion. This was no different. "Well, it's done, so you may want to get over it. I love you, and I'm out."

I watched as he pushed the door open and walked toward his car. For some reason, I couldn't move: my body seemed to be anchored to the spot he had just vacated. The smell of him was all around me, and I held the scent in my nostrils, not wanting to exhale and have it disappear into nothing.

The typical black woman went through stages of anger. Without even realizing it, I had gone through the first two. Stage one was me feeling that I had done something that deserved his cold response and constant rejections. Stage two was an overwhelming feeling of hurt, which caused me to internalize everything and feel sorry for myself. It was otherwise known as the wimpy stage. Now I was entering Stage three, the "Oh no, he didn't" stage. That just happened to be the stage where anything could happen and one was not responsible for what happened next. He had gone where no man should go and done what no man should do: walk out on an angry black woman.

Most women may not have seen his actions as all that bad, but this was not how we got along. I knew I hadn't been a saint prior to saying, "I do," but from that day to this, I had been a good wife, loving him and constantly being there. I'd put as much in New Horizons as he had and here he was dismissing me. I could only stand so many put downs and put asides.

Like a whirlwind, I stormed into my office, walked across the room to my desk, and hit the speaker phone button. I quickly keyed in the numbers for Trina's shop and paced the floor, waiting for someone to pick up. Nervous energy seemed to fill my entire chest cavity and my stomach to the point of bursting as I paced all around, not wanting to sit still.

Vicky, Trina's receptionist and substitute shampoo girl, answered after a few rings. "Hello. Divine Style Salon."

"Hello, Vicky. This is Monica. Is Trina available?" My mind continued to race, and while I didn't want to, I replayed Xavier walking out over and over again.

"She's in the back working on the books. Hold on and I'll get her to pick up." Vicky was the only one at the shop that had any real class. The rest of Trina's hires were as ghetto as they come. But the salon had a great reputation, and let anybody tell it, those ghetto women could do up some hair. Any way you wanted it, as long as you need it, and as straight as you wanted it to be. Their clientele ranged widely.

Trina's voice came through the phone line. "Hey, Monica, girl. What's going on? I wasn't expecting to talk to you any more today."

"Can you be ready to ride in a couple of hours?" I needed to get away from everything that was familiar for just a little while. My mind wandered in no one direction, but no matter which direction my mind went in, the center of the radius was the same, my feeling hurt.

"You know I can be ready, but girl, where are we going?" Trina asked.

"There's a spot in Jersey I've been hearing a lot about, and I thought we might check it out." Leaving Trina totally in the dark would only lead her to ask twenty-one questions all the way to our destination. So, I knew I had to give her a little information and hope that she would just go along.

"A shopping mall, boutique, art gallery? I haven't heard you talk about any new spots. Is it someplace we've been before? You've had us up in so many places."

"I don't think you've been to this place. But, then again, you may have. It's call the Midnight Male Revue." I reached in my purse and pulled out the laminated post-card invitation that Suzy had given me weeks ago, when I was at the spa. Her girlfriends were giving her a birth-day party there, and even though she knew I was a first lady, she'd invited me to come. I believe she'd said, "No harm will come if you just watch the tush."

"I know the place. What I need to know is, how do you? Better yet, don't answer. I'll need a couple of extra minutes to make arrangements for someone to open the shop in the morning, because if you're driving to Jersey to watch some near-naked men shake and swing their moneymakers, I'm definitely riding shotgun. If you go through with this, I know it's going to be a night to re-member." Trina mumbled something about my butt re-turning too hot for Xavier to handle as she hung up the phone, without saying good-bye.

"That's a friend always willing to go the distance," I said aloud. I had to laugh, though, at Trina's mumbled comment, 'cause unless God blessed Xavier's commun-ion wine with a dose of love potion number nine, we'd still be starting our sexual escapade at 10:00 and finish-ing up right around 10:10. That would include foreplay and two minutes of playing find the right hole. But since she didn't ask all that, then who was I to tell. Not even my best friend needed to know that her bedtime prayers should include Xavier getting his hump back and me enjoying the groove of it.

I craved the good ole days. Right now, though, I needed to get ready for our ride. I clicked the speaker phone off. And as if a silent dinner bell had gone off, signaling a heavyweight person to eat, I smiled a mischievous smile on my way out of my office, while I doubled-checked that all the lights were off and armed the alarm. By the time I checked the lock, the crisp night air had sent a chill, complete with goose bumps, up and down my arms. My smile gave way to thoughts that no first lady should have. That was exactly why I didn't want to even think about entering the red zone. I was safely standing near the yellow, and the thrill alone made the past months seem like a fleeting memory, going, going, gone.

My slick new Gucci watch affirmed that it wasn't quite six. A quick shower, a search to find something fitting to wear for a night out, and I would be able to pick up Trina and hit the interstate by eight. If traffic wasn't bad, we would be entering Jersey in time for the party. And, if I carried out what was brewing way back in the recesses of my psyche, I'd be hitting the revenge zone before the sun rose. Not physically of course, just being in a forbidden atmosphere was enough.

Chapter 12

The minute we stepped out of the truck, Trina took over. She'd noticed that I stood outside looking like someone had just led me to the temple of doom. She was probably thinking that I'd done nothing more than call her and blow some hot air because Xavier had pissed me the f-off, and yet she didn't say a word as she touched my arm lightly. I walked in with her, trying not to catch anyone's attention or look at anyone in particular, yet I was privy to the loud comments about us just waltzing past all those who had been forced to stand outside for a long time. I couldn't help it if we had an inside connection, and actually I had grown accustomed to not waiting for anything. It seemed my first lady privileges gave me access in a whole other walk of life. Imagine that. Favor in a strip club.

Suzy and a couple of ivory white chicks bounced noisily to the entrance door of the Midnight Male Revue after Trina and I showed my embossed invitation, waited a few minutes while a call was made to the private lounge, and were then allowed inside. The upscale club was actually nicer than I thought it would be. I don't know what I'd expected, but I was blown away by the décor as the entrance opened up to a well-laid-out lounge complete with well-dressed hosts, all of whom looked good enough to take home to mommy.

"Oh, Monica, you are here," said Suzy as she gave me a sloppy hug and kissed me on both cheeks. I thought that it wasn't a Swedish thing, but more of a drunk thing. This was my first sign that I should have done a Dorothy and clicked my heels three times to go home. But I had stepped out on a limb, and I'd just see how long it was going to hold me. "You come to party, yeah?"

"Well, I thought that I would drop by, and I brought a friend of mine," I said as I turned to Trina. "Suzy, this is Trina. I believe she came to see you once as a gift from me."

"Oh, I know. Good you come to party, too. Come with us," said Suzy. She and her two friends giggled and stumbled up the steps. When we had climbed to the top of the lighted circular staircase, one of Suzy's friends knocked on the door.

I was the last person on the staircase, and I leaned out to look around Trina's shoulder as the door opened to yells and squeals from a room full of women who were obviously enjoying the show. "What in the world?" I said. That was all I could say as a totally nude guy moved slightly away from the front of the door and allowed us to enter the smoke-filled, dimly lit room.

Trina turned to me and covered her mouth with her hand. "Monica, oh my God. I have been to strip clubs before, but they usually undress on a stage and almost always leave their G-strings on. If they do take it all off, the big guns they reveal are never within reach."

"Well, I could have reached out and touched that," I replied. Good sense told me that this was the second sign that I should be outside gunning my engine, head-ing across the bridge, with the wind to my back. But I reminded myself that I was here to seek some semblance of revenge. Up till now, I hadn't done anything to feel really bad about, unless you consider eyeing naked genitals bad. This was either a really different kind of strip club or every other club I had heard about was minor league, to say the least. Suzy's friends must have paid a grip for the extra bells and whistles.

Before I could say anything to Suzy, she was on the stage, dancing with two guys who actually still had clothes on. I watched as she bumped and grinded up against one and then the other. She was flinging her arms all around and she was yelling out broken profanities and they seemed to be enjoying every word of it.

Trina yanked my arm lightly and led me to a table in the corner of the room. This seemed to be the only section that wasn't surrounded by nude men, with women standing on chairs and on top of tables, trying to get to them. "Girl, can you believe this action? Your girl Suzy parties in a big way," said Trina. She began laughing at the pun. It wasn't that funny, but it was definitely true that everyone in the room was large.

"I wasn't expecting all this. I thought we would be seeing guys coming out on the stage over there and taking their clothes off and stopping at a G-string. The only really X-rated stuff I'd thought I would be exposed to is some loud, boisterous music with illicit lyrics." I tried to frown, but then I remembered that this was part of my plan. It would have been easier if they were hard on the eyes, but the club owners must have combed the entire East Coast to find these men. I would have no problem equating their looks with those of any good-looking television actor or attractive, well-known musician.

We finally caught the eye of one of the hosts and

ordered a couple of frozen virgin margaritas. If we weren't part of the crowd, at least we would look like we were. After sitting in silence and taking in the sights for a few minutes, Trina took a long sip of her drink and spoke in a rather harsh voice. "Girl, I hate to tell you, but this stuff is starting to get to me. You bring me to a place like this, and I'm not married and can't remember the last time I had some."

"I'm sorry. I just didn't think it was going to be like this. If it helps, I sleep with Xavier every night, and I've had some recently." I sighed a pregnant sigh and continued. "But this stuff is getting to me, too."

"Well, don't look now, but two guys are coming this way, and unless you have some singles or you're interested in a private show, you may want to turn the other way."

My eyes were wide open as the tall guy, who looked so exotic, moved fluidly to the music, never losing step, as he closed the distance between us. I should have looked away, should have looked in another direction, but I was cocooned in a deep, mesmerizing trance, and I could only look at his sensual face. My bottom lip fell open slightly, and I licked it to cover up the obvious reason my mouth would be open. The closer he got, the more I noticed his features. He looked to be Jamaican or possibly from Trinidad. It had to be some island. To describe him as cute would be criticizing even his worst feature, which, after careful observation, I could not readily see.

I swallowed hard as he closed in on me and held his hands out to me. I tried to stay focused on his face, but my eyes took a slow, leisurely scenic tour down his masculine chest and past his flat abdomen. Suddenly, my hands were enveloped in his and I allowed him to pull me seductively to my feet and I began to sway with him. Not close, but the distance was more than intoxicating.

I was captivated by his eyes. His chocolate brown skin glistened in the dim light, and the only facial hair was a well-shaped mustache and goatee. His head was covered with neatly trimmed dreadlocks, which were pulled together in a black and green band.

He had been looking at me in the same seductive way I had been looking at him and then he spoke. "What a beautiful woman like you doing in a place like dis?"

"My friend is the birthday girl, and I thought I'd come by." I held his gaze and couldn't help but smile as I noticed him smiling down at me.

"Dis no place for a beauty like you." He leaned down to my ear. "Where your man? I wouldn't let you out of me sight."

"He won't miss me. Besides, I only came for the birthday celebration. I allowed him to hold my hand over my head as I turned around slowly and stopped slightly, with my back turned to him. I closed my eyes and swayed my backside to the slow beat. When I faced him again, I must have moved closer than I thought, as I felt all of him rub against my thigh. It unsettled me, and my eyes jerked open as I stumbled backward.

"You okay. Me don't want you to hurt yourself." He caught me before I fell but held me closer than he should have.

I was powerless to move and enjoyed the feel of him holding me. "I'm okay. I think I need to have a seat, though. Thanks so much for the dance."

"You here for somethin', so let me give you somethin' to remember." Before I could object, he leaned toward me and placed a trail of kisses around my neck. It was so slow, and his lips barely brushed my skin there. He lingered near my ear and asked me to touch him.

I didn't want to, but when I thought of my trip across

the bridge, I thought of all that was happening on the other side of that same bridge. I thought of Garrett, and my jaw tightened as I slowly reached my hand out to encircle him. Just as my hand was close enough to encircle him, I moved my hand swiftly and quickly turned to find the table where I'd been sitting. As I walked toward Trina, my eyes were blinded with tears.

She asked if I was hurt, and when I said no, she fell in step with me as we found our way to the door leading to the outer lounge and then the one to the outside of the building. I listened as she told me that she'd seen me dancing and had assumed I was okay as she began dancing with another dancer on the other side of the room.

I unlocked my truck, handed Trina the keys, and got in on the passenger side. Under the shadow of the streetlight, I noticed a large stain on my gray slacks. The lump in my throat contracted, and like water held back by a dam for a time, tears unleashed themselves through bitter emotion and fell as if they would never stop. Trina turned on the inside light and carefully examined me, visually making sure everything was okay.

"Are you sure you're okay? Did he do anything to you?" she asked. She put her arms around me, and I responded, "No," through a hiccup and another spree of tears.

After a couple of minutes, Trina released me and wiped my face with a tissue she pulled from her purse. Somehow, I believe she sensed that my plan of guilt-free fun had backfired, and in its place, embarrassment, hurt, and anguish had slipped in, with all the emotional telltale signs that they would be staking claim to my entire being and that tonight's ordeal would replay in my mind every time I looked into the face of my husband or reached out to touch a part of him.

Chapter 13

The weather wasn't fit for anyone to be outside braving the elements to go this place or that place. After getting caught in a downpour that released its fury without mercy, I discovered that dragging myself off my sofa, where I had spent too much time, wasn't worth the effort. In short, I was disappointed. My mail was stacked neatly on my desk, but flipping through it, I found nothing there of great importance. The rain had seeped through my trench coat and had left the pants of my navy Tahiri suit hanging wet against my legs. I sat down at my desk and reached to turn the heater on to warm my legs and my damp feet. I didn't care that it was August. I had a chill, and unless I tried to warm my feet, I would be uncomfortable a big part of the morning.

Mrs. Epps came blowing in like a whirlwind. Her mouth was running and spilled out so much information, she could have provided the local radio and television stations with enough news to last for the next five days. Now, if half of what she went about broadcasting contained some truth, it might actually have some merit. However, this was Mrs. Epps, and I doubted if she carried a bone that was worth anyone chewing on. I often told Trina that when my life got so miserable that I began to go door to door to share in idle gossip that included all kinds of sordid affairs and was filled with folks' dirty laundry, she should shoot me in my foot and send me far, far away.

"You know, First Lady, we sure missed you around here," said Mrs. Epps. "The place wasn't the same without your smiling face. Pastor was concerned, too. But he did call us every day to say that you were still under the weather." She stood over my desk, going on and on.

"Well, I'm glad that I'm back. I'm going to try to stay all day, but I'll see how the morning goes." I fished in my side drawer until I found my eyeglass case. Removing my glasses from the black monogrammed case, I put them on and blinked a couple of times as my eyes adjusted to the sudden change in my vision.

"That's understandable. You don't want to overdo it. Sometimes when you have a bad cold or the flu, it takes a while to get yourself together." She sat down across from me and looked directly in my face. "Then again, cramps and female disorders can sure enough make you want to stay in bed. I knew you had to be sick when you missed church for two straight Sundays."

She was fishing to learn what my problem had been. I knew Xavier wouldn't say. In fact, he didn't really know what the problem had been himself. I'd only said that I wasn't feeling well, and while he'd watched nightly, I hadn't displayed any real symptoms, yet he would suggest that I rest. I think he knew that what ailed me was something that would not manifest itself physically.

"Mrs. Epps, do you have any messages for me that weren't included in this pile?" I didn't look up at the nosy busybody, but waited for her to verbally answer my question.

"I believe, I have a few. I'll go get them and come right back in to finish our conversation, 'cause it sure is good to have you back here. Yes, Minnie Epps is going to take real good care of you."

I had to laugh to myself, because she honestly believed the mess she was saying. She wanted to take care of me. If I asked for a cup of water, she would no doubt turn it around and say I was so weak, I couldn't even sip the water without her guiding my head to the cup. She was a sweet lady, but her assistance was not the kind of help I needed.

Minutes later, she came back and placed several other pink and white message notes on my desk. "That's all I need, Mrs. Epps. I'll call you if I need you. Right now, though, I need to return some of these calls." She remained seated and looked around like I was talking to someone else. "Mrs. Epps, why don't you go over and see if I have any messages at the church and check my mailbox over there as well?"

That got her going. She popped up and pulled her opaque panty hose up and pressed down the front of her skirt. "I sure will. I knew you wouldn't feel like walking around. Poor dear, you are probably flowing heavy."

I didn't bother to answer as she made her way out the door. Flipping through the pieces of paper, I noticed that several of the messages were from Bryce Sinclair. All of them were marked urgent and said, *Please return the phone call.* I knew I needed to call him, and yet I arranged the messages by date and went through each of them again. A few were from the same day, and the others were taken only a day apart. Obviously, whoever had answered the phone had only relayed that I was out, with no mention that I was sick or out for an extended time. But how could they have given that much information? I myself played each day by ear. If I felt like getting up and living some semblance of normalcy in my home, I did. Other days I could only turn over and beg sleep to come to rescue me from the pit I had thrown myself in.

Ever since the night in Jersey, I had been punishing myself, feeling so bad that I couldn't even stand listening to my own thoughts as I rationalized the whys. Nothing seemed to justify my being in that wrong place at the worst possible time. Today, though, I'd mustered the strength to get on with things, partly because Xavier was beginning to ask too many questions and because, after Trina came over to do my hair, I'd announced to myself in the mirror that there would be no more pity parties. It had happened, and now it was time for me to move past it. I could never tell a soul and felt bad that Trina was there to witness it, even though I knew my secret was safe with her. I had resolved to bury that night, the shame of it all, with the indiscretions I had committed before Xavier became my husband, before I became the first lady of New Horizons, and before what was changing us hung over our heads, ready to dissolve all that we were.

The phone rang a couple of times, and I quickly remembered Mrs. Epps was not in the building. "Hello. Monica Phillips."

"Mrs. Phillips, this is Bryce Sinclair. I've been trying to reach you. Did you get all the messages I left?"

"Yes, actually, I am flipping through my messages now. I just returned to the office today, so I've been playing catch-up all morning." It was the truth. I just didn't add that my return call probably wouldn't have happened today.

"Oh, well, I need to get with you to go over the second phase of the Kings Vision Program. To be honest, I was hoping to have this part done so I could go ahead and begin. I'm going to be on the road, and I wanted to get some groundwork laid before I take off."

"Well, I'm sorry I wasn't here to act as your assistant. I'm sure if you had stated your urgency to Pastor Phillips, he would have advised you to go forward with the assistance of Deacon Thomas or someone else of his choosing." My time should not be spent dealing with this man. He was working my last nerve, and we had only been talking a few minutes.

"I did discuss a few things with him, but I also told him that I wanted to run them past you. So, when can we get together?"

"Well, thanks for including me, Mr. Sinclair." I was turning papers on my desk upside down, looking for the lease agreement that I'd held in my hand moments before the phone rang.

"Look, can we have lunch and somehow start this on a better note?" He sounded a little exhausted with the back and forth game we had been playing.

"You know what? That might be a good idea. How about tomorrow?" Standing up, I reached across my credenza for the paper that I had been looking for. I didn't remember turning around or placing the paper there.

"Tomorrow? Why not today? I know the weather is terrible, and you may not want to go out, but I can pick you up around noon right in front, so you wouldn't get wet."

"That won't work for me. If you are willing to pick up something for lunch and bring it here or have something delivered here, I'll give you a few minutes to discuss phase two." This was the best I was going to do. I was not going back out in the pouring rain to meet with Bryce. To be more precise, I wasn't planning on going anywhere for anybody anymore, or at least anytime soon.

"That will work. I'll finish a couple of things with my financial advisors, and then I'll come there. See you then."

He was getting ready to hang up the phone when I realized something. "Hey, you didn't bother to ask me what I wanted to eat."

"Don't need to. I'm sure I'll include something that you like. Just leave it all to me." He said good-bye, and the sound of the dial tone hummed in my ear.

"I believe the boys will benefit from the weekly workout program I have lined up with my personal trainer. It's part of my initiative to create the total young man. Mind, body, and soul." He leaned across the table as he handed me a schedule.

"I must admit, Mr. Sinclair, this is all very impressive. I never thought about incorporating health and wellness. We've been more concerned about the educational and emotional needs of the young guys. They of course use the basketball courts and play around with the weights, but I don't think any of them actually have a workout routine." Glancing through the folder, I couldn't help but marvel at the amount of work he had already put into the program.

"Well, this is just another facet that we can include. They, of course, will be learning a lot about discipline in the workout program." Bryce grabbed a bottle of Powerade, twisted the lid, and took a couple of sips.

"That's important. Pastor Phillips will be pleased. He works out regularly. My husband can be quite a gym advocate. When we first opened the gym here, every member of the deacon's ministry was hitting the gym right along with him."

"And now?" Bryce inquired, seeming to enjoy the sidebar addition to our conversation.

I took a bite of my chicken salad sandwich, chewed a few times, and wiped my mouth before speaking. "He wore them all out." I smiled as I thought of Xavier. His morning workouts used to begin with me. He'd kiss my forehead and tell me all his plans, and when he had shared his soul, he'd whisper, as I fell back asleep, that he would always love me and share all that was in his world with me.

"He is a pretty big guy, but he looks like he's in great shape," Bryce said.

"What?" I hadn't been listening. Thoughts of Xavier had taken me someplace where Bryce, the lunch, or the phase two plans were not invited.

"I was just giving your husband a compliment." He looked at me as if I were a few cans short of a six-pack. "You were obviously daydreaming, but that's cool. I accomplished what I came here to do, and I'm in great company. A win-win for me, I might add." Bryce looked directly at me.

"Why are you staring at me? You seem to do it a lot." I stared back at him, waiting for an answer.

"Because I think you are a beautiful lady. And today I'm seeing that you aren't always hard-core."

"Why? Because I'm agreeing with you for the first time in . . . Wow, I've never agreed with you." I had to laugh. I placed my index finger beside my lips. "Don't get too excited. Tomorrow or the next day, I may come up with a reason to object."

"You wouldn't." Bryce seemed amused. He acted as if I were just joking. The poor fool had no idea that when I wanted to be disagreeable, I'd change with the wind.

"Yes, I would. So, thank you so much for lunch and for sharing your plans." I rose to my feet and began to clean up the remnants of our lunch from the new gourmet deli shop not far from the Wachovia Center. Bryce had informed me, the minute he'd sat the basket on the table, that our lunch was courtesy of the deli owner, who wanted to make sure we became one of his regular customers.

The picnic basket had included every kind of sandwich combination imaginable, and there'd even been vegetables and dip and a small fresh fruit tray. To top it all off, they had packed mini gourmet chocolate chip and oatmeal raisin cookies. Bryce had come into my office and demanded that I sit back while he placed the customary red-and-white checkered picnic tablecloth on the table and removed all the contents from the basket and placed them all strategically on the table. I'd pretended to be deep into the letter I was writing, but had kept looking away from my monitor screen as I watched his every move. When he'd announced that he was done, he'd walked over to the desk, escorted me to the nearby table, and pulled out my chair.

"Well, you're cleaning everything up, so that must be my cue to leave." He removed the tablecloth, folded it and put it back in the picnic basket.

"I really need to finish up some other things." My mind was already racing over a couple of other loose ends I needed to tie up before leaving.

"I'll set the wheels in motion before you have a

chance to object. In fact, the season tickets for the boys should be delivered via courier any minute now. As well as a package for the church that includes VIP season ticket passes for the pastor, deacons, and a couple of other key individuals that Deacon Thomas felt would benefit from hanging with the team."

I was impressed and had to voice it. "Very impressive, Mr. Sinclair."

"Glad you approve, Mrs. Phillips. Oh, by the way, I'll be on the road for a few days." He waited in the doorway for a response, and when none came, he continued. "Well, good day and enjoy the rest of your day."

I drank the rest of my Aquafina flavored water and responded, "I'll see you when you get back in town. Oh, Bryce, you're forgetting your basket." I walked back around my desk, toward the table.

"No, you keep it. That way you can return the favor of lunch." He left without waiting for my response.

Eyeing the basket and being obsessed with neatness, I picked it up, intending to place it in the closet. After folding the tablecloth, I opened the basket lid. Inside were a manila envelope and two white envelopes. Pulling the envelopes out of the basket, I wondered if Bryce had forgotten that they were there. I turned each of them over to see if anything was written on them. Neither of the white envelopes was sealed, so I looked around and then slipped the card out of the first envelope. There, on the card, was a smiley face with the words *thank you*. I opened the card and read on.

Thanks for having lunch with me. I think we make a great team. Bryce.

Smiling, I opened the other white envelope, and it was a gift certificate for weekly spa visits for the entire year, with my name as the spa guest. It wasn't the spa I frequented, but it was an even nicer one, one I had wanted to visit. Xavier hadn't seen the need to spend the extra money. By now I was blown away and took a seat at the table. I took a deep breath, not knowing what was in the manila envelope. I pulled the clasp up with a pinch of my fingers and opened it so I could slide the contents out. I held in my hand VIP season tickets. It seemed that Bryce had included me, and each ticket included access to the pregame and postgame gatherings.

The phone brought me out of the trance I was in.

Mrs. Epps had taken an extended lunch to go to the doctor, and it wasn't time for Nita to arrive. I was relieved that neither of them had been here to witness my closed-door lunch with Bryce. Each of them would have asked more questions than I was willing to answer. "Monica Phillips."

"I'll be back on the thirteenth." Before I could respond, he hung up. This man was full of himself. While I had silently wondered when he would return, I hadn't dared to ask. I mentally pushed our meeting around in my head and the peace tokens while I finished a couple of other letters.

With the Kings Vision Program in its second phase, I had a new burst of energy and continued to work for another hour. Once Nita came in, I listened as she told me what was going on in her world and I repeatedly told her that I was feeling well enough to be in the office. I tried to figure out when she had reversed roles and become such a mother hen where I was concerned.

"Nita, can you tell me something?" I turned my chair away from my desk and looked out the window as the rain continued to fall outside. I was fixated on the administrative wing of the church, as if I could see through the brick walls and into the office as my husband sat handling church affairs. I wondered why he hadn't called to check on me all day. Mrs. Epps had returned to the center and had made a point of telling me that her first stop had been to his office, to let him know that I was in the office and not looking up to par.

"Ask away, First Lady Phillips. I'm all ears," said Nita. She stopped filing the folders I had left on the file cabinet and turned slightly toward me. The earphones that were connected to the Mp3 player hanging at her waist were dangling around her neck.

I hadn't wanted to check but felt it was harmless to ask Nita a general, very generic question. "What is today's date?" Looking toward where I knew Xavier was, I waited.

"It's Thursday, the ninth." She went back to her task, without saying another word.

Chapter 14

Walking into the kitchen through the side door of the garage, I was more exhausted than I had been in a very long time. The rain continued, and all I wanted to do was take a long shower and get in bed. It didn't matter that it was only 7:30 p.m. I didn't expect Xavier to come through the door before 10:00 since it was Thursday, and almost every Thursday, there was a meeting of some sort. I usually kept up with his schedule, but then again, he usually kept me abreast of exactly what was going on. So, it would be me, a frozen pizza, and a Life-time movie.

I turned on the shower and stripped down to nothing as I paraded between our bedroom suite and the adjacent bathroom. I sat on the cushioned bench in front of the antique vanity table and brushed my hair into a ponytail. Then I removed all traces of make-up from my face and throat. My eyes were still puffy, even though I had used every known home remedy to reduce the slight swelling.

My day hadn't gone like I thought it would. I'd assumed my day would be pleasantly interrupted by my husband, and yet Bryce was the interruption. The gifts brightened my day, and I couldn't help thinking how nice it was for him to think of putting together something special like that for me. It actually made me feel appreciated. While I was still suffering from the anguish of the strip club night, I was not so naïve that I missed the comment that Bryce had made. It was actually the second time that someone other than my husband had told me he admired my beauty. The first time meant nothing, but there was something in the way Bryce said it that caused his words to replay in my mind.

After my shower, I went downstairs and pulled a small frozen pepperoni pizza from the freezer. This was one of the quick items that I kept in case I was between grocery store trips or it was late and neither of us felt like waiting for takeout or going out to get something. I could hear my cell phone ringing upstairs, but I didn't feel like running to answer the call. I figured if someone needed to talk with me, they would call the house. Sure enough, the house phone rang just as I was putting the pizza in the oven.

"Hello." I held the phone against my shoulder and started to clean the refrigerator while I waited for the pizza. My pink and white slippers slid along the floor as I moved between the refrigerator and the sink.

"Hello, Monica. I was calling to see how you were feeling." I recognized Mother Phillips's clear, even voice.

"I'm okay, Mother Phillips. I was just fixing a little something to eat since this is one of Xavier's late nights." I continued my cleaning ritual, hoping she wouldn't keep me on the phone long.

"I spoke with him earlier today, and he said he was

going to stay home with you this evening. I'm a little shocked he's not there."

"Well, maybe he's on his way." I didn't believe what I was saying myself, but I thought I would throw it out there.

"I'm sure he is. Well, you fix something quick and rest while you wait for him. Tomorrow I'll bring some soup over, and you won't have to worry about cooking anything." That was her, always a concerned woman. With all that she did for her preacher husband, I didn't know how she managed to fit us in. But I knew she would.

"Thank you so much. Give my love to Bishop, and I'll see you tomorrow." I hung the phone up as I heard the garage open. Well, this was a surprise. I still didn't believe I had anything to do with Xavier coming home early. I was finishing up the refrigerator when he walked into the kitchen.

"Hey, you. How are you feeling?" Xavier reached around me and pulled out a bottle of water.

"I'm feeling better. How was your day?" I tried my hardest to be my usual self and ask safe questions. I didn't know what he was expecting me to really say. He probably wanted me to ask why he hadn't called me today, but today was already past tense, and I wasn't planning on dwelling on the past.

"It wasn't bad, just busy. Getting this church going is taking so much extra time, but I know it will be worth it." He said it without any hesitation.

"I'm glad everything is working out. Nothing worth having is ever easy. You know that." I closed the refrigerator door and smiled at him. Was it a sincere smile? It wasn't even close, but I was going to play the role of the adoring wife to the hilt tonight. I had tried everything else, and it hadn't gotten me that far. On top of that, I needed to put everything I had into my marriage after what I'd almost done.

"I'm glad you understand. I wondered if you would come around. Maybe your rest has done you some good. Thank God for that." He took a seat at the breakfast nook and drank from the bottle of water.

"Well, I had some time to think. I'm behind you, so if that was a concern, you can put that aside." I kept my position across the room from him. It was safe. I wasn't sure what would happen if I reached out to him and saw the guy from the strip club.

"There are just some things that you don't need to concern yourself with. You were all upset about the new church, but I'm doing what is best for New Horizons. Patrick is not as bad as you make him out to be."

That was it. I wanted to go off, but I kept my mouth shut. "Whatever, Xavier. Let's just agree to disagree where Patrick is concerned."

"Well, it's under way, so you need to get used to it. By the way, I'll be going to D.C. to meet with the contractors and finish up the financing of the church. I'm also borrowing a little extra to pay off some obligations that Patrick has so that everything goes through smoothly. I'll need you to sign some papers, because your name is on all of our joint assets. I'm going to go up and shower. Is that pizza I smell?"

"How can you ask me to put up our assets to get extra money for Patrick? He should be paying his bills, like we pay our bills. I can't believe you, Xavier. I listened and bit my tongue while you stood here telling me that I needed to allow you to handle things your way. But now you are using our money to help him." By the time the last word was out, it was a scream.

Xavier never raised his voice, but I almost expected him to yell back at me. "Monica, I got a news flash for you. It's not your money. Do I need to remind you that you haven't worked a paying job since you said, 'I do'." He turned and began to walk away.

"What are you saying? I don't have a paying job because I'm busy running the community center."

"And before that? What job did you hold before that, Monica?" He stood, consuming the space in front of the refrigerator, right next to where I was standing. He was getting ready to say something else and just turned away. I walked up behind him and pulled his arm, just enough for him to turn around.

"I was helping you out with the church, not to mention trying to have a child, which we both desperately wanted." My heart felt like it was going to beat out of my chest.

"Yeah, well, that didn't work, did it? What we wanted you were unable to provide." He turned and started walking away.

"Xavier, I can't believe you. Come back in here, and tell me what you are trying to say." I took a couple of steps toward him.

He stopped and stormed toward me, and I took a few steps backward. "I've already said what I wanted to say. We don't have a child, because you can't *have* one." His words hit me like a brick. Again, he started to walk out of the kitchen.

This time I reached out and grabbed his arm. "Xavier?" I was hoping he would turn, look at the hurt in my eyes, and apologize.

"Let me go, Monica. I'm going upstairs to take a shower, and then I'm going out to get something to eat."

He continued walking and was halfway up the steps when I caught up with him.

"Not like this. You can't just walk away after what you just said." I touched his arm.

Before I knew it, he turned around and shoved me. I reached for the railing, but it was too late. My body tumbled down the steps, and I hit my head on the banister before the rest of me hit the floor. I felt a pounding in my head, and then there was a sharp pain in my lower stomach. I felt something warm between my legs. As my eyes were closing, I looked up at Xavier with a pleading look. I could faintly hear the music from the Midnight Male Revue, the stripper's voice echoing in my ears, and yet Xavier's words overpowered it all. That was all I heard before the color black overtook my thoughts, but not only my thoughts, but my entire world.

My eyes opened slowly as I attempted to pull away from the haze that had engulfed my senses. The bright light over my head blinded me for a moment as I struggled to see where I was and why I was lying flat on my back.

"Monica, you're awake. Baby, I was worried sick about you." Xavier moved closer to me and rubbed my forehead. I didn't want him to touch me.

I tried to respond, but my mouth felt like it was swollen shut. I swallowed a couple of times, and my voice came out in a low whisper. "What happened? Am I in the hospital?" I knew I was in the hospital; I just couldn't figure out how I had ended up there.

"Yes, you fell down the steps and hit your head. Listen, let me go get the doctor. She is right outside and asked that I come and get her the minute you came to."

Before I could say anything, he was out the door. I expected a portly old man, with glasses on the end of his nose, but Xavier returned with a tall, thin sister. Her white coat was starched and more fitted than the ones I'd seen most doctors wear.

"Hi, Mrs. Phillips. I'm Dr. Jacqueline Joseph, one of the staff physicians here at Thomas Jefferson."

Xavier must have introduced himself earlier, because he stood to the side and watched the two of us. "Hi. What is going on with me?" I asked. I didn't want to sound so direct, but my head was throbbing, and I was cramping like crazy.

"Well, Mrs. Phillips, first off, you have a slight concussion from the fall. We haven't given you anything major for the pain, because we needed to get an MRI done, and we've been trying to keep you awake as a precaution. We haven't been all that successful." She smiled. "But you didn't collapse on us again until after the MRI, so I was able to get the report. Keeping you awake is just standard practice for anyone that has had a head trauma injury." She began to flip through the chart. "You have some bruising at the back of your neck. I'm assuming your neck hit before your head did. I can imagine that all that is pretty bad, but I have some other bad news. When you were picked up, the paramedics noticed that you were flowing. They kept everything isolated and brought it in with them."

I looked at her, puzzled. The one thing I was not exempt from was the excess bleeding I had every month from my monthly cycle. But, when I thought back, I realized I was actually late this month. I wasn't concerned, because any amount of stress caused my hormones to go into overdrive.

"There was fetal tissue," said Dr. Joseph. "I'm sorry, but apparently, you were in a very early stage of pregnancy." She took a deep breath. "Your husband provided your medical information, and I have contacted your gynecologist. She will be coming in shortly. I'm sure she will want to perform a D & C."

I was numb. I couldn't say a word. Not only was I lying here with a concussion, but I had lost another baby. Tears began to fall from my eyes, and I didn't even want to look at Xavier.

"The headaches could continue for the next couple of weeks. I'll be giving you a prescription-strength pain reliever for a couple of days. After that, Tylenol or Motrin should help. If some dizziness or difficulty concentrating persists longer than a week, you should let me know, as it could be a sign that something else is going on." She gave me the routine spiel, but my tears had obviously touched her feminine side, because she was having trouble getting it all out.

I began to cry harder, and Xavier moved around the doctor and held me. I wanted to pull away from him, and yet I needed to be held. I needed to allow him to hold me together. I was so upset at him, and before I knew it, I pulled away. "Xavier, if you haven't already, please call my mom and dad," I said.

He looked startled. He must have thought that I didn't remember anything. "Oh, okay," he replied. "With the rush and waiting for the doctor, I haven't called yet, because I didn't know what to tell them. But I'll go and call right now." He turned and walked out.

Dr. Joseph followed him with her eyes and turned back to me, with a caring smile. "Are you okay?" she asked.

"I guess I'll have to be. That was the third baby I've lost." I hiccuped and continued to cry softly. "I want a baby more than anything in the world, and I guess, it's just never going to happen. I didn't have a clue that I was pregnant. How stupid is that?"

"Well, I'm sure your body has gone through so many changes, it was easy enough for you to miss the symptoms. There is one more thing. There is some light bruising on your chest. It looks very recent. Since you fell backward, I couldn't exactly figure out how it could have happened." I was in a private room, so she went to the door, which Xavier had left open, and closed it shut. She pulled the standard hospital bedding back and raised my back to loosen the hospital gown I was wearing. Once she placed my head back on the pillow, she examined the marks.

"Mrs. Phillips, did someone push or shove you?" she asked. She looked at me a minute and then focused on the bruising.

"No, my foot slipped, and I fell down the steps." I wiped my eyes with the hand that wasn't attached to the IV.

"I am obligated to report this as possible abuse. But if you are assuring me that it's nothing more than horseplay, I will report it as such. However, if it is more, you need to tell me. I'm all ears." She sat on the side of the bed. "Your husband looked so familiar, and so did you. It took me a couple of minutes to figure out why, but by that time he was telling me who he was. How could I have missed it? Your faces are all over town."

"I'm sure my husband invited you to worship with us some time. New Horizons is growing by leaps and bounds." I tried to sing New Horizons' praises because it was just such a rehearsed speech. I knew it was the right thing to add.

"Of course, he invited me, and I'm planning on taking him up on it. I currently go to Zion AME, but there is nothing wrong with fellowshipping." She made a poor attempt at smiling and continued. "As the director of the community center, I know you see all kinds of abuse and counsel battered women often. So, for the sake of all, don't be quiet if you know you should speak out."

Just as Dr. Joseph fixed my gown, Xavier walked back in. "Okay, Mrs. Phillips, I'm going to have them bring you something to eat so we can give you something stronger for the pain," she said. "We aren't as concerned about you falling asleep, now that we have the full report. And I'm sure with the loss and the headache, you could use some rest. I'll be in to check on you at the end of my rounds. Reverend Phillips, please make sure your wife stays calm. I know you have sent for her family, but I don't want her to be overwhelmed by anybody or anything."

Although she was giving him a warning about my family, she was really talking to him. She didn't buy the horseplay story, but because of Xavier's position and because he was my husband, I couldn't tell her what had actually happened.

Before long my parents came in, with my brothers following close behind. I took a deep breath the minute they charged at me.

My Dad moved to the side of the bed, with Ted and Malcolm. "Hey there, princess. Are you okay?" asked my dad.

"Daddy, I'm going to be fine," I replied. I fought back tears and started to cough.

My dad spoke to my mother, who was closer to the water pitcher. "Shirl, give Monica a little something to drink. I'm sure she is thirsty." A concerned look remained on his face as my mother poured some water in a small Styrofoam cup and placed a straw in it.

"Here, Mrs. Joyner. I'll do it," said Xavier as he reached his hand out to take the cup.

My mother smiled and handed it to him. My dad looked on, with a frown on his face, and said, "Lift the bed so her head can come up some first, Xavier."

Xavier did as my dad suggested. He held the cup to my mouth and placed the straw between my dry lips. I sipped a small amount, stopped, and sipped a little more. "Is that okay?" he asked.

"Yeah, thanks," I said.

Everybody stood around, with no one saying a word. Evidently, they had already received the Xavier version of the story. Although it was quiet, the tension in the room was thick. I could tell my family was anxious to quiz me and seek answers, which weren't readily forthcoming.

"Monica, I'm going to call my parents and let them know that you are okay," said Xavier. "You know they are attending a meeting in New York, and the minute it all happened, I phoned them. They are on their way back." He didn't take a breath but spoke hurriedly, which was a major switch for him. Usually, he remained calm and cool through whatever.

"Was that before or after the call you made to us?" asked Malcolm. He turned his full attention to my husband and watched him turn a little red.

"My mother happened to call me when I was following the ambulance," replied Xavier. "I apologize, but they did find out before I had a chance to call you guys."

"And tell us again why it took more than three hours for you to call," said Ted.

Mom spoke up. "Ted, you know how hectic it can be in these hospitals. You got to fill out paperwork, go in this direction for this, and then return, only to be led in another direction. It wasn't that long ago when we were here doing the same thing for your dad. Poor Xavier has been through a lot in the past couple of hours."

"Monica especially," said Xavier as he reached for my hand. I reluctantly allowed him to hold it. "I didn't want to leave her side for one minute. I do have to remind everybody that the doctor wants her to get some rest. In fact, the medicine may be kicking in soon, and she will be sleeping for a while. I'm going to go ahead and make my call, and I'll be right back."

The minute he left the room, Ted and Malcolm stood over me. We didn't talk daily, because they were always busy doing this or that, but whenever I needed them, they were right by my side. No questions asked, except the one that I knew was coming. Malcolm, being the oldest, was the first to speak. "Preacher man is gone now. You care telling us what happened back at the house?"

"Yeah, you clumsy and all, but you falling down the steps is a little hard for us to believe," Ted added, with a lot of attitude.

"If he pushed you, I'm gonna kill him and let his non-preaching daddy commit him to the ground," said my dad. My daddy was a no-nonsense man. He said what he meant and meant what he said. I knew he would have no problem knocking Xavier out cold.

"Ted, Malcolm, Dad, please. Xavier did not hit me at all," I said. "I've been having headaches for a couple of weeks. I was on my way up the steps in a hurry, felt a little dizzy, slipped, and fell back. I guess I must have hit my head when I fell, and the next thing I knew, I'm waking up in the ambulance."

What I said was true, to a degree. I had been having stress-induced headaches, trying to figure out what was going on with Xavier and me. But right now the bigger concern was figuring out how Xavier could have pushed me down the steps. He had never touched me before, had never even raised his voice or spoken a harsh word. If I had to take the stand and take an oath, I would say that the guy who had come into my house, while he might have looked like my husband, wasn't him. He was not the man I'd fallen in love with and continued to love to this day. I couldn't tell them what happened, that I was in the hospital because Xavier had pushed me down the steps and that, besides the concussion, I had lost another baby.

"You guys aren't helping matters much by talking about beating up Xavier like that," said my mom. "Couldn't you see how worried he was?" My mom was always Xavier's saving grace. Nobody could ever say anything about her son-in-law without her speaking up on his behalf. "He called me in a panic. Couldn't even get his breath."

I wanted to lean over the side of the bed and throw up. I thanked God I wasn't cut from the same trusting cloth my mom was, 'cause as of today, Xavier wouldn't be able to sell me anything that didn't come with a money-back guarantee. I still loved him, but I wasn't stupid. Who knows, I might have been able to carry this baby full term. God might have been giving me another chance, but I would never know, and I felt empty. I wanted everyone out of there. I needed to be alone.

"Enough, everyone. I'm okay," I said. "You can all

leave and let me get some rest. I know you love me, but I'm just not up to all this conversation."

"Well, as soon as the doctor comes back and give us an update, your dad and the boys can go home and let you rest. I'm going to leave a little later on," said my mother.

"Whatever, Mom," I said. I was beginning to feel drowsy and blinked a couple of times, trying to focus on their faces, which were getting blurrier by the minute.

"You must have fallen pretty hard to get a concussion," said Malcolm. He circled the bed and walked up behind our mother. "Process of elimination brings us back to preacher man."

"I told you to let it go," I said. My mom turned to him and raised one eyebrow.

Just then Xavier walked back in the room, and everyone acted like they were extras in an E. F. Hutton commercial. "Are you okay, sweetheart? You need anything?" asked Xavier.

"No, you've already done so much. I just want to rest," I replied, hoping he caught the edge in my voice.

"Well, guys, why don't you go ahead back home," said my mom as she turned to my dad. "I'll keep the car, honey, and will come home as soon as Monica is resting well." She fumbled with folding the sheet and fixing the pillow around my head.

Xavier replied, "Mrs. Joyner, I'm going to be right here. I'm not going anywhere, so you can go ahead home and take care of your husband. I insist."

"You may insist, but I'm not going anywhere until Monica is resting," said my mom. "After that, if all is well, I'll go on home."

"Okay, princess," said my dad. "If you need anything,

just tell your mom to call me, and I'll come right back over here." My dad kissed my free hand, then my cheek.

"Okay, shortie girl," said Malcolm. He touched my forehead with his fingertip. "I'll check on you later."

Ted added a comment and walked over to where Malcolm was standing with Xavier. "We will get up with you later, Xavier," said Ted. Xavier and Ted exchanged looks, with neither of them blinking.

Reluctantly, Ted, Malcolm, and my dad retreated toward the door. I watched and wanted so much to call my dad back in and tell him all that had happened. I never kept anything from him. At my worst and when everyone else was judging me, he was always there to comfort me.

"Hello, Monica. If you wanted to see me, you didn't have to go to this extreme. You could have just walked into my office," said Dr. Bennett as she walked into my room.

She'd always had a sense of humor. This morning, though, it wasn't exactly appreciated. "It was not my doing," I replied. "I would rather see you in the office any day."

"Hello, Mr. Phillips," said Dr. Bennett.

"Hello, Dr. Bennett," said Xavier. He stood up and shook her hand.

"And, Monica, I believe this is your mother," said Dr. Bennett. "I've met her at the office a couple of times."

"Yes, I'm Monica's mother. Did you come by to check on my daughter?" My mother remained in her seat but eased to the edge of it.

Dr. Bennett looked from my mother to me, and I scratched my forehead before speaking. "Mom, Dr. Bennett is here to check me out. When I fell earlier, I miscarried."

"Oh, good Lord!" cried my mother. "Why didn't you tell me before now that you were pregnant?" Mom stood up and walked over to the hospital bed.

Dr. Bennett moved back so that my mom could take a position next to the bed. "I didn't know," I said. "I was late, but I just thought it was my out-of-whack hormones. But when I fell, I started bleeding, and there was fetal tissue visible."

My mother's eyes started to water. "I'm so sorry, baby. I'm so sorry. Dr. Bennett, please do whatever you have to do. Monica has been through so much."

"Well, if you would wait in the hall, I'm going to examine her, and we will discuss what we need to do from there," said Dr. Bennett.

Mom left after Dr. Bennett told her she would be performing a D & C later in the day. She wanted to go home and check on Dad and get a little rest before coming back for the procedure.

Xavier and I didn't exchange any words once we were alone. I had questions. I just wasn't ready to deal emotionally with any of his answers, if he cared enough to give any.

When the nurse came to take my vitals, she slipped a little happy juice in my IV to help the oral pain pill. She went to get Xavier a blanket since he refused to leave my side.

I tried to listen as he chatted with the nurse. She was telling him that she was in an abusive relationship and was praying for a way out. I wanted to stay awake long enough to hear his advice to her. If I could have kept my eyes open, I'd have told her that she deserved more and that abuse was not love. But, wouldn't I be preaching one thing and doing another?

Xavier prayed for her, and after she left, he stood up and came to my bedside. My eyes were closed, and I guess he assumed I was in a deep sleep. He leaned over and kissed me gently and spoke in a whisper against the hollow of my neck. "I love you, Monica, and I'm so sorry. I never meant to hurt you or our baby. Please forgive me." I listened to his soft sobs as I drifted off into a sedated state.

Chapter 15

I jumped straight up in the bed and felt the pull of the IV that was attached to my hand. All around me, the room was dark except for the dim light over the head of the bed. My body was damp and clammy with sweat, although the room was cool. I must have been having a bad dream. I closed my eyes as parts of it flashed through my mind much too quickly for me to still any one scene. What was apparent was that in each of them, I was walking away from Xavier, and I went so far away that I couldn't find my way back.

I watched his sleeping form reclined in the chair at the foot of the bed. His blazer rested around his neck to provide what little warmth it could against the chill hospitals always had. He appeared to be just a big, soft teddy bear, and physically, he was as adorable as they came. I couldn't help but wonder whether when he awoke, the Xavier I met and fell in love with would greet me or the person who had become so foreign to me. I pondered for hours how we'd come to this. There was no sedative anywhere in the hospital that could put me to sleep long enough to keep me from thinking about my situation. I wished there was, but my wide open eyes, taking in the sight of the man I wanted to dislike and knew I would always love, confirmed it.

My heart held so much all at once, pain, empathy, sadness, and now an emptiness I never knew before overpowered me, and there was no one I could really talk to. No one would understand my dilemma. My father and brothers would tear Xavier apart; my mother, like Xavier's parents, wouldn't believe that Xavier would treat me badly; and I just couldn't unleash any of it on Trina, who had very little faith in happily ever after.

I was crying quiet tears when one of the nurses entered the room to check my vital signs and make sure the monitor wasn't malfunctioning.

She was short, with skin the color of butterscotch. Her hair was cut in a shapely out-dated afro. Her eyes were kind and sparkled, with a brightness that I noticed immediately. I took in the sight of her smock, which had colorful clowns on it. It was so noticeable that she enjoyed her job and took great pride in handling the health issues of people. When the nurse walked closer, she saw that I was wide awake. "Are you in any pain? I could get you something else to take."

"No, thank you. I don't want to take anything else. I'll be fine." I lifted my left hand, forgetting I couldn't get it all the way up to my face. So, I wiped the few tears away with my right hand.

"Your husband is Pastor Phillips, isn't he?" She turned slightly.

"Yes, Pastor Phillips is my husband." I watched as she moved around slowly, checking me out.

"Some of the nurses are buzzing around, talking about the first lady of New Horizons being on our floor.

You and your husband have such a presence here in
Philly. Listen to me going on and on. I haven't even introduced myself. I'm Eunice."

"Nice to meet you." While drifting in and out of
sleep, I'd heard Xavier talking to different people.
They'd asked for prayers for themselves and family
members, for financial blessings, for deliverance. You
name it, they'd asked for it. The world was definitely
searching for a word, and they would get it from anywhere and from whomever they could.

We chatted about the good things that New Horizons
was doing and how her nephews had been traveling
down the wrong road, but after participating in one of
our mentoring programs, they had gotten their lives together. Both were studying at Temple. I never grew tired
of success stories. I asked for their names and made
sure I added them to our tree of achievement.

"You know, Mrs. Phillips, being a pastor's wife can be
so demanding and very overwhelming. Everyone thinks
it's hard on the pastor. Shoot, they just don't know that
his work is easy because women like you make it so."
She continued to talk. "Church people can be funny.
They want to see what they want to see, and that is not
always how things are. The biggest sacrifices are made
by you first ladies that stand in the background."

I could only listen as this lady looked beyond the pale
blue hospital gown, past the first lady position, the re-
sponsibilities, the demands, the disappointments, and
saw the juggling act and the pain that had landed me in
this place.

Eunice slid my gown up slightly and checked the
bleeding. Satisfied that everything looked okay down
there, she pulled it down and placed the bedcover back
over me. "I don't know you personally, but you are a

beautiful young woman, and the spirit of the Lord is telling me that you are living in the shadow of a great man who hasn't learned to humble himself through all the fame and popularity," she said. "That's the quickest way to lose your way, and if you lose your way, can't anybody follow you."

I wanted to tell her to shut up and mind her business, but everything she said was true. It was as if she was reading from a script of our lives. I knew enough about prophecy to accept it when it came as a confirmation, and while she'd said she had nephews at New Horizons, she'd never said that she had attended our church. Still, I wasn't so out of it that I wasn't cautious and didn't immediately pray and ask God to cover me just in case this conversation took a demonic turn.

"I don't mean to be all up in your business, but can I just be candid with you?" she said. She moved close enough so I could hear her, without waking up Xavier, who stirred in the recliner a little.

"Yes, please go ahead." I didn't understand why I told her to continue, but I was eager to listen.

"You have one life to live, and God wants you to live it, activating your gifts. Anything other than that is not living God's way. You ended up here because you have been so busy taking care of him, you didn't even realize that he had stopped taking care of you. Maybe not in the traditional way, you know, food, shelter, and the like, but emotionally. It takes both to keep a marriage going, even if it's the union of a reverend and his first lady. You two are not exempt from trouble. Honey chile, you are on the devil's hit list, and he's gunning for your husband." She turned to Xavier, then looked back at me. "But you got to let him fight that battle and start seeing yourself the way God sees you."

Eunice glanced at her watch. "Goodness, look at the time," she said. "I'm going to check on a few other patients, but you take care of yourself and remember that you're a lot stronger than you think. God made you that way."

I watched her leave and drifted off to sleep, resting better than I had in a while, because I finally knew what I had to do.

I was so glad to be going home. Two days in the hospital was definitely too long. I was gingerly moving around, trying to get my clothes on, when someone knocked lightly. "Come in," I called.

Xavier came through the door, dressed in a pair of jeans and a polo shirt. It was rare that he wore jeans. His wardrobe included several pair, yet most of them remained on the hangers, with price tags still on them. "Good morning," he said. "Are you almost ready?"

I was surprised he was so early. He had stayed until after midnight the night before and had only left because he wanted to get some things ready for me at home. "Almost," I said. "Just trying to get my legs to cooperate enough to get these pants on."

"I'm sorry. I should have brought a skirt or dress. I wasn't thinking." He walked over and stood. I'm sure he was trying to decide if he should help me, or if I would yell out or, better yet, commence beating him upside the head.

"You can help me." He walked over, and I leaned against his shoulder as he helped me put my legs in the pants, one leg at a time. "Thanks."

"Have they discharged you yet?" He looked at the nearby table, scanning it for something marked "Discharge."

"The nurse should be back in a few minutes. Listen, before she comes back in, I need to tell you something." I looked at him as I continued. "I called Trina and asked her to pick me up after she goes to our house and picks up a few things for me. She just happens to be remodeling the shop and is off for a few weeks. Mom was planning on leaving for her church retreat in the morning, and I don't want her to change her plans. She was responsible for all the planning and is facilitating a couple of the workshops. We've been going back and forth about it all morning, but I finally convinced her to go."

"How is that supposed to look? I could understand going to your mom's, but to Trina's?" He paced around.

"It will look like I'm staying with my best friend so you can continue working. And since when do I care about what people think? You do enough of that for both of us. I need the extra care, and I'm sure you have things you need to do at the church. It's that cut and dry."

I turned my back to him and looked through my tote bag. We had been going through a storm for the past two days, but he was busy worrying about what people would say if I didn't come home with him. He should have been more concerned about what people would say if they found out about the reason for my fall.

"You don't have to stay over there. I told everyone at the office I would be home with you for as long as you need me. I will be going to church only on Sunday to preach the two services, and actually, I can get one of the associate ministers to preach for me if need be. So, don't worry about my schedule. I got it all covered."

"Xavier, we haven't talked about what happened the other night, and God knows, I really don't want to, but we can't act as if it didn't happen. And, more importantly, we can't pretend that the miscarriage didn't happen." I had told myself that I wasn't going to cry, but the floodgates had just opened up.

"Monica, I know what you have been trying to do, and I've been trying to do the same. I know it happened, and I can't tell you how bad I feel about it. I can't believe I allowed myself to get that outraged. I pushed you, and if I hadn't, you wouldn't have had a head injury, and you'd still be pregnant. I know you think I'm heartless, but I love you, and I never wanted to hurt you."

"So, why did you push me like that? You had to know that I would end up hurt. Not to mention what you said. Deep down you've been upset because I can't carry a baby to term. I never knew you felt that way, but you stood there and unleashed all that anger and hatred on me. I'll never be free of those words."

"Please, baby, don't hold that against me. We all make mistakes, and I'm no exception."

"I never said you were. Just let me go to Trina's for a few days, and you can keep up at the church and handle things at the community center. After that, I just don't know." I paused. "If you're worried about what to tell people, I'll call your parents and tell them I'm staying with Trina for the very reason I shared with you, the first part, that is. I can also have Nita send an e-mail to the church administration and the community center staff regarding my need for rest and where they can contact me. I'm sure they will see it as a friend watching over me."

Xavier stayed until Trina got there. He walked out to the car with us, helped me out of the wheelchair, and reached to hug me tightly. I hadn't told Trina any of what happened, and I didn't intend to, so I allowed him to hold me for a moment. I spoke to him softly. "Find your way back to me."

He stared back at me as if he hadn't understood what I'd said. He didn't respond, and to be honest, I wasn't expecting him to.

Chapter 16

I wasted no time calling everyone that was someone in our lives. I fought to keep things simple and gave them only the abbreviated version, in which I was allowing my friend to care for me so my loving and adoring husband could take care of church business and the community center. I didn't stay on the phone long with Mother Phillips, because I didn't want her to read anything into my decision to stay at Trina's. Especially since the first words to come out of her mouth were that she would have been glad to come to our house and stay with me while Xavier was at work. In fact, before I could get off the phone, Xavier's father suggested the same thing. He also added that it didn't look good for me to be at a friend's when I had family that was available to care for me. He said that Xavier needed his head examined for agreeing with my decision.

My dad was the only one that told me to do what I needed to do for me. My conversation with him lasted only a few minutes, and I felt that if I had decided to tell him everything, including my real reason for staying at Trina's, he would have encircled me in the warmth of understanding. By the time I turned my cell phone off, I could only sit on the bed and look out the window. I thought of the nurse named Eunice at the hospital. I thought of so much, when all I wanted to do was not think at all.

Xavier had called so many times, and I was tired of answering. "Girl, was that Xavier again?" said Trina. I was clicking off my cell phone as I walked into the kitchen.

"Yes, it was him," I replied. If you are making tea, could you please make me a cup?"

"I was and I will," said Trina.

"I'm going to take a shower. Just yell when it's ready."

I felt so relaxed by the time I got out of the shower. I was toweling off and walking into the bedroom when I noticed that Trina was sitting on the bed, with my tea on the nightstand.

"Special delivery," she said. She sat on the bed, dressed in a fresh pair of pajamas. I noticed Trina's eyes get big. I didn't realize that the towel wasn't covering my bruises.

"What in the world happened to you?" she cried. She rushed over to me and pulled the towel down to get a better look. While the bruises weren't as bad as they'd been initially, they were still visible.

I was trying to figure out how much I wanted to tell her. No one knew the whole story. No one knew any part of what had happened. There were some things I could trust Trina with. I was just hoping that when I entrusted her with this turn of events, I wouldn't regret it. I didn't need anyone to play judge or jury; what I needed the most was a chance to say it all out loud and hope it would grant me a little therapeutic relief.

"Let me put something on, and we will talk," I said.

I took a couple of minutes to smooth some lotion over my body, slipped on a camisole and matching capri bottoms, and returned to the bedroom.

She leaned toward the nightstand and handed me the teacup filled with tea and a wedge of lemon. "Don't keep me in suspense any longer," she said. "What happened? Did Xavier do that to you?"

"I'm here because I'm just not ready to go home." I sipped from my cup. "Trina, I didn't fall down the steps. Xavier pushed me. That's why I ended up with a concussion and why I miscarried again."

I watched the shocked look on her face. No one knew about the miscarriage except my husband and, of course, Mom and Dad. "What? Why didn't you tell me?" cried Trina. "You shouldn't be moving around so much, and I believe you should keep your legs elevated."

"I'm not in any pain, really. At least not in the way you mean. There is no physical pain that can compare to the pain in my heart. Trina, I feel so angry, and yet I know that I can't and shouldn't express it."

"Nobody is expecting you to be a saint. He pushed you, and that is abuse. I can't believe the hospital didn't file a report."

"I didn't tell them. The doctor suspected, but she didn't push the issue. He said that he didn't mean to push me. We were having a major disagreement, and Xavier became outraged. Before I knew it, he pushed me down the steps."

"He didn't mean to? What the heck are you saying? No matter what you guys were arguing about, he had no right to put his hands on you. Did you tell your dad or, better yet, your brothers? Somebody needs to go to the church and kick his butt." She stood up, as if looking for something.

"What are you looking for?" I asked.

"The phone. I'm calling your dad." She continued to move around the room and was almost out the door when I stopped her.

"Trina, that is why I didn't want to say anything. I don't want anyone to know, at least not yet. I need time to deal with this on my terms. Please allow me that." I gave her a pleading look. This was exactly why I hadn't wanted to say a word to anyone.

"I'll keep silent only if you promise me that you won't take forever to tell them." She sat back down and wrapped her arm around my shoulder. Like a little girl, I laid my head on her shoulder and closed my eyes. If Trina reacted this way, my family would be ten times worse. I wasn't ready to say a word to them, and while Trina wanted me to, I wasn't sure I could.

An entire week had passed and Sunday morning was upon me again and I was out of sorts. Last Sunday hadn't been that bad, because I was still recovering and didn't feel like moving around that much. I woke up late, and despite Trina's efforts to cook me a large breakfast, complete with blueberry pancakes, I was in the dumps.

"You want to go out and do something?" asked Trina as she lay on the sofa, with me stretched out on the love seat across from her.

"Nope." We had both showered and dressed in sweat-pants and T-shirts. In fact, I had gone through Trina's bounty of kickback clothes since I hadn't gone back to my house to get clothes. We were almost the same size, so her baggy attire fit as well as it was supposed to. My hair was brushed back, and I had put on a headband. In an effort to feel pretty, I had even put on a small pair of diamond stud earrings and had fastened my gold and diamond cross around my neck. Before I'd left the bedroom, I'd kneeled and prayed that God would work out my situation and speak to Xavier's heart. I'd also read a few passages of scripture. I couldn't sing, but I'd felt like bellowing out a few verses of something inspirational and uplifting. I'd racked my brain but hadn't been able to think of one song that would speak to my present state.

My cell phone went off, and I glanced down at it and noticed the caller was my husband. "Hello," I said into the phone.

"Good afternoon," said Xavier. "Church is over, and I thought I would call and check on you. Everyone sends their love, and they even took up a special collection for you. Sister Hilda wanted me to tell you that she added a little extra so you can buy something new." He started laughing.

I laughed along with him because it sounded just like the old bag of wind. "My favorite sister."

"I know, but she sounded concerned. I could come over and bring it to you. In fact, if you feel up to it, I'd like to take you out to dinner. Wherever you want to go. I'm sure you could stand a trip out."

"Thanks, but no. I'm on the sofa, watching a Lifetime movie with Trina." I looked over at her, and she rolled her eyes in disgust. That was another reason why I was sorry I'd involved her: if Xavier and I worked out our differences, Trina would still be hung up on this traumatic period of our marriage.

"Monica, I've been dead set against you being over at Trina's, but if you need time, as you say, why don't you stay in our old condo? Jeff and Doris closed on their house early, so they moved out this weekend. In fact, they gave me the keys after the service today. If you move into the condo temporarily, until you're ready to come home, you won't be crowding Trina, and you'll have more time alone to get yourself together."

I looked over at Trina as she continued to frown. "Thanks, Xavier. That would work out a lot better." I didn't know why I was saying thanks. It was my place, too. Then I remembered his comment about how I hadn't worked for anything we owned. I had been so busy being my husband's wife that, as intelligent and business-minded as I was, I hadn't prepared for this rainy day. I had no raincoat, no umbrella. Heck, I didn't even have a pair of galoshes.

"I'll get Trina to bring me over in the morning to pick up some clothes," I said. "Please leave the key to the condo on the dresser for me." This would actually work out a lot better, and while I knew Trina and my family loved me, the condo would give me some real time to think. Interruption and viewpoint free.

"I'll do that," said Xavier. "If it's okay, I'll call you later." He sounded so sad.

"If you want. I'll be here. Good-bye, Xavier." I hung up the phone before he could say another word, before he could tell me that he loved me, missed me, or was sorry. The more he said those things and the sadder he sounded, the more my resistance waned. I thought for a moment. That was why the characters in the movies went away to get their head together. Daily interruptions, calls, and input from others made you deal with the problem and did not really afford you a chance to work it out. If I'd had a savings account that wasn't connected to Xavier's, I'd have been on a cruise ship to nowhere by now.

Trina and I were both comfortable in the living room, still watching Lifetime, when my mother called. She wanted us to come over for dinner and wouldn't take no for an answer. I really didn't want to get up off the sofa and leave the Danielle Steel made-for-television movie I was watching, but when I told Trina that my mom had cooked chicken and dumplings, she was all ready to drive over to their place.

I fussed the entire time we put on sneakers and grabbed our purses. All the way out the door I whined. By the time I got in the car, I had given up, because Trina wasn't going to change her mind. The thought of my mom's dumplings was making my mouth water, too.

"Trina, look at me. I never dress like this to go out. Not even to the grocery store." I looked down at my clothes.

"That is sad and touching. There is nothing wrong with dressing all the way down. There is no church rule book that says you have to be in a suit every time you walk out of the house." She kept on hustling up the sidewalk, toward my parents' house.

"Well, if you say so. But a pair of jeans might have been a little nicer."

She had tuned me out completely and had opened the door of my house and was yelling for my parents like they were her blood.

"Hey, Trina." My mom came out of the kitchen, wiping her hands on her apron. "Hey, Monica, dear. How are you feeling?"

"I'm good," I said. I followed her eyes and looked at Trina like I could choke her. "Mom, I know I should have put on something else. I allowed my best friend to talk me into this casual look."

My Dad walked in from the kitchen, chewing on something. "There is nothing wrong with the way you look. This is no grand dinner. It's just supper. We do it every day around this time, and on Sundays your mom may add a little something extra."

We heard the back door open and Ted and Malcolm's loud voices. "See. This is just a normal Sunday supper, complete with our regulars, Ted and Malcolm," said my dad. We all laughed.

Ted walked through the door first, with a homemade yeast roll up to his mouth. "What? Why are you all laughing?" he asked.

"Nothing, son. I was just telling Monica that there was no need for her to dress up to come over here, that this is Sunday supper as usual," replied my dad.

"Girl, you looking tore up," said Malcolm as he walked over to where I was standing and looked down at what I had on.

"Malcolm, do I really?" I asked. I rubbed my hand over my hair and pulled my T-shirt down over my hips.

"I'm just joking," said Malcom. "You look all right. But I didn't have to tell you that. What's up with your stuck-up, Miss Prissy attitude?" We all moved toward the dining room table.

"I know you're not letting being away from Xavier get to you. You are over at Trina's, hiding out, trying to be all hush-hush about things," said Ted. "If he don't get his holier than thou act together, fu—" He turned to Mom. "I mean, forget him. You are a Joyner, so you know you will survive."

"Well, thanks for reminding me of that," I said as I took a seat beside Trina. I guess my face told the story.

I was worried about what was going to happen with me and Xavier. And sitting here in the family dining room, I felt like Xavier should be seated in his customary spot, right beside me. Instead, Trina was occupying the seat.

Malcolm had been watching me for a minute. Being the oldest, he had this thing of always wanting to protect me and Ted. Of course, Ted never felt like he needed protecting, and I enjoyed the protection that my big brother provided. It was he who had figured that Xavier must have done something to cause my fall. He'd called me every night since then, and every conversation found me closer and closer to telling him the complete truth, including what Xavier had said and how he'd shoved me. And even about the baby.

"Mom, the turnip greens are delicious," I said. I was trying to avoid being the center of attention. I felt like everybody was looking at me, ready for me to break down or show some sign of emotion. I didn't want to talk about Xavier, but I think they really wanted me to. There was such a thing as not keeping things bottled up, but I felt that there was a certain time for things to take place.

"I was going to wait a little while longer," said Malcolm, "but since everyone is here, including the foster child . . ." Malcolm looked at Trina.

"You know you ain't right. I belong as much as you do," said Trina. "It doesn't take blood to be a family." She barely lifted her head long enough to retaliate. The boys were always riding her about one thing or another and then going to her for advice, help, or for the beauty shop hookup.

"We have nothing but love for you, girl," Ted added.

"Thanks, little brother," said Trina. She smiled and gave him a thumbs-up.

"Where was I? Oh yeah, I am thinking about dating exclusively. I don't want to be a player no more," said Malcolm.

Everybody at the table busted out laughing. I couldn't believe this clown. I knew he was trying to let us know that he had found the potential one, but leave it to him to say so in a humorous way.

"So, what are you saying, boy?" Dad was still grinning as he asked his number one to make sense.

"Seriously. It's just going to be about me and Sheila," said Malcolm. "We've been seeing each other for a couple of years, and we discussed it, and for the most part, we are ready to settle down."

"So, she pretty much told you that unless you get ready to put a ring on her finger, you aren't going to be able to visit dairy land?" Ted asked.

Again, everybody roared with laughter. This time I wiped tears of laughter from my eyes. This was just what I needed. I had forgotten how much fun we had when we were all together.

"Nothing like that," said Malcolm. "I don't even visit dairy land. I may go by occasionally, but I don't stop." He winked his eye at Ted.

"So, does this mean I only have to give one free hairdo every two weeks?" said Trina. "You know, I've been averaging three or four free clients with you calling in to make the biweekly appointments. You better be glad I'm good with names and I love you. I could have blown your spot up so many times."

"That's why I love you. You gave me time to be me," said Malcolm.

"Malcolm, are you sure you are ready to commit?" I asked. It was out of my mouth before I thought about what I was saying. "I mean, do you really love her, and does she love you?"

Malcolm glanced at me and pushed his plate to the side. I believed that he was finished eating, but he probably wanted to have a second helping. My situation with Xavier was making things awkward. "I do love her very much. And I believe with all my heart and my soul that she loves me. Now, I'm just saying I want to date her and her alone. I'm not announcing marriage. This is only a mini step." He managed to smile. "But I appreciate you looking out for my heart. I always want to do the same for you."

There was a need to lighten the mood. "Trina, how 'bout I just pass you the serving bowls and you can eat out of them? That would save you from having to reach and slide bowls."

"You are too funny, Monica," replied Trina. "It's all your fault. I opened up my home to you, and you don't even have a sister's dinner done when she comes home from a hard day's work." She reached for another roll. "Tell me what is up with that?"

"Trina, I am not your keeper," I said as I popped her upside the head playfully. "Actually, speaking of living arrangements, I'm going to be moving into the condo temporarily." I looked around and held my breath. There was no time like the present, and I would have to tell them at some point in the very near future since I was going to be moving some of my things tomorrow.

Mom was the first to speak. "Oh, okay. Well, Malcolm and Ted will help you." No one else said a word. It was as if each of them was a member of a psychic network and had seen this coming.

"We have your back, and we're behind you," said

Malcolm. He winked an eye. I was about to shed a tear when Dad silently mouthed, "I love you."

"Honey, I'll go in and get the dessert," said my dad. He rose from the head of the table and went into the kitchen.

"What's for dessert?" Ted questioned, pushing his dinner plate to the side.

"Actually, we have two desserts. Zerenda dropped off two sweet potato pies, and I made a triple chocolate cake," replied my mom. "She just got back. In fact, she cut her vacation short so she could be here for Monica."

"She called me the minute her plane landed and made me promise to rest."

Mom was an excellent cook, but she was known locally for her desserts. That was one skill my grandmother had passed on to both her daughters. Auntie Zee could create desserts that could grace any magazine page. I was going to take some sweet potato pie with me, but I couldn't wait to taste the triple chocolate cake.

After we finished our desserts, we went into the living room. Of course, the boys had filled their bellies and were ready to leave.

"Monica, call us when you are ready to move your things," said Ted.

"Yeah, the earlier, the better. My boss man doesn't like it when I'm late for work," said Malcolm as he looked over in Dad's direction.

"When I was your boss man, you didn't come to work on time," replied my dad. "Turning the business over to the two of you may mean spending my legacy to hell."

"Cliff!" Mom looked at him. She knew he was joking, but she didn't like for him to curse.

"We does a good job, and you know that," said Ted.

He laughed on his way out the door. "Monica, holla at us in the morning."

Pulling a cap over my head I set out with Trina to move some of the small items from my house to the condo. Ted and Malcolm had already moved the heavier things. I kept telling myself that I didn't need to carry much, that it was just temporary. But when I thought of the things I needed to make myself comfortable, and I stared at the empty space they'd left in our house, the move started to feel more permanent.

I was glad the condo was only a short distance from the house. We were able to move what I needed in about two trips. Trina didn't want to leave me, but she had planned to go to a hair show that evening.

"Monica, I can stay here with you and help you unpack and put everything away," said Trina. "The show is not that important, and besides, I'm sending two of my stylists there, anyway. So, they will come back and give me a full update."

"No, I don't want you to alter your schedule for me. I'll be fine. And if you help me unpack everything and put it all away, I won't have anything to keep me busy. And more than anything else, I need to be busy," I said as I stood beside the kitchen table. "You guys have lifted and moved all the heavy stuff, so it's not that much. I won't overdo it. I promise."

"Okay, if you say so. But call me if you need anything. And if you don't want to spend your first night here alone, I'll come over."

"Trina, I'm a big girl. And this place is not new to me. I lived here for a while, remember?"

She tapped her head, like she had forgotten. "That's right. Okay, then I'm leaving. Call me."

I hummed as I began to get things in order. The condo was pretty spacious, and the only reason we'd moved was because Xavier had felt, as the pastor of New Horizons, we needed to move on up, like Weezy and George.

By four, I was exhausted. Trina was an early riser, and we had started out around five that morning. While I loved my friend dearly, I wasn't a morning person. On top of that, I wasn't able to sleep that well at her place. There was a lot of truth to the saying that there was no place like home, and I was hoping that since this was my old home, I was going to be able to sleep like a log. I still needed to go to the grocery store, so I fumbled through the condo until I found my cap and sunglasses.

Not wanting to venture far, I stopped at the Acme around the corner. I parked a distance away from the entrance and hiked it across the parking lot. I was dressed in a pair of old jeans, an oversized T-shirt, and sneakers. No one would be able to ID me by looking at my clothes. I had had to search a while to locate these old items. I believe, the last time I wore them was when I had had the bright idea that I would paint my own living room. What started off as an exciting, liberating project ended up a major nightmare. My dad ended up coming over to rescue me in the midst of paint cans, brushes, and plastic drop cloths. I could still see his face as I opened the front door, with my face and half my body covered in dynasty gray paint. If I learned nothing else that day, I learned that contracting the job out was an excellent concept. I was all for outsourcing, even if it was on a small scale.

I removed my sunglasses and rushed through the

store in record time. By the time I got to the counter, I was loaded with everything I needed.

Before I moved my grocery cart forward the straw-berry blond cashier asked, "Paper or plastic?"

"Plastic, please." I removed my items and placed them on the conveyor belt, organizing them as I went along. I did this more to keep my hands busy and my head down than to control what went in what bag.

"Seventy-nine dollars and thirty-seven cents," said the cashier. She smiled and waited for me to swipe my credit card. Xavier hadn't cancelled any of my credit cards, and I'd even noticed this morning, after calling to check my balance, that money had been deposited into my account. I wanted to call and thank him, but reminded myself that it was not just his money. It really was my money, too. I'd worked at the community center since it opened three years ago, and even before that, I'd been busy at the church almost every day. After the board of directors said that the grant included a salary for a director, I'd accepted the position but requested that the salary be put toward funding the center. I'd done it for the center, and I'd done it for my husband.

I pulled my SUV into the private area and parked it in my designated parking space. After a couple of trips, I had taken everything in.

I began to assemble the ingredients I would need to prepare a quick dinner. I sprayed the baking pan with a little Pam, seasoned the chicken, and placed it in the pan. Knowing that I was going to take the easy way for a while, I removed the Uncle Ben's wild rice microwave package from the cabinet and placed it on the counter, with the plan to cook it when the chicken was almost done.

A hot bath was in order, so I delayed putting the

chicken in the oven so I would have time to linger a little and enjoy the luxury of something so simple. I walked through the living room and down the hall. There were two bedrooms, in addition to the large master-bedroom suite, because even in the early years, Xavier and I had planned not to delay having a child. I stood in the doorway of the first room, which we had envisioned as a nursery, and looked around. I wondered what our life would have been like if we had remained in this condo. What would have happened if he hadn't become a preacher? More importantly, what if I hadn't miscarried twice? And what if I hadn't lost this last baby. If Xavier hadn't pushed me down the steps?

Too much depression was not good, and I walked farther down the hall and into the bedroom. I couldn't resist yielding to the urge to be sad one more moment as I removed my clothes and rubbed my hand over my flat stomach. I climbed onto the bed and cried for all that I had lost. The long bath would come later; I'd rest a minute and take a shower, eat my dinner, and go to bed.

My cell phone rang several times and finally stopped. The chime went off, letting me know that someone had left a message. I rolled over and pushed the sheet back a little. Yawning and stretching, I was relieved that I had slept through the night and hadn't experienced any dreams or night sweats.

I reached for my phone and played the message, and I couldn't believe it was him. I hit replay and listened again. Somehow, Bryce Sinclair had cajoled someone from the center into giving him my cell number. Right off the bat, I could think of two people that would do such a thing, Mrs. Epps and Nita. It probably didn't take much.

My phone rang again the minute I put it back on the nightstand. "Hello," I croaked. I coughed once to clear my throat and thought that I should probably take something to avoid coming down with a cold. That would be the last thing I needed.

"Mrs. Phillips, this is Bryce Sinclair. I have been trying to reach you for a couple of weeks. Is everything okay?" he asked. I almost thought I heard real concern in his voice.

"I'm fine. I haven't had a chance to contact you." I was slow in responding because I wasn't sure what he had heard.

"Well, actually, I was in church the Sunday that Pastor Phillips announced that you had fallen and were at home recovering." He waited for me to say something.

I began to go through the motions, weaving a story as I went along. While I was in midstream, he stopped me.

"Mrs. Phillips, I'm not going to let you do this," Bryce said.

"Do what? What are you talking about?" I was confused and irritated.

"Unless you and Xavier have moved since the last time I dropped some papers off to him, there is no reason you should have been shopping near Luke Road, so let it go." He continued. "I just happened to see you yesterday going into Acme. I didn't follow you, because I didn't want you to have to create a story on the spot. Which, I just learned, is not your strong suit."

"I've never been one to think on my feet, especially when my story is built upon nothing but falsehoods," I said.

"Lies. Call them what they are. 'Falsehoods' makes it seem way too pretty. Look, do you want to talk?"

The question was out before I had a chance to say

something about him calling me a liar. "I guess we can go over the Kings Vision Program." I had e-mailed Xavier and told him that I would be handling some of my duties at the center. This program was one of the things I had included in my newly organized workload. I didn't want too many people to see me out in public and ask why I hadn't come back to church yet, but there were things that I could do from the house and via fax and e-mail.

"I don't want to talk about the Kings Vision Program, and I don't think you do, either. I want to talk about you. You obviously are trying to stay down under, but since I caught a peek of you, you can at least tell me what is going on." He was blunt.

I was tired and had to admit there was so much I couldn't tell Trina, or anyone else for that matter. I guessed I could use a listener. "I may consider it."

"I've got a late practice today, and since you do go out, you can meet me at Five South Bank Street around nine tonight. You know, in the Old City area."

"What's at Five South Bank Street?" I thought about it and couldn't come up with a thing. I knew the area was well known for its nightlife, but I wasn't sure if the place was a lounge or restaurant or both.

"You'll see when you get there. It's not like I can meet you in your usual circles, so this place may be a little different from what you are used to."

"You are enjoying my incognito status, aren't you?" I couldn't believe he was finding humor in my having a limited radius. He was willing to listen, and for that, I wouldn't fuss about the locale.

"Monica, are you going to be there?" He was quizzing me like I was a student that needed to answer a question while standing at the blackboard.

"Yes, I'll be there." I didn't know why I was saying yes, but I was saying it just the same.

"Good. I'll see you then." He hung up the phone, evidently on to emotionally torture his next victim.

As I rolled on my side, I looked out the nearby window and tried to gauge what the weather was like outside. I didn't trust the weather report. If they said it would be hot, it would be cool, and if they said it would be cool, it would be hot as all get out. I thought of the ending of our conversation. He'd called me Monica. Not Ms. or Mrs. Phillips, but Monica. I hadn't corrected him, because it had sounded good coming from his lips. Refreshingly good.

Chapter 17

It had been more than a month, and I needed to shop. Plain and simple, I was yearning to spend some money. The pin that popped the balloon in my shopping equation would be the reality that my money was limited. I wasn't sure how long Xavier was going to give me access to our assets, so until then, I'd have to be frugal. I expected he would continue to allow me access to our accounts, because if he was nothing else, he was an excellent provider; however, my spouse was no longer predictable.

Instantly, it came to me. There was someplace I could go, and it wouldn't require an exchange of money for services rendered. I was brilliant. I could get a few hours of pampering and be treated like the queen I knew I was. Searching for my cell phone under the pile of clothes I had placed on the end of my bed, I located it and hit a programmed button to quick dial the number.

A lady with a high-pitched voice picked up the phone. I didn't recognize the voice. "Could I speak to Trina please?" I said.

"Hello, this is Trina," she responded in a cheery, customer service voice.

"Girl, it's Monica. Look, I need to get a makeover like yesterday, and I can't come into the shop, because half of New Horizons goes there. So, come up with a plan." I knew she would argue at first, but I'd win her over.

"You are always expecting the almost impossible. But because of what you are going through, I'm going to bend without complaint. I'll pack up what I need and be there in an hour. Just make room for me and my stuff."

"No problem. Oh, and would it be possible to get a manicure and a pedicure?" I knew I had just pushed a button.

"I'm ahead of you. I'm going to ask Dynasty to come with me. She is my new trainee. Now, can I go so I can get everything together and make sure Dynasty doesn't take any more walk-ins?"

"I love you." She was the best, and she really knew how to put a smile on my face.

"You, too. Now get off my line. You are so bad for business."

My hair had never looked so good. I had been staring at my reflection for the umpteenth time. Xavier had never wanted me to cut my hair, and Trina had always raged about how long it took me to grow out my hair to a decent length, so I had always allowed them to win the battle. But today I'd won the war. I was sporting a short, razor-cut bob. It looked and felt so carefree, and I quickly resolved that it was just what I needed. She had even added a few highlights, which brought out an alluring edge that I didn't know I had. Taking one more look in the mirror, I thought, *You go on, girl*.

* * *

I arrived in the Old City area sooner than I thought I would. So, I decided to drive around to kill time. I had to admit that Bryce was right. This was an area that I never ventured into, and I relaxed a little, knowing that no one Xavier and I knew would see me meeting a handsome and buff guy who just happened to be listed in today's paper as one of Philadelphia's hottest and most popular men. Right after I had spoken with Bryce this morning, I had stumbled to the door and had got the paper from outside. Over a cup of hazelnut Starbucks coffee, I'd read away, and there he was in all his fineness. As married as I was, and even if I'd been blind in one eye and not able to see with the other, I still couldn't have missed what I saw before me. Even though the photo was in black and white, it only confirmed what I saw the first day I met him in my office and what I couldn't miss when we had lunch.

I pulled my Lexus into the parking lot across from the address he gave me and glanced around. There it was, the Five Spot. He had invited me to a club of sorts. Well, I was here, and I wouldn't turn around and go back since I had gone all out to prepare. I pulled the lighted mirror down and checked my make-up and my hair. I had done that at the last red stoplight, so I knew nothing had changed, and yet I looked at myself from both sides. I even checked my teeth to make sure there was no lipstick on them.

With all that done, I checked the digital display, which told me it was 9:10. Arriving too early would make me appear anxious, and I didn't want that. On time would send the message that I was predictable. But a few minutes late said, "I'm worth waiting for." I stepped out of the truck and looked down at my outfit. I was dressed in black cuffed slacks and a black-and-white Empire tunic, with kimono sleeves and a neckline that showed just the right amount of cleavage. The Nine West sandals I chose were a great accent for the outfit. Silver jewelry hung from my neck and my ears. My watch and tennis bracelet hardly ever remained in my jewelry box, and neither did my wedding ring. But after my hospital visit, as wrong as I knew it was, I had left my ring in the cushioned box.

I didn't look like I was going to a church meeting or the office, but more like I was hanging out. That was exactly the look I was going for. As I walked, I left a trail of my exotic fragrance in the air, and I could only smile to myself. My hips swayed to the rhythm my heels created against the pavement as I approached the entrance of the Five Spot.

Hearing footsteps behind me, I turned slightly and looked up into Bryce's smiling face. "Trying to sneak up on me?" I asked.

"No, I watched you sit in your vehicle, checking the time, making sure you were going to make a fashionably late entrance." He continued to smile and touched my lower back, allowing me to walk in before him.

While he paid the cover charge, I had a chance to observe him. He was dressed in black slacks and a white shirt. The outfit was simple, but I knew it had to be a famous label, because the garments hung on him like they were made to be worn by someone with money.

We were seated at a table in a cozy corner, and still, Bryce had plenty of room to stretch his legs and relax against the cushioned back of the seat. When the server came over, he ordered wings and chili fries, claiming he hadn't eaten for at least a couple of hours and was starved.

Our conversation was relaxed and we talked about

light stuff and he joked about this and that. Before long, I was chatting and eating from his plate while I sipped on a ginger ale. I had assumed that he would order something harder than soda, but after he ordered a ginger ale, too, he told me that he didn't drink or smoke.

I had thought I would feel funny talking to Bryce and listening to music that was different from what I was used to. When the conversation turned personal, I was so comfortable that I shared everything, and he listened without speaking. Once I had finished, the burden of keeping it in lifted, and I was grateful for an ear that wasn't attached to a body that wanted to pay lip service.

"Would you care to dance?" Bryce asked.

"It's been years, and I don't even know if I still remember how to," I answered quickly and hoped he didn't press the issue.

"Well, tonight I'll take a rain check, but the next time we play therapist and patient, I'm going to expect you to grant me at least one dance. It would only be fair. Deal?" He reached out his pinky.

"Deal." I laughed and wrapped my pinky around his.

We talked a while longer, and I finally announced that it was way past my bedtime, and I needed to get home. I read disappointment in his face, but I had gotten what I had come for. Someone to listen to me vent. I was going across town with a burden lifted, and that was worth the trip.

Bryce insisted on following me home, and I didn't object. He said he would just drive past and wouldn't turn in or anything. He was concerned only for my safety.

True to his word, once I signaled and turned into the condo development, he drove away in his Mercedes SLK.

Before I could get out of the truck, my cell phone rang. "Hello."

"Monica, I had a really good time. Thanks for joining me and for allowing me to listen. Sleep well." With that said, he hung up.

I floated through my front door, and without turning on the lights, I headed straight to my bedroom. I could still smell the scent of him, and a strange urge settled below my waist. It hadn't happened in a while, and I wasn't sure I wanted to feel any urge. I just wanted to feel without the hurt.

Slipping out of my shoes, I turned on the light in the bedroom and walked to my dresser. I began to take off my jewelry and place it in the jewelry box, and there, in the cushioned box, was a reminder. I was still a married woman.

The very next morning, bright and early, my cell phone went off. I was nestled between the sheets and woke, with a giggle in my throat. I didn't even want to imagine who was calling, because I knew exactly what and whom I'd been thinking about before I'd closed my eyes and drifted into sleepy land.

"Dag, this better be good." I didn't bother to open my eyes and normally wouldn't have answered the phone like that. I had no clue who it was and just wanted to go back to sleep and reclaim whatever it was I'd left in dreamland.

"My, aren't we grouchy in the morning. Didn't you get enough sleep?" Bryce's deep, rich voice came through the phone.

Instantly, I was awake. "It's early, and you are the reason why I'm grouchy. But, since I'm up, what can I do for you?" I resisted the urge to smile because somehow I thought he could hear what he couldn't see.

"Glad you asked. My car needs its yearly maintenance, and they are picking it up as we speak. Can you give me a ride to the airport?"

"The airport?" I confirmed what he'd said.

"You know, the place with the big planes, all the noise, and ticket counters." He laughed.

"You are too funny for it to be so early. Give me your address, and I'll be there." I grabbed a pen and was ready to write.

He rattled the address off to me, and I was ready to hang up the phone.

"Monica, aren't you going to ask me what time my plane leaves?" He was still laughing.

"What time, Bryce?" I had to laugh with him. The boy had thrown me off, and I believed he knew it.

"At ten a.m. So, you have just about three hours to get over here. See you when I see you."

I pulled up to the gate and gave my name. The tall, well-groomed gentleman checked a pad and waved me through. I was impressed. Of course, Bryce would live in the plushest neighborhood in the area. It had taken me a minute to get here, but the beauty of it all alone was worth my rising early. Finding his house, I pulled around the circular driveway. He was walking out, dressed in jeans and a 76ers T-shirt.

"Good morning, sweetness," he said. "You look good, even though I woke you up so early." He placed his bags in the cargo area after I popped open the trunk.

I held my breath as he came back around to get in the car. When I heard the car door close and watched out of the corner of my eye as he put his seat belt on, I exhaled, and there was the smell of him again. "Good morning yourself." I wasn't going to look at him. Not yet. I couldn't. I counted to ten, and between each number, I said silently, *I'm a married woman.*

"Monica, could you look at me for a moment?" He touched my arm, and a chill ran down my spine.

"What?" I questioned but didn't stop the car.

"Look at me." He touched my arm again.

I had only gotten to the end of the driveway when I put my foot on the brake and slowly turned to him. By the time my eyes met his, the remainder of the ice had melted away from my heart, and I felt it. I could honestly feel something. "I'm looking."

"And I'm seeing." He leaned toward me. I thought he was going to kiss my lips, and again, I held my breath. Instead, he touched my cheek softly.

"Thanks for coming to get me. Now you can continue," he said. He put his sunglasses on and began to play with my Sirius radio system.

We were cruising along and had just passed an intersection near the church when I spotted them. I could recognize that long yellow Cadillac anywhere. "Jesus Christ!" I yelled.

"What's wrong?" Bryce sat up in his seat and looked around. "Is it a cop?"

"No, it's Sister Hilda and Sister Sadie from church. They are in the long yellow Cadillac that just pulled out at the light."

"Do you think they saw you?" He started to turn around.

"Don't turn around. They are right behind us, and knowing those buzzards, they are straining to see who is in the truck with me." I speeded up and ran the next light.

Bryce started laughing. "Monica, don't look now, but they just floored the Caddy and are hot on your tracks." He was almost on the floor in a fit of laughter.

"Bryce, this isn't funny. I've got to lose them." I was nervous because I knew they were going to spread the news of this innocent drive to the airport like wildfire. Hilda was driving the big car so fast, the bumps in the road were causing their gray heads to hit the ceiling of the car.

"Maybe they will think I'm Xavier." He started to turn around again.

I hit his hand. "You think? The last time I checked, Xavier was high yellow, and you are a chocolate Milk Dud. Now turn back around."

"Chocolate? I'm offended. You could have at least said milk chocolate or creamy chocolate. You just gonna call me chocolate just like that, huh?" He was enjoying every tortuous moment of the car chase and my nervous reaction to it.

"Bryce, stop tripping. What am I going to do?" I was almost crying.

"Seriously, they are catching up with you. So, you may want to make a sharp right turn and stop driving like Miss Daisy is in the backseat and get your money's worth out of this Lex. You got some horses under the hood, and you need to use them."

As he suggested, I made the sharp right turn and hit the gas, throwing us both back in the buttery leather seats. It worked, because I glanced in the rearview mirror and watched as the long yellow Cadillac tried to maneuver the sharp turn and ran up on the curb.

By the time we got to the airport after our detour, Bryce was holding his side in a fit of laughter. I couldn't help but laugh with him. I pulled up to the unloading area and waited for him to get his things together.

"Girl, that was too funny," said Bryce. He was taking his stuff out of the back. Once he was done, he came back to the passenger door. "Seriously, are you okay?"

"I'm fine. Go ahead. You're going to miss your plane." I smiled and pointed toward the entrance of the airport. "I saw the e-mail about how you are taking a few of the boys to the game. I'm sure they will have a blast."

"I think they will. But I'd gladly pay a late fine if I could catch a replay of the last hour. You be easy on those turns."

"Get out now." I couldn't believe how funny he was.

"If you need to talk anytime, just give me a call. Miss you." Before I realized what he'd said, he was gone.

How could he miss me? At first I thought, *Nah,* but after last night, I couldn't miss it. He was a good person, and I could use an extra friend. I had listened to Xavier, and the only person I had in my friend circle was Trina. I had called Liz a couple of times, but she kept making excuses for why she couldn't come to see me, and why I couldn't come to see her. The last time I talked with her, she just came right out and said Patrick didn't want her to go near me.

When I pulled into the condo parking lot, I found Xavier in my space, standing beside the church van. Why he was driving it, I couldn't say. This was indeed a rare occasion. I did know why he was there. Obviously, Sister Hilda and Sister Sadie must have gotten the Caddy off the curb and rushed back to the church to spread the word. They hadn't even bothered to use the grapevine channel but had gone straight to the top.

I pulled next to him and reached in the backseat to get my purse. I hadn't done anything wrong, so I wasn't going to take any mess from him. Now, my thoughts were different, but no one was privy to those. Only the man above.

"Monica Joyner Phillips, what in the hell do you think you are doing?" he yelled. He was in my face the minute I climbed out of the truck.

"Hold up. What did you say?" I couldn't believe he was using that word, and I couldn't believe that he was raising his voice at me yet again.

"Sister Sadie came into the office, without knocking, telling me you were gallivanting around town in my truck with a man. And I doubt very seriously that it was Ted or Malcolm. In fact, it wasn't, because I called them." He was standing in front of me.

As calmly as I could, I spoke. "You care to come in? If you want to talk to me, you can do it inside. Outside is not the place." I was steaming and didn't want it to show.

Once we were inside, he continued in a rage. "Who was in my truck?"

"Your truck? I'm sick of this ownership thing. The title says Monica Joyner Phillips. At least it did the last time I checked."

"I gave it to you," he huffed.

"That's the operative word. Gave!" I placed my purse on the kitchen counter and turned to get a bottle of water. "You want something to drink?"

"This is a serious matter, and you're offering me water?"

"Look, I gave Bryce a ride to the airport." I took a seat on the sofa and reached for the remote.

"Bryce Sinclair?"

"Yes, Bryce Sinclair. His car was due for maintenance, and he needed a quick ride to the airport. End of discussion."

"The discussion is far from over." He paced around the room like a caged animal. "Why would he ask you? The man could have called a driver, and I'm sure he has more than one vehicle, and several women at his beck and call, for that matter. Why would he need my wife to take him to the airport?"

I was so carried away, I hadn't thought of Bryce as having more than one car or a number of women eager to carry him anywhere. "Are you finished?"

"Not yet. You haven't answered my question." He sat next to me, and I could almost smell his rage, which oozed from every pore of his being.

"Xavier, this is not the first time a man has been in my truck. I've taken Deacon Thomas and some of the others across town, to the post office, to meetings. Not to mention that Deacon Fooks and I went to New York for three days, and I drove. So, why are you tripping? I still work as director of the community center, and at your request, Bryce and I work on the Kings Vision Program together. In fact, my boys are already on their way to Denver."

I was glad I had read the memorandum this morning, since Bryce hadn't mentioned it last night. At least, it seemed that I was aware of what was going on. I continued. "But it is nice of you to remember that I'm your wife. You didn't remember that when you pushed me." I nervously took a sip of water. The rage in his eyes was the same rage I'd seen when he pushed me down the steps. Maybe he was on some kind of drug. *No,* I thought. *This black man is crazy.*

"You think I have no say because I made a mistake. I

can take all you have, and you're playing word games with me."

"You can take whatever you want, but that's not going to break my spirit. I've spent weeks trying to get myself together, because I couldn't figure out how the man I love could hurt me. I lost our baby, and you are here questioning me about who was in my car. You should be doing all you can to mend the broken pieces of my heart. If you think you can take everything, go ahead. The truth is, Pastor Phillips, I don't have anything left for you to take." My heart raced.

He looked at me through narrowing eyes. "I'm sorry. I didn't mean to upset you. But can you imagine what people are going to say, and what they will think?"

"It doesn't matter if you know the truth."

"Yes, but it will affect the ministry if people think you are running around town with another man. You are the first lady, for Christ's sake."

"But I've told you what I was doing. Isn't that enough?" When he didn't answer, I went on. "I think you need to leave, and when you realize what's important, let me know."

He slammed the door shut. Obviously, opinions mattered more to him than convincing me that together, we were bigger than our problems.

Chapter 18

That was the straw that broke the camel's back. I wasn't cheating, and yet he'd acted as if I was. All I'd done was find a friend, someone that made me forget my problems. I wasn't crazy. I knew Bryce was into me, but I hadn't entertained it. That night at the strip club, I ran out. All in the name of love and honoring my marital vows. For what? So I could be accused of doing something I hadn't. Unbeknownst to Xavier, I was still a God-fearing woman. Nothing was going to change that.

The phone rang, and I decided to just let it ring, then grabbed my purse and pulled it out of the side pocket.

"Monica? Are you okay?" Bryce was on the other end, although the connection wasn't great.

"No. Xavier just left, and as I suspected they would, the sisters ran right over to his office and told him that they saw me with someone."

"And I hope you told him it was me."

"I did. But it didn't stop his rage." I rubbed my temple and closed my eyes, trying to shut the headache out. It had been long enough for me to be headache free, and still the headaches continued to come and go. I knew I was supposed to let Dr. Joseph know, but I just kept praying that they would go away and that they weren't a sign of a serious ailment.

"He didn't do anything crazy, did he?" Bryce yelled over the static.

"No. Listen. You are breaking up. I'm okay. Just call me when you land." I was going to lie down and hope my headache subsided.

"Hey, why don't you join us."

"What? How?" I wasn't sure I was hearing him.

"On the next plane. Haven't you ever done anything spontaneous? Just pack a bag. There is a first-class ticket waiting for you at the airport."

"You were sure I'd say yes?" I was irritated. Someone else was doing all the planning and controlling.

"I was hoping. I knew you were going to catch some heat for the drive to the airport. And at the last minute, I just went ahead and got an open ticket."

"It's not going to get better, is it?" I asked, praying he had an answer.

"I'm sorry, baby. But, I don't think so. Hop a plane. The next one leaves at six, and you'd be here by ten twenty. I'm sure the boys would be glad to see you, and you can help Davidson out and be an official chaperone."

"Okay. I'm on my way." I hung up the phone. It didn't make sense that I was leaving Philadelphia to go to Denver to watch a game. An honest assessment of my life of late would have indicated that nothing was making sense.

I packed a couple of suitcases. I was closing the door on all my problems, at least for a few days. There was one thing I needed to do before I left, though.

I drove to the community center. I'd remembered that

there was a missionary meeting at two o'clock in the conference room.

I walked through the doors of the center right on time. Mrs. Epps looked like she had seen a ghost, and I spoke and continued on toward the conference room. I swung the door open, and all the ladies in the room turned around.

"Good afternoon, ladies. Don't bother to get up. I'll only need a few minutes of your time. I just have a quick announcement before the meeting gets started." I walked to the front of the room and stood between Sister Sadie and Sister Hilda. "I'm actually here to save you time. I believe I can take care of agenda item number one."

Everybody circled around the table, looked down at their agenda sheet, and stared at each other, with puzzled, bewildered expressions.

"This morning there was a slight accident," I said.

Some of the ladies grabbed their chest and asked if someone was hurt or had died.

"No, ladies, no one was injured. You see, Sister Sadie ran her Cadillac into a curb because she was chasing behind me," I said. I watched the shocked expressions. "Let me explain, I gave Mr. Bryce Sinclair a ride to the airport. An innocent ride to the airport, and like two insane people, they chased us all over town at high rates of speed. Now I continued to drive because I refused to give the two nosy busybodies anything to talk about, and yet after they ran their car up on the curb, they interrupted Pastor Phillips and told him that I was running around town with another man."

Sister Hilda was getting ready to speak, and I motioned to her to wait. "No, let me finish," I said. "Now, you all know that your pastor is a God-fearing man and wouldn't tell you to entertain idle gossip. That is exactly what he told a few of you in this room when Sister Sadie was admitted to the hospital last year for an emergency procedure. He didn't want anyone to believe the ugly rumor that some type of device had broken off in an intimate part of her body. Nor did he want you to believe that Josie, Sister Hilda's housemate, is more than just her friend."

Sister Hilda and Sister Sadie grabbed their chests. Sister Hilda was the first to speak. "They were just rumors. There wasn't any truth to any of that."

"I know what you're saying, and Pastor Phillips didn't want any of us to gossip and spread rumors about that," I said. "So, I know he wouldn't want you to gossip about the affairs of our lives." I turned to look directly at them. They had assumed that he would be outraged. Instead, he'd been hurt that they would bring something so petty to his attention.

I went on. "I have nothing to hide, and neither does the pastor. We are having problems, and we both felt it might help if we gave each other some space, so I've moved out temporarily. And because I love him and want to salvage our marriage, I am following the word of God, which says to separate yourself for a season. I want to ensure that he gives his all to you, his congregation, without dealing with our issues. With God's help, we will work out our differences."

By this time Mrs. Epps was standing in the door of the conference room, with her mouth open so wide, she could catch a fly.

I looked at my watch and saw that I had to leave. "Any questions?"

No one said a word. Then Nita walked out from behind Mrs. Epps and started to clap. After a second

Mrs. Epps joined her, along with the ladies seated around the conference-room table. Everyone except Sisters Hilda and Sadie.

"Thank you," I said, turning to the sisters. "Ladies, I'm turning the meeting back over to you two. God bless you real good."

On the way out the door, I stopped at the buffet table that held their luncheon items. I examined the table, picked up a napkin, speared half of a chicken salad sandwich, and walked out. I winked at Nita, and she could only grin.

I felt so good about what I'd just done, and it was actually long overdue. As I figured, Xavier was leaning against my truck. Obviously, Mrs. Epps had called him. "Not again," I muttered. I took another bite of my sandwich, my appetite disappearing.

"What are you doing?" He was still angry.

"Damage control. Get an update from the ladies, because right now I'm on my way out of town. If you truly need me, call my cell." I wiped my mouth with the napkin and ran my tongue over my teeth.

"Where are you going?" He didn't budge but continued to stand in front of my door.

"I need to get away." I reached in my pocket and pulled my keys out. I hit the keyless remote and unarmed the doors. I'd tell him my destination later, if he decided to calm down.

"Is that all you're going to say?" He still didn't move.

Nita was standing at the door and finally came out. "You need anything, First Lady Phillips?"

Xavier smiled at Nita and moved away from my door. "Hello there, Nita," he said. "It's nice to see you. How is school going?"

"It's fine," replied Nita. She was still looking directly at me.

"Nita, sweetheart, I'll call you." I said. I winked at her and got in my truck and drove away. Even though I would be dealing with five teenage boys, I still felt the trip would do me good.

I walked through the airport, exhausted from the plane ride and with my head still throbbing like crazy. I scanned the area and was a little upset that I didn't see Bryce. Then, as was becoming a custom for him, he walked up behind me.

"Hey, beautiful, are you waiting for someone?" he asked as he leaned over my shoulder.

"Actually, I am." I looked into his eyes and immediately felt the warmth. I felt some of the tension ease, and for the first time in a while, I could breathe easier. Yes, it had to be the new location.

"Xavier called me and asked about my needing a ride." He took my arm, and we began to walk to the baggage claim.

"And what did you tell him?" I was still looking up at him, trying to gauge if Xavier had upset him.

"That you were kind enough to help me out." He stopped as we reached the baggage claim area. "But that's not what I wanted to say."

I was almost afraid to ask, but I asked, anyway. "What did you want to say?"

"That he had a good thing, and he shouldn't throw it away or let people come before what is important. I mentioned that someone could take his place."

"Like I got men knocking down my door." I pointed out my luggage, and he pulled it off the rotating belt.

He looked at me again with those same piercing eyes, and as if on cue, his smell engulfed me again. "Monica,

I'm knocking." His eyes lingered on me, and he ran a finger along my forehead and down the side of my face. It was the exact area where my head throbbed, and instantly, the headache was gone.

He grabbed the last piece of luggage and placed it on the floor and pulled the handle out so that he could roll it behind us.

We rode in silence to the hotel. Bryce finally broke the stillness that had settled in the rental car. "Monica, don't get quiet on me. You had to know from day one that I was into you."

"Thinking and knowing are two different matters entirely." I couldn't deny that I had seen it in his eyes. He hadn't tried to hide it, and it was impossible to miss.

"Well, it's out there. Don't be afraid of it." He touched my hand, the warmth of his palm touched my being.

I tried to speak, but no sound came out. The words drifted so far inside me, I could only look at him and hope that he had some knowledge of sign language.

"Monica, I'm willing to wait. No strings attached. And I don't want you to perform any act to get, maintain, or keep my affection. It's there, it's real, and isn't going anywhere."

"I'm scared." It wasn't much, but finally something came out.

"I know, but you had to know that the minute he hurt you, everything changed. Not only in our eyes, but also in the eyes of God. Just try my friendship on and see if it fits." He smiled. "And, girlfriend, I've been watching you for a while, and your friend circle is small. One more can't hurt."

"Thanks a lot." I smiled, but the truth hurt a little.

When we arrived at Hotel Teatro, I waited patiently at a distance while Bryce stood at the counter, taking care of everything. We got in the elevator, behind the bell-man who was carrying my luggage. Once we were in, the bellman used a key to program the elevator to go to the top of the building. The ride up was quick, and the elevator doors beeped twice and opened wide. The bell-man smiled and allowed us to get out of the elevator first. I followed Bryce to the end of the hall of the most beautiful hotel I'd ever seen and watched him insert a card into a door.

The door opened to a suite the size of my living room at home. Bryce threw the card on the table and turned to me. "You like?"

"I do." I walked around, checking out everything, and then went back into the sitting room and stood beside him.

The bellman put my luggage in the adjacent room, and after receiving a tip, he left the suite.

"I'm tired and have a long day ahead," said Bryce. "My suite is across the hall, and the boys are down the other end of the hall. I believe Donaldson is going to take them to breakfast, and he has a couple of things planned for them. So, don't feel like you have to get up right away. I'm sure they will leave you with enough energy." He walked to the door of my suite, and I followed a short distance behind him.

"Bryce, I don't know what to say to you." I felt like crying all over the place, but the tears wouldn't have been attached to any real emotion, just a mixture of left-over stuff that needed to go.

"Then don't. Monica, I'm glad you came. Now go to bed and sleep well." With his back to me, he added, "Monica, I love you already."

He didn't turn around to check if I'd heard him or if I

understood the simple words he'd allowed to escape from his lips.

I closed the door and leaned my back on it and listened as the words resounded in my ears. I couldn't misinterpret the statement or the meaning behind it. In fact, since I'd stepped foot off the plane I'd felt it. And it felt so right.

Nervous energy would not allow me to sleep. I looked at the nightstand and noticed that it was only 10:00 a.m. The time change didn't even mess with my psyche. I wondered if Bryce was up across the hall. He'd said he loved me, and deep down, something told me that I should believe him, that I could even trust him.

I reached for my robe and put it on. I didn't bother to slip my feet in my slippers but walked over to the window. The view was breathtaking. The sky seemed to swallow the top of the mountains. Photos had not done this place justice. And I was here with Bryce. Okay, that was it. There was no way I was going to be able to sleep.

I slipped into the bathroom and brushed my teeth. After reaching for my facial cleanser, I took my time and thoroughly cleaned my face. I'd been so exhausted when I entered the room last night, I hadn't even showered or removed my make-up. After I cleaned my face, I splashed some Mac toner on my face and started the shower. I turned it on hot and hoped that my skin could take it.

I took my robe off and placed it on the hook behind the door and dropped the matching gown on the floor. I touched my stomach tightening my muscles as I looked in the floor length mirror and twisted the end of my gold belly button ring that had a solid gold heart hanging on the end of it.

I covered my head with the shower cap and stepped in. The hot water flowed over my body and I turned around a couple of times. The water was too hot but I didn't touch the control; I let it beat against my body as if I was punishing myself. I hoped that so much of what was could be removed through each moist thump against my body. And wouldn't it be a relief if all of it could swirl around several times and disappear down the drain leading to nowhere in particular, but with no possible way of returning.

Turning the water down, I lathered my puff with a couple of dabs of Donna Karan perfumed gel. Repeating the process a couple of times, I turned the water off and blindly reached for the towel on the rack. Drying off only took a couple of minutes and I immediately followed with my ritual of baby oil, body butter, and then perfumed lotion. I left the steam-filled room and sat on the bench in front of the mirrored dressing table. I fixed my hair, making sure every piece was in place. I was almost sure that Bryce would be up soon and may even want to go out for a while before the game. I quickly dismissed the thought, when I realized that his teammates were probably in the same hotel and definitely in the same vicinity and that he may not want them to see him with yet another woman. Suddenly doubt loomed and told me I was crazy if I thought I was the first and only one that he had treated this way. Not the only first class ticket receiver and not the first to hear those golden words released on the wings of passion and delivered straight to the heart of his potential prey.

My entire dressing process slowed considerably. There was nothing to really rush for. He was just making me feel better and helping me through a difficult time. He wasn't new to community service and volunteering. I was probably his summer project.

I finally completed dressing. And decided on a pair of jeans and a fitted T-shirt. I put on the new pair of white Nike sneakers I had bought some time ago and had never worn. I eased the door open and Bryce was sitting on the sofa looking at something on the television.

I was pleasantly greeted by his contagious smile, which always seemed to be in place. "Good morning." He lifted the remote and clicked the television off. "I thought I heard you move around earlier and then things got quiet, so I thought you had went back to sleep."

"No, I've been up for a while. I just assumed that you were still sleeping." I had brought the same doubt-filled thoughts into the room with me.

"I couldn't sleep knowing you were on the other side of the room." Bryce stood up and walked over to where I was still standing.

That was not a half-bad idea if he wanted to get close to me, because I had no intention of joining him on the sofa. "I'm sorry you couldn't sleep. You have a game, and I'm sure you need to be well rested."

"Well, the regular season is over, and these are just summer-league games, so I don't need any extra energy. My body is used to functioning on little sleep. I'll make up for it later." He didn't move from in front of me and was obviously waiting for a reaction or a response.

When none came readily, he spoke again. "What's up? I thought we ended our late night on an upbeat note." He turned and reclaimed his spot on the sofa. "I wasn't expecting you to come out and run into my arms, but I was expecting you to be just as happy to be here with me as you were last night."

"I'm sorry. I just was thinking that maybe I made a mistake in joining you here." He appeared disturbed by my lack of expression and even more so by my comment. "Look, I know that you could be here with a long roster of women, and I don't want any of your friends or teammates to think I'm just a groupie. Well, I guess I am, in a way, because we can't be—"

He interrupted me. "Is that what this is about? Come over here."

I obeyed because I really wanted to hear what he had to say. "You're here because I asked you, and in case you didn't hear me loud and clear the last time, I love you. Now, as far as the roster of women is concerned, that has never been how I roll. My friends and teammates will meet you as my special friend. When we are clear about you resolving your marital issue or dissolving your marriage, then the introduction will change to more adequately reflect our situation."

"So, what are you saying?" I'd heard him, and yet I needed it broken down in layman's terms.

"I tell you I love you, and you have a short bus moment." He rubbed his hand over his face. "Monica, I want you here. I want you around me all the time. I'm going to wait for you, and I don't think I'd do that if I thought we were just going to be buddies, partners, good friends. I'm in this to win this."

"Oh." I smiled.

"Is that all you are going to say?" He mocked me. "Oh."

"I'm hungry. Can we grab something to eat and sight-see a little before the game?" I moved beside him and playfully bumped his arm with my elbow.

"Back to your in-control self." He bumped me back. "I like that."

After we had lunch at the ESPN, Zone, we acted like

typical tourists. Of course, this wasn't Bryce's first time in Denver, but he had never taken the time to really check the city out by day. We did all we could in the short time we had. The Botanic Gardens were so beautiful, and the mixture of all kinds of plants took my breath away. My green thumb shined through as I strolled through the gardens, pointing out plants and flowers that I recognized.

I couldn't believe the weather. I don't know what I was expecting. We took in the scenery of Denver under clear, pleasant skies. It was seasonally warm, and I enjoyed every minute of what we did. Of course, he saw right through me when he pulled the rental car into the parking garage near the Denver Pavilions. I had already scoped out the tourist brochure and knew that they had some shops up in there. Once the car came to a complete stop, I didn't wait for Bryce to come around and open the door for me. I was out of the car and rounding the corner of the parking garage.

"Monica, why are you in such a hurry?" He did a quick jog to catch up with me. "I mean, we did a leisurely stroll around the gardens. We window-shopped as we walked hand in hand downtown. Now you got smoke coming out the sides of your Nikes. What's up babe ? Did you have a Flo Jo moment?"

I slowed up and allowed him to walk in step with me. "If I tell you, will you promise not to trip?"

"I promise." He looked like he was all ready to ride me, but I went ahead and told him.

"I'm an occasional shopaholic. And since my separation, I haven't even been by a shopping center, strip mall, boutique, no Mart of Wal, no Kmart. Bryce, I haven't swiped a credit card for anything but groceries or toiletry items at the pharmacy." When I had told him my trials and tribulations, I looked up at him with sad, puppy dog eyes.

"Oh, my God, you're suffering from withdrawal." He wrapped his arm around me and held me tight. "When you turn Wal-Mart into a name that sounds French, it's got to be serious."

"It is. It's not like I spend a whole lot of money on shopping." I bit my lip a little and decided to retract my statement. "Actually, I spend a whole lot. Impulsive? Yes, sometimes. But that is how I get my thrills."

"Is that the only way?" We began walking again, at a much slower pace than before.

"No, but you will never find out. Now come on. If my credit card isn't declined, I'm going to go get my shop on." I pulled at his hand.

"Wait a minute." He stopped again.

"What, Bryce? I told you, I'm jonesing. Help a sistah out." I folded my arms across my chest and glared at him.

"You don't need to use his money. I'm fronting this fix. Everything you need from this point on is funded by me." He put up his hand when he noticed I was getting ready for a rebuttal. "Now when you get your life back on track, you can get a j-o-b and begin to have your own cards. I know that will make you happier than depending on anyone."

I couldn't help but feel all warm on the inside. In short, he was a good man, and he was right. I needed to get my life back. Out of impulse, I stood on my tiptoes, and I kissed his cheek. It definitely wasn't the kind of kiss that would make the earth shake and tremble, but I felt it sealed our friendship.

"Did you feel the earth shake?" he asked. He was still close enough for me to kiss him again.

"Sweetheart, it didn't, but it could." With that, I was back on my hunt for red-hot bargains and even something that was well out of my price range but that, suddenly, I could afford without guilt.

For two hours I shopped, with Bryce on my heels. He was the ideal shopping partner.

I came out of the dressing room, and Bryce didn't remind me of the husbands that grew tried of their wives' shopping and would find a chair to rest in. He stood right outside the dressing room, waiting for me. "That looks good on you. But I like those pants with the coral blouse," he said. "That isn't bad, though, so get both."

"Are you sure?" I looked at myself in the mirror and turned around to try to get the back view of the blouse I was trying on.

"I am. Now, I also think you need to get that black pantsuit. It looked really good on you." Bryce turned and picked up a sleeveless zebra-print top. "This would be perfect with it."

I looked at him and couldn't believe that he was having as much fun as I was. "You are too much."

"I've been told that before."

I tried on the other outfit, and then we looked around in Saks. If I picked something up and turned it around a couple of times, he would take it out of my hand and tell me I should get it. Before I knew it, our arms were filled with packages. Bryce dropped off our bounty at the Saks customer service desk and asked that the things be delivered to the hotel. I said "our bounty" because he was shopping as hard as I was. He knew all about my addiction, because it takes one to know one.

We had just enough time to get back to the hotel, shower, and change. I stood in front of the mirror, looking at the full effect of the third outfit I had tried on. Bryce had already called the room for me to hurry up. He had to understand, I needed to look good. I stood looking at one other outfit, and it came to me that it was one of Xavier's favorites. In fact, he had picked it out. I knew that I couldn't always feel blue or down whenever I thought about what was or even what I was going to do once I got back to Philly. It wasn't going to frighten me anymore. My time on earth wasn't in my hands, so it was going to be all good.

The packages had been delivered, so instead of wearing something old I decided that I would wear one of the outfits that Bryce had picked out. Rushing to change yet again, I reached for my shoes in my bag. One last look in the mirror, and I was ready. I knocked lightly on the door and heard Bryce say, "Come in." He was standing at the window, looking out over the city. He was dressed in a sharp navy suit, which looked good from the back. The front view could only look better, I decided. He turned around, and I was absolutely right. Bryce looked good.

"Well, you definitely were worth the wait," he said. "That outfit looks good on you. Davidson and the boys are waiting for us downstairs, so let's be off."

"We probably shouldn't go down together. You should go ahead, and I'll see you after the game."

"Monica, we talked about this. Now come on."

When we reached the lobby, it was filled with noise and plenty of people standing around. As I walked out of the elevator, the boys yelled and ran up to me. I walked up to Davidson. "They are so excited about the game," I told him. "Thanks so much for chaperoning my men."

"It's my pleasure. They are a great group of boys," replied Davidson.

With a hand gesture, Bryce beckoned me over to where he was standing.

"Me?" I said in a low voice.

"Yes, Monica. You," said Bryce. I walked over to where he was with three other guys. "This is Monica Phillips, the director of New Horizons Community Center and a very good friend," said Bryce.

The tallest guy, whose complexion resembled Xavier's, reached for my hand and bent down to kiss it. "So nice to meet you, Monica. You are a very beautiful lady," he said. The other two guys nodded and looked me up and down.

"Enough," said Bryce. He placed his hand at the small of my back and walked me back over to where my crew was standing. "Until later. Wish us well, and cheer real loud for me."

Chapter 19

The ride back on the plane was over much too soon. It was so different from the plane ride to Denver. I flipped through *Ebony* magazine and chitchatted with the boys, who were seated in the aisles next to and in front of us. He had leaned his head against the headrest and was snoozing lightly. Bryce must have been born smiling. I shook my head as I watched him, because even in his sleep there was that same sheepish grin.

Once we were inside the airport, we realized that we had to be cautious—not that we hadn't been in Denver, but this was Philly, home of the buzzards.

"Monica, did I sleep the entire plane ride? My neck is stiff," said Bryce. He rotated his neck around a few times.

"Yep, you were asleep before the plane could lift off the ground." I stepped on the escalator with the boys, and he followed.

A silence fell between us as we handled the business of collecting everything we had brought and the things we had added. I wished we were back in Denver, and although I didn't voice it out loud, I believed that he knew what I was thinking. My face showed all the signs of someone that was unsure of what would come next. I had told myself that coming back shouldn't shake me up, but now that we were here, I wasn't sure that all my self-talk had worked.

"I guess, I can't catch a ride home," he said.

"Funny. But if you want me to, I will," I said. "I can't possibly be followed twice. And, besides, we aren't creeping around."

"I know, but we can do without the accusations. So, I'm going to ride with Davidson and the boys." He called ahead for a van to pick us up. "I'll call you as soon as I get settled."

The house phone began ringing off the hook the minute I unlocked the door. Someone must have me on visual, because the timing was impeccable.

"Hello," I said into the receiver. I didn't bother to look at the caller ID. Too out of breath to stand after hauling my stuff in, I sat down in the chair near the telephone.

"Hi, Monica. Did you just get back in town?" Xavier's voice was a lot calmer than the last time we talked.

"Yes, actually, I just walked through the door. Am I under surveillance? Is that how you dialed me at just the right time?" I started to laugh. Bryce's sense of humor was contagious. I would have to tell him that.

"No, you are not." He sounded sedated. Almost like he had indulged in something that mellowed him out.

I wanted him to say something else. When he didn't, I cleared my throat. "So, Xavier, is there something on your mind? Something else you need to say?" I had a feeling he knew I was in Denver with the boys and Bryce.

"I've missed you, Monica, and I need to see you," he stated, without mixing in a lot of idle chatter.

"You saw me right before I left town," I responded. I didn't want to mix in unnecessary words, either.

"I've had some time to really think. Nothing is the same without you, Monica, and the truth is I can't breathe."

I couldn't believe he'd said that. "One of my last vivid memories of a conversation with you sort of took my breath away as well."

"Maybe I deserve that comment. But deep down, you know I love you, Monica. I know you know that."

"Look, I got a little jet lag. I do need to see you, but now is not the time. How 'bout I call you later on?" I was hoping he would allow me to end the call peacefully.

"No problem. I'm not in the office. I've been home for the past couple of days. So call here or on my cell phone. Oh, by the way, do you need anything? I noticed that you haven't taken any money from our accounts and there hasn't been any credit card activity for the past couple of days, so you must need some cash?"

"Actually no. I'm okay. I'll talk to you later, Xavier." I shouldn't have said that, but then again, I should have, because it was the truth.

I had just finished taking a nap when the phone rang. It wasn't really a nap, because anything longer than two hours was sleep to me. I reached for the phone on the nightstand and put it to my ear, hearing only a dial tone. Still, a phone continued to ring, and I realized that it was my cell phone. I checked to see who was calling. Bryce's name came across the display.

"Hey, you. What are you doing?" I said. I turned over

on my back and looked up at the ceiling fan as it rotated slowly, providing a light, airy flow throughout the room.

"I just finished talking to my mom. Monica, my grandmother passed away a few minutes ago."

I swung my legs over the edge of the bed and got up. "Oh, Bryce. I'm so sorry. Are you okay?"

"No, not really. I'm on a guilt trip because I knew she wasn't feeling all that great, and I kept putting off my trip to see her."

"Don't do that to yourself. I'm sure she understood." I didn't know what else to say. Even as a first lady, I always had trouble comforting someone in their loss. Saying that your loved one is in a better place, joy comes in the morning, look to the hills—none of that seemed sufficient in the midst of experiencing the loss of someone you love. I knew because I had been on the receiving end of the same and very similar words.

"I'm going to be leaving for South Carolina in a couple of hours." His voice was so serious, and I wasn't used to it. But I definitely understood, he was in the middle of a crisis, and humor was not the ticket out.

I didn't even know he was from South Carolina. I couldn't remember if we had talked about it. "Are you catching a flight?"

"Yes, I need to get there as quickly as possible. My mother is a basket case. They were very close. In fact, my grandmother had been living with my mom for the past year, ever since she fell and broke her hip."

"Bryce, this is going to sound crazy, because I feel like I should already know. But what part of South Carolina are you from?" I held my breath, realizing that there was so much I still didn't know about him, and it didn't matter.

He did manage a chuckle before he answered, "I'm

from Wampee. But for you folk that need to know the big name, I'm from North Myrtle Beach, South Carolina."

"A South Carolina boy. It figures. You have some southern ways about you." I smiled, thinking of his mannerisms.

"I've heard that a time or two before. Look, Monica, I'm going to pack, and I'll call you before I leave the airport, the minute I land, when I get to my mom's and every hour after that."

"You just go and be with your mom." I wanted to ask if I could go, but I knew it wasn't a good time for me to go to Wampee. And besides, what would I say? "Hi. I want to be your son's woman, and I just happen to be married, and to a preacher, to boot."

"Monica, I love you." He hung up. It was almost as if he wasn't ready for my response or feared that it wouldn't match his sentiment.

Before I could unpack my things, the doorbell rang. This must have been my day for interruptions. I left my suitcase in the hallway and hoped it was someone selling something that I didn't want. There weren't that many people that knew I was here. Xavier wouldn't be crazy enough to come over after I told him I would call later, but then again, he was a walking endorsement for the not so sane.

I stood on my tiptoes so I could see through the peephole. It was my dad. I was more surprised than completely happy that he was standing on the other side of the door. After unlocking the dead bolt, I opened the door wide. "Dad. What a surprise."

He hugged me as I moved to let him in. "It is okay for me to come see my daughter, isn't it?"

"Of course. You don't even have to ask." I took a seat

on the sofa and patted the cushion beside me so he could have a seat there.

"I was on my way to check on a repair job that Ted is working on, and since I was just down the street, I thought I'd take a chance that you were back from your mystery trip."

I looked at my suitcases, which were still in the hall-way. "Actually, I've only been back about an hour."

"And your trip was good?" It was if he knew I had been up to something no good. He always came at me this way when he knew something. But in this case, there was really nothing he could have known. Unless he had been spending time in the heavenly connection chat room.

"It was very restful. That's basically why I went. I really needed to get away." I told the truth. There. That should get him off my heels.

"You know, Monica, I've always taught you not to run away from your problems. The thing of it is, they don't go anywhere. They are still there for you to handle." He leaned back against the cushion of the sofa.

"Who you telling?" My dad had me talking to him like we were young, hip partners. I felt like adding what Nita always said when I was dropping wisdom on her. "You ain't never lied."

"I don't know exactly what went down with you and Xavier. But I know you wouldn't be over here if it wasn't something serious. If you are in the right, all I want you to do is stand your ground. If you yield and he's in the wrong, wrong is all you'll know for the rest of your life with him." He stood up to leave. My Dad didn't play. He was a hit it and quit it kind of man. He didn't waste time. He came, he spoke, and he was out.

"Thank you, Dad. I needed to hear that." I kissed his cheek and rubbed the lipstick off that my lips left behind.

I ran a few errands after I unpacked. I didn't have to worry about being spotted, since everyone at the church knew Xavier and I were living apart. I drove across town to my usual repair shop and dropped off my laptop. Then I grabbed a crisp chicken salad from Ruby Tuesday and drove back to the condo.

Bryce called, and we only talked for a few minutes before he had to go. Family members were already starting to drop in, and he needed to chat a little and make some other calls to relatives. I knew the next few days were going to be hard for him. So, I wasn't really expecting him to call me as often as he had promised before he left town.

By the time I had tidied up the house and eaten my salad, I was ready to do something other than look at the four walls. It had been all I'd wanted to do for a while, and now I couldn't stand the silence. I guess life was funny that way. I decided to call Trina and let her know I was back. We had been chatting for more than an hour about everything and nothing when she told me that Xavier had been calling her almost every day.

"He misses you, Monica." She acted like she was telling me something I should already know.

"And you believed him." I didn't want to hear her sing Xavier's tired old song. "Besides, when did you join his fan club?"

"I didn't. But by the fourth visit and the thirteenth call, I guess he wore me down. You know, he don't really care for me, so for him to use me to get you back, he must be either desperate or he has lost his mind."

"I doubt very seriously if he's desperate." I was going

to say more, but I left it at that. "Look, I've got to go.
Someone is at the door. Holla later, girl."

I didn't wait for her to respond. The minute I put the
phone down, the door bell rang again. I looked up.
"God, what in the world is going on? Am I speaking
things into existence or what?"

I pulled down the back of my baby blue Tinkerbell
T-shirt and moved swiftly to the door. I didn't bother to
peek this time, but unlocked the door and pulled it open.

"Hello, Monica. I came by to check on you." Mother
Phillips was standing all prim and proper at my door.

"Mother Phillips, what a surprise." One more surprise
and I was going to see if I could go someplace where no
one knew me at all.

She didn't wait to be invited in but took several steps
until she was all the way in. "This place looks the same
as when you and Xavier first moved in."

"Yeah, the tenants didn't do a lot of changing. I guess
they must have liked my style and flair," I said.

"I'm sure. You have always been a great decorator. Do
you mind if I sit for a few minutes?" She looked at the
sofa and waited for me to offer.

"Oh, I'm sorry. By all means, have a seat." I stood because I knew I had to offer tea or coffee, and knowing
her, she would say yes. "Would you like something? Tea
or coffee? I believe I have some crackers, cheese, and
maybe a little fruit."

"That sounds nice," she responded and removed her
short-sleeved blazer.

She was acting like I had invited her to spend the night.
I'd said crackers, cheese, and maybe a little fruit. I'd expected her to choose the crackers and cheese or the fruit.
Now I had to make some tea and cut some cheese and
fruit. It was not the way I wanted to spend my evening.

We exchanged pleasantries, like we always did. We always got along. I wasn't so sure about now. I really didn't know what Xavier had told them and what rumors had been left for them to pick up like mail.

"Look, Monica, I came to talk about you and Xavier." She touched my hand. "He is going through a rough time. I don't know if he mentioned it, but he hasn't preached for three Sundays and hasn't even been going to handle the daily affairs of the church." Sighing, she continued. "I believe that he is depressed and that he misses you."

"Mother Phillips, I spoke with Xavier earlier today, when I returned. We will be talking sometime this week. Now, what we decide is up in the air, but there is so much that you don't know." I didn't want to get into it.

"I know more than you think I do. I've been where you are. I'm not suggesting that you stay, and I'm not suggesting that you go. That is my son, but he has become proud and arrogant, and that is hard to deal with."

"I feel a big part of this has to do with me not being able to carry a child to term." There. It was out, and from the look on her face, I could tell Xavier had never said a word about this last miscarriage. "I wanted more than anything to give him a child, but I couldn't. Over time, I guess, it made him bitter."

"Please don't feel like it's your fault. There is no one to blame, only God knows why. If my son can't see that, and if he can't see that you are the glue that keeps him and his ministry together, then I feel sorry for him." She wiped a tear that had fallen on her cheek and reached for my hand.

Chapter 20

It had been seven whole days since Bryce had left to attend his grandmother's funeral. So many things were coming up, and with every call he made, I felt so bad for him. My emotions were running rampant. One minute I thought about Bryce confessing his love for me. The next I thought about Xavier being depressed. Then there were my feelings somewhere in between. That was, perhaps, the hardest part, since I didn't know what I felt deep down.

Surprise filled me when I answered my cell phone one evening and a lady asked to speak to me. I held the phone away and double-checked that it was Bryce's phone number on the display. My first thought was that someone he was seeing must have found my number in his phone and decided to call and tell me to step off.

"Monica dear, this is Bryce's mother, Betsy." Her voice sounded a lot younger than I figured she was.

"Oh, this is a wonderful surprise. I'm sorry to hear about your mother. I've been thinking of you two and keeping you lifted in prayer." I was as nervous as a school-girl talking to the mother of the guy she had a crush on.

"Thank you. And thank you for the lovely arrangement. Bryce has been anxious to get back to Philly, and although he hasn't come right out and said so, I think it has a lot to do with you."

"I would rather he be there to make sure you have everything you need. This can be a very difficult time, and you two should draw from each other's strength." I didn't mean to sound so holy, but I guess, what's in you is bound to come out of you.

"Well, I'm not going to hold you. I just wanted to thank you for the arrangement. And for the smile on Bryce's face. He's talked about you nonstop to me and everybody else." She chuckled softly. "So, I know you must be a special lady. Please come to visit real soon."

"I will. And thanks for calling."

"Well, Bryce wants to talk with you." After a brief second, his voice came through the phone.

I relaxed as he entertained me and told me about all the crazy things his relatives were doing. Listening to him was like listening to a song that you wanted to put on repeat. You knew the lyrics, upbeats and down tunes, and yet you still wanted to hear it over and over again.

It was a little after eight when Trina called and suggested I get out of the house. I hadn't realized it, but I hadn't been out and about since Bryce left. My only outing had been to the convenience store to get milk and a liter of soda. I had stretched the contents of my refrigerator and knew I was going have to replenish things soon.

"Girl, I'm not up to going out. And where in the world would we go?" I said. I was in the middle of the living-room floor, polishing my toenails.

"Didn't you go to the Five Spot with Bryce not so long ago?" She threw it in casually.

"Yes, I did." That I should have kept to myself. You had to be so careful about what you shared with people. Some things had a way of coming back to haunt you.

"Well, let's go there. Actually, I've not been. It might be fun." She continued. "Come on, what else are you going to do?"

"Nothing. And that's the way I want it," I replied and blew on my toes. I could hardly bend over and knew it was due in part to all the food I had pigged out on while I was in Denver. Bryce had had to coax me into eating. He'd noticed that I had lost weight and felt that I needed to make sure I ate regularly. The trouble was, the regular eating was showing.

"You're waiting for Bryce to call and he could be up to just about anything. Did you remember that he's not your man?" She stopped the minute the last word came out.

"That wasn't necessary. Don't you think I know that he isn't my man? Bryce and I are really good friends. That's all you need to know." She was my girl and all, but that was exactly why I didn't share everything with her. The best of friends said the wrong thing sometimes. That stuff had been known to ruin the best of friendships.

"Look, let's just go out." She continued. "You call Bryce and tell him you are hanging with me."

"I'll meet you there around ten." I was going to go because, frankly, I was bored stiff. But she had still pissed me off, and I wasn't going to be riding in the same car with her. The way I was secretly feeling Bryce, I might have a flashback about her comment and knock her upside the head.

By the time I walked up in the Five Spot, it was

10:30. Even with the added pieces to my wardrobe, I hadn't found the right outfit to put on. I wasn't trying to impress anyone but myself. And maybe Trina. I wanted her to see how good Bryce's friendship looked on me. I didn't want her to hate or anything like that, I just wanted her to see that I was making it just fine.

I spotted her sitting alone near the center of the room. I pointed her out and walked behind the hostess. "Hey, Trina." I bent down near where she was sitting and hugged her. I wasn't even pissed anymore. After I hung up from Bryce, I was as mellow as I needed to be. "I'm sorry I'm late. I had a struggle just trying to get out of the house."

"Well, you look absolutely radiant." She smiled. "He becomes you."

See, that was what I was talking about. She noticed. "Whatever. I'm starved. Did you order anything to eat?"

"I was waiting for you. I only ordered a virgin frozen strawberry daiquiri."

"Oh, okay." I got the server's attention. "I'll have the same thing she is drinking. Make sure it's virgin. And bring me the beer-battered shrimp and Cajun fries."

He looked at Trina,. "I'll have the same," she said.

We talked about my trip to Denver and about my plans to look for a job. I loved the center, but I knew I needed a paying job. I had decided to take Bryce's advice and carve out a life of my own. Regardless of what happened, I would need my own life.

"So, when is Bryce coming back?" she asked.

"Trina, I love you, boo. I really do. But I'm not going to talk about Bryce tonight. Any other subject, and I'm game. We are out to have a good time."

"And we are having a good time. I just want what is best for you," Trina stated, with a sincere look on her face. She looked behind me, and I assumed that the server was coming back to see if we wanted anything else.

"Hello, Monica." A deep voice spoke my name, and it sounded a lot like my husband.

I turned around slowly, and there he was. "Xavier, what are you doing here?" I said. I couldn't believe my eyes. You could have knocked me over with a feather.

"I came here to talk to you," he said. He pulled a seat from a nearby table and positioned it beside my chair.

"Let me guess. You were in the area," I said. I looked over at Trina. She looked everywhere but back at me.

"Trina arranged this only because I asked her to," he said. He looked over at Trina. "Thank you, Trina. I owe you."

"Look, Monica. I only did it because I think you two should talk," said Trina. She could hardly look at me. "I'm going to leave. I'll talk with you later."

I didn't say anything but looked toward the dance floor and watched people sway to the beat of the music. Imagine my husband, the anointed and appointed Rev. Xavier Phillips, up in the Five Spot. This was something that Sister Sadie and Sister Hilda would live for. Personally, if he wanted to talk to me that badly, we could have got together in the parking lot of the church, in the church, at the community center, at our condo, or in our house. This place reminded me of Bryce, and up until the time Xavier had walked in, I'd been reminiscing about our time there together. I wasn't even seeing Trina. I felt like Xavier had violated my memory. I was more than ready to go.

"Look, I came here because I thought that you would see me differently," he said as he looked around him. "I lost my way, Monica. I was so caught up in being a pastor that I forgot how to be your husband."

"And now you say this?" I pushed my food away, suddenly full.

"I'm hoping it's not too late. You mean the world to me, and I can't stand not having you beside me. Not in my ministry and not even in my personal life. I can't eat, can't sleep. I'm miserable without you, and I've been such a fool, thinking that I was pleasing God when I wasn't honoring who he gave me."

"I don't know, Xavier." Tears began to fill my eyes. He was saying everything I wanted to hear. But why couldn't this stupid fool have said it months ago?

Luther Vandross's "If Only for One Night" began to play. "Dance with me?"

"What?" I looked at him like he had lost it.

"Dance with me. That was our song back in college. Do you remember that?" He was using the past.

"I remember that it was our song. But do you remember that you're a preacher?" I raised my eyebrow in disbelief.

"I'm your husband."

"You probably don't even remember how to dance." If nothing else, I could dance with him and get a good laugh.

He got up and reached for my hand. Together, we made our way to the dance floor. Xavier pulled me into his arms and I nestled my head against his chest like I used to do and we moved together. After a few movements, it all felt the same. He hadn't lost it, and my sigh let him know that. He held me tight, and I could feel his breath against my forehead. This was how it used to be. This was something I missed. I never felt as close to him as I did when we became one on the dance floor, moving in sync and creating a perfect rhythm, which was about more than just the music.

As if he read my thoughts, he spoke. "Monica, this is

how it used to be. This is how we fell in love." His voice was low and needy. "I knew I'd love you for a lifetime, the minute I realized that we were a perfect fit."

We danced off and on the rest of the night. Our conversation after a while was like old times. My appetite even returned, and I ended up eating half of his bacon cheeseburger. Gone was the stiff, businesslike, and no-nonsense preacher, and in his place was a carefree man who was just in love with being in love.

Good night wasn't easy, because feelings had been stirred up. But as we stood in front of the condo, we continued to reflect, and he began to make promises, and I wished that he could keep them.

Xavier deposited me on the doorstep and wanted to come in, but I had to draw the line someplace.

"I'll talk with you tomorrow," I said. I tried to smile and unlocked the door and went in. I leaned my back against the door because I couldn't figure out what end was up. Now I was going to have to take another trip to sort this out. Before I could move from the door, my dad's conversation played back in my head. And so did the things the nurse had said before I left the hospital.

My cell phone rang, and I assumed it was Xavier, letting me know that he was home "Hello," I said.

"This is Bryce's girlfriend, Sandy. I just wanted you to know that Bryce and I are back together, and that is pretty much the reason why he is not back in Philly. When he does get there, he won't be alone." The call ended and the mysterious caller was gone. Still the words reverberated in my ears.

I was so hurt. I knew that I shouldn't jump to conclusions, but why would this unknown woman lie to me? What would she have to gain, besides maybe weeding out the competition? I couldn't deal with another hurt. If I was going to go through changes, then I would remain with my husband.

And that was how I ended up standing outside the door of my old residence, using my key, ascending the steps of my house, and opening the door of the bedroom I had shared with my husband.

Xavier didn't seem surprised when he saw me standing in the doorway. He was lying on my side of the bed. He never opened his mouth, never even blinked, but threw back the sheet, exposing his nude body, and waited for me to get in.

I thought of Bryce, and then I thought of Sandy, who'd said she was coming back to Philly with him. It all hurt, and I was mad that I had even believed that it was possible to be loved by him. Maybe Xavier was all I deserved. Even with the changes he carried me through and even the ones that would come. Cycles had a way of repeating themselves; I wasn't so naïve that I didn't know that. All that I had done and all the things I had tried to hide had brought me to this crossroads. Who was I to think that I could take a different path, travel along the high road?

The man lying in front of me was my husband; he belonged to me. There was a piece of paper somewhere in this house that said so. He was the man God gave me, and obviously, God wanted me to endure like a good soldier. So, yes, I removed my clothes, with tears in my eyes. I got in bed and rested my head against his pillow. Xavier leaned up on his elbow, and I watched him through misty eyes as he traced an invisible line between my breasts, over my stomach, and through my belly button, and then he stopped. He told me he loved me, and then he turned off the light. In the stillness of the night, sharing the bed we had lain in so many times, with the weight of all that had gone bad with us suspended over me like a black cloud, we made love and I cried.

Chapter 21

I woke up the next morning, and Xavier had already left for the gym. He'd whispered to me on his way out that he would see me when he got back home. I'd acted as if I was in a deep sleep because I didn't know how to react to what he had said. He was already assuming that I was back to stay. I hadn't said anything like that, but actions speak louder than words. My entering our room, climbing in bed, and allowing him to make love to me had sent a message that all systems were go.

How could I have been so careless? Now, in the light of day, my reason for coming to my house last night wasn't a good one. It was like running into the arms of the second guy because the first one turns his back on you. Xavier should not have been my rebound piece. For God's sake, what was I thinking?

I picked up my pillow, which Xavier had laid his head on, and held it to my chest tightly. Closing my eyes, I waited for something. I needed to feel something. I had made a vow, and I had accepted his hand, and in front of our family and friends, we had said that we would keep that vow. Wasn't that enough? If I remained with

Xavier, it would have to be enough. But two wrongs don't make a right.

As wrong as it all was, I cared about Bryce. I hadn't meant to open myself up to him, but I had, and right now I needed him to say something, anything. Before I could change my mind, I leaned my body out of the bed and reached for my bag, which was tangled up in my clothes. Pulling my cell phone out of my bag, I noticed that it was dead. I looked at the cordless phone on the nightstand and decided to chance making the call from here. Xavier never checked the phone bill, so the chances of him knowing that I had called Bryce from here were slim. I dialed and waited for Bryce to pick up. All kinds of thoughts rushed through my head. How could I ask him about this Sandy person when I just made love to my husband, whom I was no longer with. If I had never left Xavier in the first place, the attraction between Bryce and me would have never had a chance to become anything more than that. This web I'd managed to weave had all the makings of a women's fiction novel. The right person could develop my story and sell it to a publishing guru, like the one at Urban Soul.

"A groggy-sounding female answered the phone. "Hello."

I leaned my head, trying to ascertain if it was the same voice from last night.

I heard a deep voice in the background say, "Who is it?" The woman on the other end said, "No one is saying anything."

I didn't need to listen anymore. That was the same woman that had said she was Sandy, and the deep voice belonged to Bryce. I ended the call.

She was telling the truth. Why else would she answer Bryce's phone so early in the morning? It didn't take a rocket scientist to figure out that if he was close enough in the background for me to hear him through the phone, they were together, and because she sounded like she was asleep, they were in bed.

I dropped the phone beside me. Pulling my knees up to my chest, I put my head on them and cried again. For allowing myself to get close to Bryce, even though I knew we could never be. For knowing what I had to do. And for knowing that my heart would ache until it isolated itself from what had made it feel so good. Because of the good it had felt, my life would never be the same.

For the next few days, I walked around in a daze. I didn't answer any of the calls that came from Bryce's cell phone. The next week, I started receiving calls from his house, and still I didn't answer. I knew it could have been him, but then there was a chance that it could be Sandy.

Life was complicated enough for me. Ever since the night I spent with Xavier, I was living out of two houses. While I knew that Xavier and I were probably going to end up working things out, I wanted to make sure that the problems that had existed between us were resolved. We had lost our way, and the raw truth was that I had fallen out of love with the person that Xavier had become long before Bryce came into the picture. I wasn't always able to say that, but I knew it was the truth.

Xavier didn't say anything about me spending days at home and nights at the condo. I guess because if it seemed like I was coming back, he wasn't going to make any waves. I hadn't slept with him since that night. The feeling I had after we made love wasn't the kind of feeling a wife should have after making love to her husband. I wasn't clear where things stood, and my two residences weren't making things any clearer for me.

Xavier did make some changes. One of the major ones was dissolving the partnership with Patrick Garrett. The church in Delaware wasn't going to be, at least not with the name Xavier Winston Phillips attached to it and not with any of our money. Yeah, we resolved the me, mine, and our thing, too. I presumed we were working toward being on the same page.

I was walking to my truck, with my head down, one late afternoon when Bryce came up beside me. I jumped. "God, you scared me," I said.

He looked a little thinner. I wished that I could say that absence had not made my heart grow fonder, but Bryce standing before me confirmed that it had. This up close and personal look at him only revealed to me that I had memorized his features and tucked the information away for safekeeping. "Hello, Monica." He didn't smile.

"When did you get back?" I asked.

"I got here Sunday. So, today is Tuesday. That would make it two whole days. Forty-eight hours. You get my drift. But you wouldn't know that, because you haven't been answering either of your phones. At least not any of my calls. Caller ID may very well be the worst invention for someone who doesn't want to be reached."

Without responding or reacting to what he'd said, I blurted out, "Who is Sandy?" I tried to wait and see if he was going to say something.

"Is that what this is about? Why you didn't answer my calls? Why Xavier called and told me that you were going to move back home, and that you had slept with him?" The look on his face immediately told me that there was no Sandy and him.

"She said that you two were getting back together. That she was coming back to Philly with you. Then, when I called you early one morning, she answered the phone, and I heard you in the background." I was stumbling over my words.

"There is a Sandy, and she just so happens to be my ex-girlfriend. What started out as a visit to check on my mom ended up as her attempt to win my affections. I told her about us, and she said she understood. That same night, my cell phone went missing. She returned it the next day. She'd picked it up, thinking it was hers." He paused. "As far as the voice you heard, all I can say is, it wasn't me. I could give you a theory, but it would lead to the same outcome. Sandy is crazy enough to have planned the whole thing."

"I didn't know what to think, Bryce. She was so convincing."

"Look, let me help you out with this. I told you I was in love with you, and I meant it. I don't play games. I also told you, I was willing to wait, and I have. There is no Sandy. She wants me, and I told her that I wanted you. That ended all that. She planted the seed of doubt in your head, and you thought that if there could be no us, then maybe it was time for you to go home. The Monica I've gotten to know in the last couple of months wouldn't give into Xavier that easily, but the old Monica would think that she should hang on, even when there isn't anything to hold on to.

"I know you are scared, and this is a big decision. Xavier is your husband, but you made a mistake that night. You slept with him only because you thought I didn't love you. This may sound crazy to you, but I'm confident enough in what I know you feel for me to label it a mistake that shouldn't have happened. Monica, you need to decide where your heart is. No matter if it's with me or Xavier, you deserve to be happy, and that is all I've ever wanted for you."

"Bryce, I—" He interrupted before I could finish.

"Monica, you are caught between two worlds and only you can change that." He took both my hands and pulled me toward him. "I've got to go back to South Carolina tomorrow because my mom is scheduled for surgery. I'll be on the road after that, so it will be a week before I'm back in Philly. Monica, as long as there is a chance, I'm not giving up on the possibility of us. But you have to be free to love me. And right now you aren't." He kissed my cheek and walked away.

Chapter 22

"Monica, I'm so pleased that the funding went through. I know that you are excited to start the renovations on the house. I believe it's going to help a lot of women in this area." Councilwoman Jennings stood and reached to pick up her briefcase.

"I believe it will, and you can't imagine how excited I am. There is definitely a need for the counseling services, and providing transitional housing is perhaps the best part of it all." I spoke from the heart. I wasn't just proud to provide another service to a community through New Horizons. I guess that was for obvious reasons. Going through some changes with a spouse and having no place to go could be so traumatic.

"Reverend Phillips must be very proud." She began walking toward the door.

"He sure is. His philosophy has always been all about bettering. The pastor is fueled by a passion to better the community. This is just another avenue, and there are many more to come."

"I'm sure. Oh, by the way, how is the Kings Vision

Program coming along?" she asked, with a concerned look on her face.

"Very well. We had some delays, but things are going very smoothly." Whenever someone mentioned the Kings Vision Program, I couldn't help but think about Bryce. As a result, I was sure the enthusiasm I had about the program wasn't reflected in my voice.

"Well, I'm going to leave and let you work to keep making things happen. But you take care, and if you need any support, you can always call on me." She leaned toward me and gave me a businesslike hug.

"Thanks for all your support. We do appreciate you and your many efforts. You take care. I know you get your spirit fed well over there at Bethel, but please come join us for service sometime."

"I sure will. I don't want to be a spiritual creeper, but I've heard that you all are feasting on the Lord, and that if I come and enjoy one service, I'll be ready to turn in my AME card." She started laughing.

"Well, you know we'd be glad to have you." I laughed along with her. Because the truth was that many of the old parishioners were now the new parishioners at New Horizons. We were being accused by almost every church in the city of stealing their members. While many thought we should have been insulted, we were happy, because the central goal should have been that if someone was being fed, that was all that mattered. Where they chose to spend their Sundays and leave their tithes shouldn't have mattered. But to many pastors and their trustee boards, it did. If they didn't get it together, they'd be trying to bust us up in Heaven by calling for denominational separation. Moses, Paul, Luke, and John would end up having to escort them out.

I glanced at my opened organizer on my desk to see

what else I had to do today. It was around three and if there wasn't anything else pressing, I was going home to enjoy a few hours alone before Xavier got there and demanded more attention than I really wanted to give.

We had reconciled. In fact, this Saturday would mark the fifth month of my return. Why? That was complicated and yet simple. I needed to give us one more chance. My heart was saying one thing, but I thought about my promise not only to Xavier, but to God. And my going back was the right thing to do. When I married Xavier, I not only committed to him, I made a commitment to God, and that was more important than anything else. Even my happiness. So, I guess you could say, I made a sacrifice, and I was going to give it my all.

I thought of Bryce more times than I should have. That day in front of the condo was the last time I saw him. As difficult as it was, and as many times as I picked up the phone, I never contacted him. I knew I could never give him what he needed, because thoughts of who I really was would always plague me. I prayed, fasted, and cried many nights and finally realized that there would always be a part of me that wanted to be with him, a part that craved him, and that all of my heart wanted to love him. But we were not to be, and I had to accept that. I didn't look at it as Xavier winning. I turned away from Bryce not because of the love I had for my husband, but because of the love I had for God. At the end of the day, when all was said and done, and I closed my eyes and waited for the commencement of tomorrow, that was all that mattered.

Rubbing my temple, I felt the onset of a headache. I couldn't understand it, but whenever I thought of Bryce or gave the state of my emotional existence a lot of thought, I would end up with a headache. Many times it caused me to stop everything and get in bed. The headaches had gotten so bad that I had to see a specialist, who labeled them migraines. I didn't want to think about it, but I guess my decision to stay, although right, made me sick.

"First Lady Phillips, I need to go over to the church and pick up something from Sister Connie," said Mrs. Epps. She stood over my desk, eyeing everything on it.

"Okay. Go ahead. I'll answer the phones. I don't have anything else, so when you return, I'm going home." I had been away from the church and the community center, but some things hadn't changed. Mrs. Epps was as nosey as ever. It was just her and me now. Nita had started at Temple and only came by every now and then. We used Sunday service to catch up.

"You want to go home and fix a special dinner for Pastor. That is so nice. He's been so happy since you came back to him. I guess it don't matter that them nosey church people thought you were having an affair and running around like a harlot. I told them so many times that you were a good, God-fearing woman. It didn't matter that you was in your car with another man, riding all over the city like you weren't married. You can ride with whomever you want to ride."

I had to stop her. "Thank you for believing in me." I smiled. "Go ahead and pick up what you need. I'm sure Connie is waiting on you."

This was what I'd had to put up with for five months. But at least now they were speaking to me. When I first returned, I couldn't even get a nod. They acted like I had some disease, something they could catch just by exchanging a kind greeting with me. It took so much strength just to walk up in the church on Sunday and to try to function like nothing had ever happened.

Xavier said he understood, but how could he? I was the villain, and he was the fearless leader who, according to them, had done no wrong. On top of that, for the first month of my return, his sermons talked about love, forgiveness, and endurance. If he talked about the prodigal son one more time, I was going to lose it. While he said it wasn't personal, when I quizzed him about why he brought that particular bible story up so many times when there so many others that needed to be brought to light, he replied that God had laid it on his heart so heavily. That was bull. He was talking about me, and everyone in the church knew it.

"Monica, are you here?" Xavier came through the door and kicked his shoes off while removing his tie.

"I'm right here." I walked out of the bathroom, dressed in a black teddy, complete with a pair of those high-heeled slippers with the fur on top. I had been doing a little extra to keep things interesting. But it was also because I needed a jump start. It had been that way for a while. Many times I didn't even want to make love, but I was here, and he was my husband. In a word, submission.

"My, my, don't you look delicious." He closed the distance between us in a few quick steps and circled me with his arms.

Before I could breathe, he was attacking my mouth. It was always rough. Even the way he made love to me. Like he was punishing me. When I finally got up the nerve to ask him about it, he said that he just couldn't seem to control himself, and his love for me was just bringing out a different kind of passion.

"Hold up. What have I been telling you about this

rough thing? Sweetie, I'm fragile, and you have to handle me like a piece of fine glass."

"I'm sorry, girl. I just get so excited." Xavier placed my hand on him and cracked a grin that was more unnerving than sexy.

"Excitement is good, but slow passion is better." I should have recorded what I just said so I could just push play. I had to say it every time we made love.

Xavier began to remove his clothing. When he had removed the last piece, he asked me to do the same. I slowly came out of the slippers and seductively removed the teddy. I looked in his eyes as lovingly as I could while I slid the thin fabric down my body. In the middle of taking it off, I turned around slowly and dropped it around my ankles and lifted my feet out of it one at a time.

"Do you like what you see?" I knew I was teasing him.

"You know I do, but I can show you better than I can tell you."

Xavier pulled me to him. While sitting on the edge of the bed, he pulled me onto his lap and pulled my body down on him. Before I could get adjusted to him inside me, he began to move. Slowly and then a little harder. I leaned my head back and grabbed his shoulders. That was when he put both hands on my waist and began to slam into me. I started to squirm, and he held me tighter. I opened my eyes and looked at him. I couldn't speak, because I couldn't believe what he was doing. This wasn't making love to me.

"Xavier, you're hurting me."

"I can't stop now, baby. It feels so good."

He slammed harder and harder. After another minute, he yelled out and clawed at my back. When he finished, I swung my leg around and got up. Moving away from him, I watched as he acted like what we just did was normal. He didn't even look up at me or tell me he was sorry for being so rough. He turned the comforter and sheet back and climbed into bed.

I walked to the bathroom and closed the door. Leaning my back against the door, I tried to pull myself together. Every step I took brought a pain between my legs that was almost unbearable. I turned to the linen closet and removed a towel and reached to turn on the shower.

When I thought the water was hot enough for me, I opened the shower door and stepped in. I grabbed my bath puff and squeezed some shower gel on it. I began to lather myself. When I got up the nerve to wash there, I wanted to yell because it felt like something there had broken. A surge of pain went through my midsection, and I looked down to see blood flowing down my legs.

Chapter 23

I pulled into the parking lot of the church. I needed to talk to Xavier. After last night I couldn't even stand to kiss him when he left this morning. After my shower last night, I'd cleaned myself up and put on a nightshirt. I had had every intention of telling him what he had done to me, but when I walked back into our bedroom, he was sound asleep. I stood over him and watched him for a few minutes. I was hoping I was wrong, but what I saw on his face was a smile. Obviously, our love-making escapade had made him very happy. I couldn't have disagreed more, because it made me sick in more ways than one.

Just as I was getting out, Nita came running up to the truck. She must have seen me from the community-center window. "First Lady Phillips. You look so good." She hugged me and held my hand.

"What's with the compliment? I don't feel my best today and know that I don't look all that good." What I said was so true. I could hardly get out of bed. My morning started off slow, and I really didn't want to leave the house. But I was determined to talk to Xavier before I went to see my doctor.

"Well, since you know I'm up to something, I'll go ahead and spill it. I want to go to the social this weekend, and my mom is dead set against it. I need a dress, and she is definitely not going to give me the money." She looked at me with pleading eyes. "And I was going to ask you."

"You can stop there." I put my purse on top of the hood of the truck and pulled out my wallet. I pulled out two hundred dollars and gave it to her. "Only because I love you and you are the child I never had."

"I love you; I love you; I love you." She clutched the money to her heart.

"I know you do. Now go on somewhere and leave me alone," I joked and playfully hit her on the butt.

"I'll call you later." She hugged me again and kissed me on the cheek.

I watched as she waited for traffic to pass, and then she ran across the street. She was dressed in her usual attire of T-shirt and jeans. Some things never changed.

I wanted to ask her where Mrs. Epps was, but there was still a chance that I would run into her. I walked into the church and made the turn that would carry me to the administrative wing. Everything was neat and tidy. The smell of freshly vacuumed carpeting and Pledge was in the air. Ms. Handy must be in the place, handling her business. You could always tell when it was her week to clean. Some didn't take cleaning seriously, but Ms. Handy cared about her profession, and it reflected in her work.

Connie wasn't at her desk, so I peeked into Xavier's office. He wasn't there, but his computer was still on, so I knew that he couldn't be far away. I walked back out and started toward the conference room. Voices came from the room, so I knew that he had to be in there.

I took a seat in the chair near the conference room, deciding that I would wait. I removed the *Charisma* magazine from the nearby table and began to flip through it. There was an article on first ladies that caught my attention. We were growing in number, according to the article, but yet we had no real voice. I flipped back to where the article began to get the name of the person who wrote it. I might have to e-mail her and let her know that she was right on the money with this one.

When the conference-room door opened, Xavier came out, laughing. I remained seated and waited to see who he was meeting with. Out popped Deacon Thomas and Rev. Garrett. I wasn't going to think the worst, and because I was free, kindness filled my heart.

I stood up. I removed the sunglasses from my head and placed them in my bag. "Hello, Pastor Phillips, Deacon Thomas, and Reverend Garrett," I said.

"Hello, First Lady Phillips. It's good to see you," said Deacon Thomas. "You are looking beautiful as usual."

Rev. Garrett rolled his eyes. Nita had told me how he was telling everyone that I was carrying on behind Xavier's back, and that I was no good, and that it had all started when we were in college. I never confronted him, because he didn't deserve even an acknowledgment from me that I remotely cared about what he said. "Well, well, if it isn't Monica Joyner Phillips." There was a long pause between my maiden name and my married name. "What brings you by?"

I was going to need to count down from ten because he was going to catch a case. "I came by to see Pastor

Phillips. But it's always good to see that you are still amongst the living. There is so much sickness and disease going around. You did hear that Diane Dixon from Temple Hills died last week." I watched the shocked look on his face. This was a lady that I knew he'd had a fling with, but I knew he didn't know her status, because her family kept it hush-hush. "Yes, she died of AIDS, and her husband was diagnosed not long after her and isn't doing good at all."

Rev. Garrett looked like he was going to pass out. "Frat, I'll get with you later today, "he said. "I believe leaving in the morning for Delaware may be a better idea."

I looked at Xavier, and he could only look away. "Hey, First Lady Phillips. You look so good," he said and smiled weakly. "Let's go in my office." He acted like the memory of last night was just that: a memory and, obviously for him, a good one.

He asked if I wanted something to drink. I declined. "They are removing the carpet in the den this afternoon," he said. "I went ahead and set up a time for them to come, since you have already picked out what you want."

"Xavier, don't do this." I sat in the chair across from his desk. "What's going on with the church in Delaware?"

"What do you mean?" He busied himself with opening a letter with a letter opener.

"You told me that you were dissolving the deal with Patrick, and I walk in here today, only to find him in the conference room. Then the man is so cocky, he insults me and then drops the bombshell that you two are going to Delaware in the morning. Unless there is something else going on there, it's got to be about the church."

"I never said that I wasn't going through with it. I said I would consider changing my mind about it." He folded the letter and looked directly at me. "Oh, I authorized a fifty-thousand-dollar wire transfer to Patrick from our account at Commons Bank. There will be another next week."

"I can't believe you." I stood up. "I've spent so many sleepless nights worried about our situation. Wanting to make sure I was giving us all the opportunity we need to make things work. I've been bending over backward to make us work."

"Things are on the right track, and I thank God for that." He must have told himself this a lot, because he sat there like he believed it.

"There is something wrong with you. You lie to me and say you didn't. You make love to me like I'm just your whore. And you probably don't even care that you hurt me so bad last night, I'm bleeding like crazy. Everything you have ever stood for has become a mockery to you. And I no longer want to be a part of any of it. You'll be receiving papers from my attorney." I thought that this moment would cause tears to fall, but what I felt was more like disappointment.

As if I were moving in reverse, I walked through the door, down the hall, and out of the church, and Xavier never tried to stop me. He still thought that he had time and that things were working out. We were definitely going someplace, but we were not on the same track.

"Monica, you never did anything wrong. You shouldn't feel guilty about what happened between you and Bryce, because you never let it get to that point. You made a sacrifice, and God will honor you for that. But you have to believe that God doesn't want you to stay in a loveless marriage." Auntie Zee handed me another tissue. "He allowed you to experience this pain so that you could make a decision. I know it wasn't an easy one, but no one told you that the road you would travel would be easy."

I cried harder. After I left Xavier's office, I'd managed to get to my doctor's appointment, only to be told that I would be in pain for a while. My doctor asked repeatedly if I'd been raped, because of all the scarring. I just told her that my husband and I had gotten a little wild. With a look like she didn't believe me, she wrote me a couple of prescriptions. I needed to talk to someone, and once I started my car, I knew exactly who I needed to see.

"I tried to work things out because I wanted to honor God through my marriage with the man that he had given me. But I failed."

"You didn't fail. He did. You were given a chance to do things decently and in order. You ended that chapter, but now you have to close the book completely so you can start a new one."

I wiped my eyes again. I knew that they were swollen because I could barely see. "I understand. Get Uncle Joe on the phone."

Auntie Zee went with me to get my things from the house. This time I cared less about removing a lot of my things. Everything there reminded me of him. So, I just took the majority of my clothes and some other things I needed. Once he was served with the papers, I would come to get the rest and figure out the what next.

I wanted to go back to the condo, but Auntie Zee said that he would go there, and that although the place was as much mine as his, I would still be holding on to a part of him. So, with that wisdom dropped on me, I got in my truck and followed her back to her house.

I kept waiting for my phone to ring that night, but it didn't. Obviously, Xavier didn't care as much as he said he did. Or he was still in denial and was thinking that just like before, I'd be gone a while and would come back. He just didn't know that it was over, and I was relieved. I'd gone back for the wrong reason, and to be honest, I was still in love with Bryce. But that was another story and one that I didn't even want to think about. When and if I talked to him, it would be with a clean slate and a fresh start. If I went to him, it would be as Monica Joyner. I wouldn't be rebounding. How could I when, emotionally, I had never left?

Uncle Joe proved why he made the big bucks. By the end of the week, Xavier had been served papers. Uncle Joe didn't think it would take me long to have the whole thing resolved, to get my part and my life back. The painful part was telling him everything—the good, the bad, and the ugly. I couldn't leave anything out, because he was afraid that Xavier's attorneys would dig and turn over every rock to make me look like a lowlife. They were not planning on making me look like the adoring first lady. And on top of that, because of our prominent position in the community, all eyes would be on us, and especially on me, because they had labeled me as having a history of leaving and running around. That I never did, but when I told Uncle Joe just how far I had gone with Bryce, he told me that the only thing I didn't do was actually have sex with him.

I had to admit that some of the things Uncle Joe

brought to light made me feel like I was in the wrong. It wasn't about materialistic gain for me. I just wanted out, to be free to move on. In essence, I wanted my life back, and I didn't mind fighting Xavier for it. Whatever it took, I was going to make it.

The phone rang, interrupting my thoughts.

"I got the papers, and I don't want out of our marriage. This has already gone too far, and we need to stay together for the sake of the church."

"Xavier, that's not a good reason to stay together. I just want to move on with my life. The good part of what we shared will always be a part of me, but you have just become someone I don't know." I rubbed my forehead, feeling a headache coming on. Would I ever be free of either Xavier or these headaches?

"Xavier, do you still love me?"

"What?"

"Do you still love me like you used to?" I had to ask. Uncle Joe had told me to limit our conversations or not talk to him at all, but I had to know.

"Yes, of course. We have a ministry to keep going. Bishop Watson wants us to go on a couples' conference cruise and serve as co-facilitators. There will be a lot of big names on the ship. You'll need to get a new wardrobe. I want you to look your best."

After the call with Xavier ended, I clicked the phone and waited for Uncle Joe to pick up. He had told me that I needed to let him know when Xavier contacted me. "Hey. It's me," I said into the receiver.

"Hey, baby girl. How you feeling?" Uncle Joe sounded rushed, as usual.

"I'm okay. Xavier just called."

"I figured he would. He was served papers at the church. They had the nerve to ask me if I wanted to wait and have him served at home because of his status in the community." He paused. "They must have been crazy. I don't care about his status in the community. I know you didn't want your auntie Zee to tell me, but, Monica, what he has been doing to you for months is crap. I may be old, but loving isn't supposed to hurt."

I had pleaded with Uncle Joe to go easy, but he had reminded me that they were going to attack me. So, he wasn't planning on cutting them a break. It would have been perceived as a sign of weakness, and that wasn't how he played the game. Uncle Joe went in it to win it.

"I know you got to do this, but I wish I didn't have to handle all the publicity this thing is going to get me." I exhaled.

"Just stay strong, and let me handle the heavy weight."

"Uncle Joe, thank you so much, and thanks for letting me stay here. As hard as all of this is, being here gives me a sense of security." I loved my parents dearly, but right around now, they would be talking about my situation nonstop. At times I needed a quiet refuge, just to fuel me enough to make it through the difficult moments. And there were plenty of those. "You know, I thought that Xavier and I would last forever."

"I know you did. He was your husband, but I don't believe he was your soul mate. The good news is, the one for you is still out there, just waiting for you to find him. You can do that now, because you've found yourself."

"I owe you so much." I knew I could never repay him for all that he had done and, most of all, for providing the shoulder I needed.

"Monica, you are my baby girl. This one is on me."

Chapter 24

Trina was helping Nita out from under the dryer. "Girl, these straws you wanted so badly caused my carpal tunnel to act up," said Trina. "I hope this fellow you are going to the cabaret with is worth it."

"Trina, he is worth the straws and a whole lot more," replied Nita. She stood, with her hands over her heart, like she was reciting a moving piece.

"I hope that whole lot more doesn't include anything that would cause me to beat you upside the head," I said. I was only half joking. "I don't want to have to come up on that campus and hunt him down."

"Oh, it's not like that, First Lady Phillips," Nita said. "He is a good guy, and he goes to church."

"Everyone that goes to church isn't necessarily a good guy," I replied. Didn't I know that. There were some in the church that were worse than those in the world. I could write a book on the subject. But my situation was still a little different. Xavier hadn't been a bad person in the beginning. It was just that success as a pastor had gotten to him.

I couldn't believe that even with the upcoming legal

stuff that we would go through, he had managed to get invited to speak on the same platform as T. D. Jakes. Now, when I heard that, I thought I would lose it. How could he even feel comfortable getting up there with the ultimate heavy hitter in the television ministry? I didn't know how he pulled it off. Trina had said that I should call and tell somebody in the Jakes ministry all about Xavier, but what would be the use? And besides, I didn't roll like that. I believed that God would deal with him. My concern was not about Xavier's spiritual being; I didn't have a heaven or hell to put the man in. I had more of a personal trinity concern—me, myself, and I.

"I know," replied Nita. "And I thought about Pastor Phillips and what you're going through with him. It's so hard dating, and it's even harder dating saved. But I'm going to always pray and ask God to lead the way. I know that's the only way I'm going to meet the man that will become my husband."

"Yes, but that is a long way down the road, isn't it?" I asked.

"Definitely," replied Nita. "I need to finish college, and I want to get a graduate degree. So, Mr. Right will have to wait for me. I believe I'm worth it." She turned around and looked in the mirror after Trina sprayed hair spray all over her head.

"Keep that thought, and don't let nothing or no one change it," I said. If she kept that thought, I knew that she would be one of the ones that would make it to the happily ever after. She was like a daughter, and I wanted her to have the best life she could. While her mother didn't understand the extras and was old school, without thinking that she was going a bit overboard, I was stepping in to make her life somewhat normal.

"So, First Lady Phillips, what do you think?" asked Nita. Trina turned her around in the chair to face me.

I stood up and walked over to her. "I think you look absolutely wonderful," I said. "This guy is not going to be able to take his eyes off you."

"I hope not. I didn't spend three hours here for him to be looking all up in someone else's face," replied Nita. She sucked her teeth. There it was. She was going above and beyond because there obviously was a little competition somewhere.

"Oh, well, let's be off. There is something else we need to get before I drop you off on campus," I said. My wheels were already turning. She was going to wear a pair of shoes that she already owned. She didn't want to take any more money from me since I had bought her dress and jewelry. But since I was a shoe person, I knew she definitely needed a new pair to jump over the competition. Shoes could make or break an outfit, and we were getting ready to step up the pace so she could make a lasting impression.

"Hey, Monica, you have a big day tomorrow. Are you still coming to talk a while?" asked Trina. She was waiting for her next client to take a seat in her chair.

I turned and responded, "Yeah, I probably will."

"Well, I'll be tired. So pick up a pizza or something. And maybe some ice cream," said Trina

I smiled. The small things made me happy these days. "I'm already on it. Cold Stone was already on my list for tonight."

"Malcolm, I can't believe that I'm on my way to court." I was more scared than I thought I'd be. Getting up early did nothing more than allow me more time to hang my head over the toilet.

"Well, by the end of the day you will be able to move on with your life," said Malcolm. "That's got to be a good feeling."

"That's what we thought weeks ago, only to get to court and find out that Xavier's attorneys had opened Pandora's box. I can't even believe that he sat there and allowed them to paint me as a slut. I was so embarrassed. Not just for myself, but for you guys. I know that he is upset with me, but I don't deserve to be treated like this. He expected me to take the little money offered on the table and run. It's not about the money. Now it's more about my reputation."

"Is that really why you didn't settle?" Malcolm asked.

I was puzzled. "Why would you ask me that?"

"Well, I thought maybe, and I'm just saying maybe, you were afraid to move on. I know you've been giving it a lot of lip service. But over is over. And once you accept what is offered, it's over. Are you afraid of that?"

"At one time I would have said that I was. But now I'm not afraid anymore. I've given it my all, and the bottom line is, I stayed too long."

"So, what's up with this Bryce person? I mean, you kept saying that he was just a friend, but according to the record, you two were more than friends."

"I love him, Malcolm."

"Hold up. That is the present tense."

"I know. I went back home because it was the right thing to do, and I gave it my all. The sad part is, I never stopped loving Bryce."

"Did you guys—"

"Stop!" I hit him on the arm. "I never slept with him. You can fall in love and love a person with all your heart, mind, and soul and never touch him in that way." I smiled. "But my mind. Now that's a different story. There I've made love to him every moment of every day."

"Hey, that's enough. TMI. Too much information. I'm your big brother, and I don't need you to give me the X-rated. Even if it's just something in your mind. I'm not asking you anything else. For the rest of the drive, just be silent. Jesus Christ, wait until Ted hears this." He mimicked me. "I've made love to him every moment, every second of every day, over and over and over."

"I didn't say it like that."

"It's the way I'm going to tell it. By the time I deliver it, I, of course, will have jazzed up the version even more, and Ted will be riding you. You know, he never stops once he gets going."

"You'd do that. Even though what I shared with you was personal and very private. And not to mention the fact that I'm going through a very rough time. I can't eat, I can't sleep, and my hair has been falling out."

"You don't look like you've lost any weight, you look well rested, and your hair has always been nappy. So I'm still telling." He laughed.

I couldn't help but join in with him. For these few fleeting moments of our drive to the courthouse, I felt some relief. Laughing was very good for the soul.

I watched out of the corner of my eye as Xavier entered the courtroom lobby with his attorneys. Bishop Phillips and Mother Phillips walked behind him. They both looked in my direction and gave me a slight smile. I wasn't surprised that Mother Phillips smiled; we talked almost every day, and she knew exactly what was on my mind. I hadn't kept anything from her. And even when the worst came out at the last hearing, she still said she understood, and I would forever be a part of her family, even if I wasn't married to Xavier. Now, Bishop Phillips's smile was unexpected. He hadn't uttered one word to me since I left the last time and filed for a divorce. I heard rumors that he was Xavier's biggest supporter, but no one had said that he was trashing me, and to me, that was a good thing.

Uncle Joe walked up to where I was standing with Auntie Zee, Mom, Dad, Trina, and my brothers. A short distance away, Nita stood beside her mother and Mrs. Epps. I knew Nita and her mom were here to support me, but I wasn't sure what side Mrs. Epps was leaning on. She was known for talking out of both sides of her mouth. If that held true, then at least half of what she said would be on my behalf. I'm sure a lot of other church members wanted to be there to see and hear what was going on, but for the most part, it was a closed hearing, with only a select group of people having access. It didn't really matter, because I knew the minute the judge cracked her gavel, the news would be hitting the streets. My grandfather used to say that there were three ways news got out: telegraph, telephone, and tell a nigger. There were a few of them here, so the news was as good as told.

"Monica, now this hearing will go pretty much like the last," said Uncle Joe as he pulled me to the side. "Now, you know that I met with Xavier's attorneys yesterday. We are all on the same page. So, unless they go in there and pull a rabbit from their behinds again, it all should be pretty cut and dry."

"Do you think they will bring anything else up?" I asked.

At the last hearing, Xavier's attorneys had come in

and told the judge that the reason Xavier and I were having problems was because I had been having affairs. They said that the indiscretions had started even before we got married. Documentation was presented that indicated that I had slept with three guys when I was engaged to Xavier. This was only partly true: there were actually four, so one must have gotten away from them. They had somehow found out that Bryce had purchased a plane ticket to Denver, and I, of course, had gone. They left out that I had chaperoned for the boys. That part didn't surprise me, and I had even told Uncle Joe all about it.

What did surprise me was when they stood in court and disclosed the details of the night I had traveled to the Midnight Male Revue and had been part of a private show. I could only put my head down. I was so ashamed and embarrassed. But, for the life of me, I could never figure out how they had found out about that. I had even tracked Suzy down in Michigan. She had moved there a couple of months ago. When I questioned her, she told me that she hadn't talked to anyone about my being there, and she added that she was so drunk that night, she didn't remember me being there at all. Uncle Joe blew up about that. He told me that I should have told him about it so he could have been prepared to respond. When that information was shared in court, Uncle Joe had stood there, looking stunned.

"Is there anything else?" asked Uncle Joe. He looked straight at me, with a not-so-pleasant look on his face.

"No, Uncle Joe. There are no more skeletons. My closet is clean." I pulled my sunglasses off and placed them in my purse. I had kept them on as long as I could, trying to hide my eyes. They were swollen from allergies, but I knew people would assume that I had been crying.

He touched my chin and tilted my face to the left and then to the right. "Your eyes actually look a little better today. Did Dr. Jarrett give you something to keep you calm? Not that I expect that you will need anything, but I would rather be prepared than have you endure another hospital stay."

"Yes, he did. I took it after breakfast this morning, so I should be fine."

I didn't like the idea of taking an antidepressant at all, but when Auntie Zee noticed that I couldn't sleep, she took me to the doctor. I felt they were ready to put me on suicide watch, because of the type of questions he asked. I felt like my symptoms were justified. If someone was airing your dirty laundry and fighting you in court, you'd feel blue, like you didn't want to get up in the morning, and tired all the time, and you'd have an overall feeling of unhappiness. Those were stupid questions, and I wanted to tell him so. But, instead, I took the medicine and left.

I kept telling Auntie Zee that I was going to take the pills, but I didn't. Finally, she sat me down and told me that I was acting silly, that if I wanted to get better, I should accept whatever help I could get, even if it came in a pill form. I told her that my biggest fear was getting addicted. Her response was simple. She asked where my faith was and said that God wasn't going to let that happen. She said I should just be careful and not depend on the pills, but should not be afraid to take one if I needed it, either. After the first pill, I had to agree with her; however, I could see how people got addicted, because after the dose kicked in, I believed that I could fly.

The court officer came out and told us it was time to

start. Everyone filed into court. Xavier's crew went first and then my crew. I walked behind Uncle Joe, and as he extended his hand out for me to take my seat, I did so. Once I sat in the oak chair in front of a table with the same oak finish, I turned and looked around. Mom and Dad were talking to each other, Auntie Zee blew me a kiss, and Ted and Malcolm winked. Great and small minds think alike. I caught Trina's eye and couldn't read her expression, but I gave her a weak smile, anyway.

I didn't want to look on the other side of the room, because, quite frankly, I didn't know what I would see. I knew what I wanted to see, and that was empathy, but I knew that wasn't possible. So, I didn't chance a glance in that direction.

Before I had a chance to say a quick prayer, the judge was ready to come out, and we all had to stand up as she entered the room. She was a tall lady who looked to be in her fifties, and she had short blond hair. A pair of wire-framed glasses was positioned on the edge of her nose, and she wasn't smiling. I watched and listened to the preliminaries and waited for the important part.

Both of Xavier's attorneys were called to the front and Uncle Joe went forward, too, with a folder under his arm. I watched as he shared the contents of the folder with Xavier's attorneys and one of them turned beet red. Uncle Joe then gave the folder to the judge, who took a minute to scan its contents. There was a verbal exchange, a couple of raised voices, and then, as if accepting whatever Uncle Joe had said, the older attorney who represented Xavier nodded his head affirmatively.

Making his way back over to the table, Uncle Joe sat down and leaned back in his chair. He tapped his index finger on the table. Obviously, this was a legal thing, because I couldn't tell if he was pleased with what had just happened, on the edge, or mad as heck.

The judge began to talk. "I have read over the documentation, and I am told by both of your legal counsels that both of you are in agreement this time around. The said property at 4945 Laker Avenue in Wilmington, Delaware, with the deed recorded under the names of Patrick Garrett, Xavier Phillips, and Monica Phillips, is to be sold and the proceeds equally divided between the three parties, or one of the parties may retain the property and pay a third of the value of the property to each of the other parties within a certain period of time, as specified by this court, and they may retain ownership of the property after said amount is paid in full."

Xavier looked at his attorneys. The older one leaned toward him and was talking and using hand gestures to explain something.

The judge cleared her throat and continued as she looked over the rim of her glasses. "Secondly, the 2006 Jaguar is titled in the name of Monica Phillips and will be retained by Monica Phillips." I had assumed the Jaguar was in Xavier's name, since I hadn't signed anything.

The judge went on. "And, finally, the following is stated in the agreement that was set forth before the aforementioned additions were made. The residence at 3930 Pond View Lane in Huntingdon Valley will be under the sole ownership of Monica Phillips. The condominium at 4050 Lakeshore Drive will be under the ownership of Xavier Phillips. The assets acquired by the two since their union will be split equally, with each half totaling two hundred fifty thousand dollars. One last thing. Monica Joyner Phillips has also requested to retain the use of her maiden name, Joyner. Since both parties are in agreement, I am granting the petition for divorce. Court is adjourned."

I turned to Uncle Joe and hugged him tight. "Oh, my God, I can't believe it's over. I wasn't expecting all of that."

He held the folder in his hand. "When you hold the ace, the game tends to go down a different way. I told you that this one was on me. I wasn't about to let him walk out of here a rich man and see you leave with just the shirt on your back."

"I feel bad, though. I know he wanted to keep the house, and to be honest, I really don't want to stay there. It would only remind me of him." I would have been happy with the condo for a while. And I had assumed that was what I would end up with. I would have stayed there until I could afford to buy something else.

"Don't feel sorry for him. He has some hidden stuff I didn't even mess with. You got what you deserved, and so did Xavier. Come on. I need to listen to Zerenda tell me how wonderful I am."

As I backed away from the table and followed behind Uncle Joe, Xavier came toward me. Uncle Joe stood in front of me. "No, Uncle Joe, it's okay," I said. "I'll let him speak his mind, because this will be the last time I have to listen."

Xavier rolled his eyes at my uncle and stepped around him. "I'm sorry it ended this way, Monica. I wasn't trying to make you look bad. It was just business. But your uncle is a cutthroat lawyer. I guess he still has a hood mentality."

"You can say whatever you want. I got what I deserve, and in the end, so did you," I replied. "I'm sorry if I hurt you, and I wish that things had ended differently between us. I will always care about you, because you were my husband and a big part of my life for so long. But this is the end of the road. I'm not bitter, and I'm big enough to say that I wish you the best. You have New Horizons, the community center, the new church with Patrick, so you will recover from all this. On top of that, you have a bunch of people at the church that love you and respect you. Don't mess that up. I kept your reputation intact when I could have blown you out of the water like you did me. But, it's all good, and things will be just fine."

I really meant every word I said to him. I had to be the bigger person because he was standing there like he could knock me out. There was no reason for us not to be civil. I wanted Xavier to understand that his position should mean more to him than hurting me or getting even.

"Whatever," Xavier mumbled and started to walk away. "Oh, by the way, I guess you were wondering how I found out about the Midnight Male Revue?"

"I really don't care, and it doesn't matter." This time I turned to walk away.

"Tell Trina thanks for everything." Patrick walked up just as he mentioned Trina and they both laughed.

I was floored. He had to be joking. I knew this was probably not a good time to confront her, but I was so hurt, I couldn't wait. I stood there, apparently looking so shocked, everyone moved in on me.

"Are you okay? What did he say to you?" said Mom. She was looking at me and waiting for me to answer her.

Malcolm was the next to speak. "See, I'm going to have to go on over there and whip his butt. And I was trying not to do that, but he is just going to have to take this whipping I got for him."

"I'm right behind you. I ain't never liked the yellow

punk, no way. A thug in pulpit clothing," said Ted. He stood beside Malcolm, and they both turned around and looked Xavier up and down.

"Stop. He was just expressing his disappointment in what he lost," I said. "I'm just ready to get out of here." I tried to smile.

"Let's get you out of here then," said my dad as he reached out for my hand.

Everyone was chatting and planning to go out to get something to eat. I wasn't feeling much like eating. My plans included going back to Auntie Zee's, taking a long bath, and curling up in bed with a good book. I wasn't even up to watching a Lifetime movie. What I had just been through definitely could top the best of them.

Once we got outside, I slowed down. "Hey, Trina, can I talk with you for a minute?" I said and gave her a sugary smile.

She was wedged between Ted and Malcolm. "Sure," she answered.

"I just wanted to thank you for all of your support. You have been more than a friend," I said.

"Girl, don't even mention it," said Trina. "All I do, I do because you mean the world to me. I can't remember a time when we weren't friends, more than friends, actually. You are my sister."

"Yeah, that is why I believe in giving credit where credit is due. So, I wanted to thank you so very much for telling Xavier about the Midnight Male Revue." I stared right in her eyes in case she was getting ready to lie. Knowing her so well, I could tell when she was lying or avoiding telling the truth.

"Monica, I—" She looked like she wanted to pass out.

"No, don't even worry about it. I don't know why you

did it and what you wanted to gain. I'm just glad that he told me. If there is one thing I wanted to accomplish today, it was to end all the lies. Living a lie, staying in something because of a lie, and maintaining something that stands on a lie. Trina, that would be this friendship."

"I'm sorry. Let me at least tell you what happened. You got to understand my situation."

"I don't have to understand nothing. And you are sorry, but not sorry for hurting me like this. You came to court the last time, when they brought the whole thing up, and you never said a word. I stayed at your house that night and cried on your shoulder, and you never even told me that you had something to do with it. What were you thinking? Did you do it because you wanted Xavier?" I had never thought of that, but standing before her now, I thought anything could be possible.

"Your life was so perfect. Xavier deserved so much, and I just wanted to be there for him." Tears ran down her face, and she didn't even try to wipe them.

"So, you wanted to be me. You thought that if you told him, you'd be the next first lady of New Horizons. Girl, get away from me before I forget that you ever meant anything to me."

"Monica, please don't hate me." She started to walk after me.

Turning around, I held my hand up like it was a stop sign. "I don't hate you. I feel sorry for you. And if you want Xavier, he's free now, you helped him divorce me."

Chapter 25

"Monica, you've been working on this house all day," said Auntie Zee. "Don't you want to get out and do something? I could use a little R & R. I'm not as young as I used to be." Auntie Zee was seated on my new sofa.

"Okay, I'll take you out. If I don't, you might tell Uncle Joe that I'm a slave driver," I replied. I wrapped the coral-colored silk scarf around the rod and adjusted the ends down the sides of the window. I stepped down from the chair and walked to the middle of the floor so I could check to see if the scarf was even.

"Is your mother still coming next week?" Auntie Zee asked.

"I'm afraid so. You know she is only coming because you've been down here with me all week. You'd think she'd get tired of being so jealous of our relationship."

Auntie Zee had come down to help me move into my new house. It was all new, and I was extremely excited. I knew I didn't want to stay in the house that Xavier and I had had together. And after a couple of months of living there and of soul-searching, I decided that living in Philadelphia, with Xavier on every billboard, radio station, and early morning Sunday television broadcast, was impossible. I knew it was time to relocate. I searched locations, did Internet searches, and even went on a few interviews before I decided on a location. Once I had that narrowed down, it took another three months to find the ideal house. So, just one week ago, I left the City of Brotherly Love and moved to New Castle, Delaware, to a new gated community. While I didn't need a large house, in order to even stay in this area, I had to settle for a house with five bedrooms. It was crazy, but at least I would have plenty of space for company. The tripped-out thing was, it reminded me of the house that Bryce had in Philly. It had a circular driveway, the same layout, similar ceilings, and a sunroom. I knew he would crack up if he saw it.

"Well, you just work her like you're working me, and I'm sure she won't stay long. I've thought about calling your Uncle Joe more than once. I hope he's not expecting me to do anything extra in the bedroom next week, because after this workout, I won't be able to hang off the chandelier like I do every Monday and Wednesday night."

The doorbell rang, and I checked my watch. It was probably the delivery person with my big-screen television. "Oh, that's nasty. I'll never look at a chandelier in the same way again." I threw a pillow at her on my way to the door. Through the glass door, I could see someone standing at my door, with a bunch of flowers.

I threw the door open and giggled. They were probably from Daddy or the boys. No one else knew I had moved, and so far I hadn't seen any neighbors that looked single and available.

"Monica Joyner?" the deliveryman asked.

"Yes, that's me." I took the two arrangements from

him and placed them on the round table in the middle of the large foyer.

"Could you sign here please?"

"Sure." I scribbled my name on the line. "Wait. Let me get you something."

"No. Actually, it's already been taken care of."

"Oh, okay. Thank you." I walked him back to the door and locked it the minute it closed.

"Auntie Zee, look. Someone sent me two beautiful arrangements. Not your typical roses. These look all exotic and alluring." I leaned down and inhaled the sweet fragrance deeply. It tickled my nose, and I smiled.

Auntie Zee came into the foyer. "Oh, aren't they pretty. Go on and check who sent them. That cheap brother-in-law of mine wouldn't have paid no money for flowers. Now he may send you a little cash for groceries, but that's about it."

"Daddy is not that bad. You have always teased him, when you know he has a giving heart." I started laughing while I opened the first card. I knew my dad was tight, but I didn't want to agree too quickly with her. It was much more fun holding out and debating the issue with her.

"You know I'm telling the truth. Never mind your tight daddy, girl. Who sent the flowers?" Auntie Zee was peeking over my shoulder.

"I don't know. This one doesn't have a name on it. The card is completely blank." Turning it over, I noticed that nothing was on the other side, either. I reached for the other card and noticed that this one was blank, too. "This is crazy. Who sends expensive, exotic flowers and doesn't sign the card? Looks like they don't want the receiver to thank them. It must not be from a man."

"You know that's right. If they send some flowers, they expect to get more than a handshake."

"Well, so much for finding out. Let's go shower and I'll take you out to dinner and I may even take you to the movies."

"You sure know how to treat a woman." Auntie Zee moved gingerly. Maybe I shouldn't have worked her so hard.

"Why don't you wear the new outfit I got for you yesterday?" We had decided to make a quick trip to the mall since it was down the street from Home Depot. The contractors had put in a side-by-side refrigerator, and I wanted to get one with French doors and a bottom freezer. I had also decided to change the range.

"I sure will. I was going to wait until I got back home, but there is no time like the present. Tomorrow is not even promised to us, anyway."

"There you go, dropping wisdom. Go take your shower before I change my mind and call Domino's."

It was only fitting that Auntie Zee and I spent her last day with me at the place where we spent our first day and the place that made us the happiest, the mall. The mall here in Delaware was pretty nice, and the great thing about still being close enough to Philadelphia was, I could go there anytime and shop at Franklin Mills or King of Prussia. Not to mention, by taking a two-hour drive in the other direction, I could enjoy some Maryland and D.C. shopping. Life was just so wonderful.

I knew that I was going to be lonely once Auntie Zee left, and even more so when Mom pulled out the following week. I had no one else lined up to come to visit with me. I had even called Nita to make sure she received the check I sent her. Spring break was the only time that she could pencil me in for a trip. And even then it was a toss-up between time with me and time in Miami with her friends. I wasn't a betting woman, but I wagered that she would be hanging on the beaches of Miami in a two-piece.

I dropped on the bench outside Bath & Body Works. I couldn't believe this was the same woman who had threatened to tell Uncle Joe that I had overworked her. She had just run through the mall like she was a member of the Olympics. Sticking her head out of the door of the store, she yelled. "Hey, it's three for the price of two. You still like that vanilla brown sugar stuff?" She waited for me to respond.

"Yes, I sure do." It wasn't vanilla brown sugar, but before I could correct her, she was off to make her purchase.

When she finished, I looked up at her, hoping she would be ready to go. "Auntie Zee, you want to go in any other store?" I slipped off my leather mule, crossed my leg, and rubbed my foot.

"I was hoping we could just drop in Macy's for a few minutes. After that, we can go. I promise." She looked at her watch. I couldn't believe she was all of a sudden concerned about the time. I thought she had come with the intention of staying until closing.

"Okay." I picked up our bags and moved slowly behind her. I wondered if she had been doing that speed walking thing with some of her friends back home.

We had looked at almost everything in her size and everything in my size. And still she was looking through another section, pulling out things she thought would look nice on me. "Look at this one, Monica. This is so pretty. You have got to try this on. The color is just right for this time of year. I have a charity function next month, and I'd love to see you stroll in with this on."

I circled the rack and looked at the pale blue Evan Picone suit she held out. The blazer was fitted, and the skirt was slightly flared. I did like it a lot, but I could easily take it home, and if it didn't fit, I could bring it back one day when my house was empty and I had nothing else to do. "It's nice." I looked at the size. "It's a size eight, and it looks like it should fit. I'll go ahead and get it, and if it doesn't fit, I can bring it back later."

"Come on and humor me. Try it on. This is the last store we are going in tonight."

"I'm going. I'm going." I took the outfit and walked toward the fitting room. She was getting on my nerves with all this shopping. I shocked myself. I never thought I'd be tired of shopping. It must have been because I had been decorating my house and buying house stuff for so long that I was all shopped out. I prayed that it wasn't a permanent thing. I removed my mules, slipped my jeans off, and pulled the blouse over my head. Turning, I looked into the mirror. The wonderful thing about dressing rooms was they allowed you to see yourself from all angles. I was still trim, with everything in the right place. That was good to know, seeing that I was a single woman who was about to have another birthday in a month. I hadn't thought about my status in a while. Life had become so busy, and I had been so focused, I really had not thought about the word *single*.

I would be starting my job next month as director of public relations at the University of Delaware. My first paying gig, and I was ready to start. It seemed that all the work I did for the New Horizons Community Center had paid off. I was good at what I did. I always knew that, and so did all the people that gave me a glowing letter of recommendation. When word got out that I was relocating and had asked a few people for recommendations, almost everyone that I had ever worked with was sending them left and right. What a blessing.

I pulled the skirt on, zipped it up, and slipped into the blazer. It fit great, and I had just the right blouse to wear with it. My head was down as I walked out of the fitting room. "Auntie Zee, I like it, but I was just noticing that it's a little shorter than the skirts I usually wear."

"I think the length is just right."

I jerked my head up, and there stood Bryce. "Bryce, oh my God! What are you doing here?" I said. I stood there with my mouth open. He looked better than ever, if that was possible. He was dressed in a pair of jeans and a short-sleeved Ralph Lauren polo. I couldn't close my mouth.

"I'm your substitute shopping partner, and I'm sorry I'm late, but I got stuck in traffic."

"So, this was a plan, and Auntie Zee brought me here and had me up in every store, waiting for you to show up and relieve her." I tried to put it all together. I couldn't be mad at her. Heck, with Bryce standing before me, looking all good, I would only give her all the money in my wallet and my Cold Stone Creamery coupon.

"That is the size of it. Why don't you go put your clothes on, and I'll tell you all about it." He smiled.

"Okay." I didn't say another word but retreated to the fitting room. I closed my eyes the minute I walked in and closed the curtain. It was Bryce. Bryce was here in Delaware, and he had been talking to Auntie Zee. It had been almost sixteen months since I'd seen him. I wanted to call so many times. I'd even started to go to a game, but I could not get up the nerve to do it. I didn't want him to think that I was rebounding. Why would he want me after I had been with Xavier again? So, I didn't call, and I didn't let him know that I was free, and yet here he was. I prayed that this would be my second chance. I knew second chances didn't come that often, but if this was mine, I wasn't going to mess it up.

After he told me that I would have to ride with him because Auntie Zee had taken my car and gone back home, I climbed into the front seat of his Escalade.

"This is different," I said. "The last time I rode with you, you were sporting a Benz."

"Oh, I still have a Benz, but not the old one. I just bought a new one a couple of weeks ago. This I bought yesterday."

"It's nice. I know I could never push anything this big, but it looks good on you." I looked over at him and tried to read his mind.

"So, what do you think of this area?"

"It's nice. A little smaller than Philly, but it's nice. I love my house. I guess that is the best part of it. And since I'll be working at the University of Delaware, things are not so bad."

"You with a job? That is so good. I knew things would come together for you." He checked his mirror and merged into traffic.

"Bryce, how much do you know?" I was curious, and since I was ready to spill my guts, I wanted to know where I should start.

"As always, Monica, I know everything. Auntie Zee has such a wealth of information. I even know that your favorite toy at the age of two was a Winnie the Pooh." He chuckled.

"Oh, I'll kill her. I can't believe she told you that."

"She did more than that. When I get back to Philly, and as soon as I have time, I'm invited over to her place to see the famous Winnie that used to sleep with you."

"Bryce, there is so much I need to tell you, so much I want to say." I felt a lump in my throat. I was happy to see him, but I felt bad that it had been sixteen months since we'd seen each other. And it was all my fault.

"There is a lot we need to talk about. But as I said, Auntie Zee has given me a play-by-play."

"Tell me, how long have you known Auntie Zee? I never introduced you two to each other." I was puzzled. I knew that during the time that I was sort of with Bryce, I hadn't taken him around any of my family. No one knew I was really seeing him. At that time I didn't think it was right, because I was married. Of course, I would have loved to show him off, to tell everybody that this man was in love with me.

"Since right around the time you filed for divorce. She tracked me down, and when she mentioned your name, I was all ears. After that we kept in touch, and she would let me know how you were doing."

"I can't believe that."

"Well, believe it. She is my auntie Zee now, too. She was looking out for me, even though you didn't know it."

He signaled and made a right turn. "Bryce, do you know where I live?"

"I sure do. Girl, when are you going to learn that I know everything? Nothing escapes me."

"You are too much."

"So I've been told."

"I feel like I'm at a disadvantage, because you have kept up with me, but I have not been privy to anything that has been going on with you."

"Was that by choice?" The smile that had been on his face and in his voice suddenly left.

"I was afraid to reach out. And I assumed that you would think I was rebounding. I went back to Xavier because it was the right thing to do, and even though I tried to make it work, it didn't."

"Did you ever think about me?"

"All the time. There were times when I'd be alone and I would hear your voice. Sometimes I'd even smell you. I felt at times like you were haunting me or at least haunting my thoughts."

"I'd never haunt you. I guess you were thinking of me because I was thinking about you. Every day for the past sixteen months."

We pulled into the estate, and when Bryce rolled the window down, I waved at the security guard, and he waved back and opened the gate.

"All of this is so familiar," said Bryce. He smiled and winked his eye. "Which way?"

I slapped his arm. "Like you need to ask."

Bryce maneuvered the truck around the corner and turned into the last lane. Slowing down, he turned into my circular driveway. "This is too much," he said.

"I thought you'd seen this already." I thought that somehow Auntie Zee had brought him to my house.

"No, I only knew where the estate was and the street name and house number. I didn't know you went to the contractor and told them you wanted a house just like that of the fine Bryce Sinclair, starting shooting guard for the Philadelphia 76ers."

"I didn't say all that. But it is designed just like your house. The only room that may not be an exact duplicate is the master suite. In all the time that we hung out, I never entered your bedroom."

I thought of all the times I had wanted to. I still couldn't believe that we had had so many chances, and neither of us ever went that far. Bryce never did more than give me a quick kiss on the cheek. This was a man's man.

"You had entered my bedroom, just not in the physical."

He turned the truck off and sat there for a minute. "Are you coming in?" I asked. I really hoped that he would. I still wanted to talk to him. I wanted to tell him everything I was feeling, and I wanted to tell him that I loved him.

"I was hoping to. But if you're tired, I'll understand. It's so late now. I was going to get a room someplace in hopes that you would have breakfast with me before I head back to Philly."

"I want you to come in."

He removed the keys, closed his car door, and walked around to my door and opened it. We joked with each other all the way to the front door. Once I unlocked the door and flipped on the nearby light switch, Bryce busted out laughing.

"I thought you were exhilarating. This is too much. The only difference is the way our houses are decorated," he said.

"That's about it. But I had to do a better job of decorating, because I have a lot more taste."

"Same old Monica."

"Would you have it any other way?" I asked. I began to feel comfortable around Bryce. It felt like old times. I also couldn't believe he was here with me. I led the way to the living room and took a seat on the sofa. I thought he would sit across from me, but instead, he relaxed against the cushion right beside me.

"Actually, I wouldn't. I've missed you. I've missed you a lot." Bryce reached for my hand and pulled it to his lips, kissing it softly.

"I missed you, too. Bryce, I'm so sorry."

"You don't have to be. I know that you did it for all the right reasons. You are forgetting the one thing I told you to do."

"What did you tell me to do?" I looked at him with a puzzled look on my face. I had no idea what he had told me. I mean, I remembered almost every conversation we had ever had. But I couldn't pinpoint one particular thing. He would at least have to give me a date and time.

"That day in front of the condo. I told you to come to me when you were free."

I remembered that day clearly, and now that he had brought it to my attention, it was crystal clear. "I remember it very well. It's been playing on repeat for all these months."

"If you had called me when you went to stay with Auntie Zee, you would not have been free. Even after the divorce, it was all new, but deep down, you weren't free. It's taken finding your independence, moving on with your life, and even deciding that in Philly you were still connected somehow. You are living in a different state, driving a new car, and getting ready to start a new job. Now you are free, and even if I get back in my truck and never see you again, I'll still be proud of the woman you are. A woman with worth."

"I do feel free. It wasn't an easy journey. But it has been worth it. Life has come full circle, and for the first time, I had no help getting here. I got here on my own. The only assistance I had was from the man above. He led and I followed. I think, for a while, I had the who does what out of order."

"Monica, can I kiss you? We've never kissed." He put his head back against the sofa.

"No, Bryce, we have never kissed, and I'd like nothing more than to live out my fantasy."

Slow enough to take in every movement, he reached toward me and tilted my face to his and kissed my mouth lightly at first. Then, suddenly, his tongue touched mine as if it were the commencement of a slow dance. Within seconds, we grooved them together, and I experienced ecstasy. When he pulled away from me, I could hardly breathe. My eyes felt like they were crossed as I tried to look at him.

"Monica, you mean the world to me, and I love you so very much."

"Bryce, I love you, too. And I've wanted to tell you that for so long. But it just wasn't the right time. But now I can tell you and not fear that it's wrong."

He kissed me again, and I realized that my body was coming to life in a way it hadn't in forever. "We are going to be great together."

I could only smile as I listened to him. "Bryce, there is one thing I need to tell you. There is something that you need to know."

"What is that?" He looked into my eyes and waited for me to share.

I inhaled and put myself out there. "I'm not perfect." I exhaled and looked at him as I waited for a reaction.

Smiling at me, he replied, "Monica, I never asked you to be."

Epilogue

"Come on and put your foot in this shoe, please," I pleaded to the little, brown-eyed child. Her hair was combed neatly into two ponytails, held in place by purple ponytail holders. Even though the ponytails were positioned high on the sides of her head, they hung down to her shoulders. She whined and rubbed her eyes as if she were still sleepy.

"I told you to stay in bed last night," I said. "But, instead of doing that, you wanted to stay up and wait for Daddy to get home."

She was a daddy's girl. I was good for all of life's little necessities, but she made it obvious that her preference was her daddy. Hands down, to her, he was Santa Claus, the Easter Bunny, and Cupid. I didn't mind at all. Watching the two of them together was always a treat. So many people thought that she was actually our birth child; she had been merely a few days old when we brought her home. Since that time, she had become our angel, and I was so in love with this little girl. In a few days, she would be celebrating her second birthday, and I believe, my husband was just as excited as she was. I had to keep reminding him that a child's party was not supposed to be on the same scale as her future wedding reception. But he wasn't hearing it.

"Mommy, I don't wanna put on," she complained, right before sliding down from my lap and running out of the den and into the hallway, with one shoe on and only a nylon folded anklet with lace on the other foot.

"Bryce, are you in the kitchen?" I called. I waited for him to answer. Leaning against the sofa cushion, I rubbed my back as I tried to get up.

"I'm in here, and so is Bianca. One shoe short, but she is in here." I heard her giggling, and the minute they came into view, there she was, sitting around his neck.

"That's exactly why she doesn't listen. You are playing with her. She thinks that you are a large toy." I couldn't help but laugh as she continued to giggle and showed her two front teeth, which had the cutest small gap. The dimples in her cheek looked like the Pillsbury Doughboy's dimples.

"I am whatever she wants me to be. You just need to realize that she has beaten your time, and this little lady has all of Daddy's heart." He bent down and pulled her over his head and placed her little frame on the floor.

"Oh, please. I know she is Daddy's angel, but I still rank. If I didn't, my stomach wouldn't look like this." I finally managed to stand up and rubbed my stomach, hoping that our son would decide to keep still, at least for a little while.

I guess this was proof that medical science was not always right. I was told after the last miscarriage that I would never have kids. Bryce and I had resolved that since we couldn't have kids, we would adopt. That was a decision we never regretted. But just when we had settled into a comfortable three-person family, I became sick with what we both thought was the flu. After several visits to the doctor, at the insistence of an older nurse who said she could swear I was pregnant by the telltale signs, I gave in and took a pregnancy test. Imagine my arriving home and announcing to Bryce that I didn't have the flu and would continue to have periods of nausea because I was pregnant. I thought he had lost his everlasting mind, the way he ran through the house. Before I could calm him down long enough to talk to him, he was already on the phone with his mother. The next call he made was to his auntie Zee. The two had become so close, you would have thought by watching them, they were actually mother and child. I was glad. My two favorite people deserved to love each other as much as I loved each of them.

"Baby, are you okay?" Bryce gave me a concerned look as Bianca held his hands and was swinging back and forth. He picked her up and moved over to the sofa, next to me.

"I think so. It's my back. You know that this baby is getting so big, it seems all the pressure is on my back and down here." I pointed to the lower part of my stomach. Although I was having a rough pregnancy, I would never complain. I had prayed and asked God to just help me go full term and allow the baby to be all right. I was two weeks away from my due date, and since my pregnancy was labeled high risk, I had appointments so often, I thought I lived at the medical center. But things were going smoothly.

"I know you are determined to go this morning, but you can always stay home. I can even take Bianca with me. Mom would be more than glad to keep an eye on her." At the mention of Bryce's mom, Bianca started yelling, "Meme!"

Bryce's mom had moved here only a year ago. There wasn't anything to keep her in South Carolina. And after we got married, she was visiting so regularly that she fell in love with the area. I would always adore Mother Phillips, but Mom was a one of a kind. From day one, she refused to have me call her anything else except Mom. Bryce and his mom were so close. It was interesting to watch them have a disagreement, because the minute they voiced their differences, they were all hugs and were telling each other they loved each other..

Bianca was her first grandchild, so you can imagine. She allowed her to do anything and everything. So, if Bryce was talking about Mom watching Bianca, it could easily be the other way around.

"No, I need to be there. I'll be okay, and if I start to feel bad, I'll just get up and come back home." I pushed to put a smile on my face. The truth was, I wasn't convinced I would be okay. I had been experiencing pains all morning and I didn't want to alarm him. This was a special day for him, and I wanted to be there more than anything.

"Okay, if you say so. I'm going upstairs to finish dressing, and I'll come down and watch Bianca so you can finish dressing." Bryce disappeared down the hall and up the steps.

"Mommy, me want somethin' to drink," said Bianca as she pulled at my skirt.

"Okay, just let Mommy take her time, and I'll go in the kitchen and get you something to drink."

"Yeah, Mommy gonna get me drink." Bianca fell in step behind me as I walked into the kitchen.

I watched her at my side as I walked into the kitchen. She opened her legs wide and held her back as she walked along beside me.

"You are not funny. How can you mimic Mommy that way? You are too much." I burst out laughing the minute I saw her put her little tiny hand on her back. This wasn't the first time she had done anything like this. Obviously, today I must have looked a little more humorous.

It took me so long to get ready. I worried that I would make Bryce late. I stood in the mirror and tried to comb my hair. The style I was going for just wasn't working, so I pulled out a brush and brushed it all back and put it in a neat bun behind my head. To make it look a little fancy, I placed a rhinestone comb on the side. Looking in the mirror, I was pleased. I decided that it looked like I was going for an elegant appeal. The real truth was, I couldn't do anything else with it. But no one had to know that. By the time I pulled the maternity jacket on over the stretch sleeveless tank, I was completely out of breath. I looked at my shoes, then my feet, and my shoes again, and I knew that they were not going to work. Not only were they not going to work, but I wasn't going to be able to put them on. I sat on the bed and lay all the way back. After I did that, I tried to roll my body to the edge of the bed so I could lean over and get the shoes. It didn't work. "Bryce, can you come up here," I called in disgust.

In just a minute, Bryce came up the stairs, carrying Bianca on his hip. "What's up, baby?"

I started crying. "I can't put my shoes on." The tears flowed down my face, and I cried so hard, I started having hiccups.

He placed Bianca on the bed, beside me. "Baby, you got me, and I can put your shoes on. Don't cry. You are making me and Bianca sad." He looked over at Bianca.

"Mommy, don't cry," said Bianca. "Me don't have shoes on. Me don't want you sad." She got up on her knees and wiped my eyes with her hands. She kissed me on the lips. "All better."

Bryce got down on his knees and put my shoes on. "Okay, your shoes are on. You okay now?"

I couldn't stop crying. It was like a wave of sadness had settled over me. "Nooooo."

He smiled. "What's wrong now, sweetness?" He was such a patient man. "You got to stop these big crocodile tears. Baby, tell me what's wrong."

"I got to pee." In the midst of my tears, the sadness lifted a little, and I started to laugh.

"Did you do it on youself?" asked Bianca as she pulled at my skirt, looking to see if I had wet myself."

"No, sweetheart. Mommy didn't wet herself." Bryce helped me up, and I slowly walked to the bathroom.

After a couple of more bathroom trips and a change of shoes, we made it out the door. I was thankful that the ride didn't take that long. I felt terrible that the morning had been so hectic. I didn't want Bryce to be late, and yet I knew that he didn't care about his tardiness. Bianca, I, and our unborn son were his world. That was the one thing I was told every night as I cuddled in his arms and fell asleep.

"Are we there yet?" asked Bianca as she leaned over in her car seat. She must have had a mileage chip on the inside. The minute she reached her restless mile marker, the questions started.

"We are almost there. Can Daddy's big girl be nice and quiet until we get there?" said Bryce as he glanced at her in the rearview mirror.

"Yep. Me big and nice," said Bianca. She didn't say anything about being quiet. While most people wouldn't think anything about that part being left out, I knew it meant she had no intention of being quiet, and that after just another mile, she would ask the question again.

We finally pulled into the parking lot, and Bryce swung the car into the designated parking space. "Okay, girls. We are here," he announced.

"Good. I'm glad," said Bianca. She started pulling at the car seat and trying to get it to open up and let her out.

We were walking toward the church, and I looked around and felt so proud. If anyone would have told me that my life would unfold like this, I would have told them that they were crazy.

"Tell me, husband, do you miss playing ball?" I asked Bryce. Two years after we were married, Bryce sustained a knee injury, and even after months of physical therapy, it was not the same. After some soul-searching and a lot of disappointment, he decided to retire rather than risk the chance of making it worse.

"Actually, no, I don't. My family is expanding even more," replied Bryce. He reached over and rubbed my stomach. "And I couldn't ask for a better career now. I believe that even though I played ball, this was always my destiny. I'm content, happy, and blessed."

We walked through the side entrance and exchanged greetings with several people.

I tapped Bryce on the shoulder and leaned in to whisper. "Bryce, I'm going to the restroom."

"Oh, okay." He kissed my cheek and leaned down to kiss Bianca.

After we had made our bathroom run, I made my way to the sanctuary. It wouldn't have been church if someone didn't stop me to talk about this or that. There was something about a pregnant woman that made people want to stop and talk about their childbirth experiences, reveal how good or bad those experiences were, and tell me what I was going to have to endure. Despite my telling some of the older ladies that it was a boy, and I had actually seen him on the sonogram, they were sure that it was a girl, and possibly two of them because of my size.

By the time we got to the pew where Mom was sitting, I had to go to the bathroom again. But because the service was getting ready to start, I told myself that I could wait.

"Hey, Mom," I called. I leaned over and kissed Bryce's mother on the cheek.

"Meme," cried Bianca as she jumped into Mom's lap and started planting kisses all over her face.

"Oh, you missed your grandmom, and your grandmom missed you," said Mom. She kissed Bianca back.

The ladies sitting behind us made comments about how pretty Bianca was and how sweet it was that she was giving her grandmother so much loving.

"She is very affectionate," I responded.

Mom leaned over and asked, "How many candidates do we have for baptism?"

"I'm not sure," I said.

"Is Bryce already back there?"

"Yeah, he is." I looked around. The church was packed with visitors as well as the regular membership. The service would begin right after the baptism. So, a few would probably leave after they saw their loved ones get dipped in the water.

Just then the candidates came out. I watched Bryce walk in and grinned a wide grin. He was so handsome, and while I'd always thought it, the best thing about it now was, he belonged to me. Our exchange of vows and small ceremony on the beach in Jamaica proved that I had said, "I do."

The baptism went by relatively quickly, and the service began after everyone was dressed.

I watched as the pastor of Temple Hills Baptist walked up to the pulpit. "Good morning, church. What a blessing it is to be in the house of the Lord and to witness the baptism of these saints. There is something about new beginnings, and they are embarking upon a new life with the Lord. I want to honor God, who, of course, is the head of my life, and I honor my wife, Leading Lady Monica Joyner Sinclair. I always say 'leading' and not 'first,' because for me, there will never be another."

Suddenly, I felt a gush under my skirt. I leaned over to Mom and tried to speak calmly. "Mom, my water just broke."

"Oh my goodness," said my mom. Before she could do anything, Bianca stood up on the seat of the pew and yelled at the top of her lungs. "Daddy, hurry! The baby wants out."

Mom helped me to a standing position, and I listened as Bryce told his congregation that our son was ready to be born. I thought, how right he was. There would only be one leading lady for him. Whenever someone asked me if had seen it coming, referring to Bryce becoming a pastor, I would answer that God got jokes. While I was told as a child that I would spend my life as a pastor's wife, I thought that it had been short lived when I divorced Xavier. But now I knew that this was the life that they were referring to. I had my soul mate, and I was a preacher's wife. I was getting ready to give birth. The best part of it all was that I wasn't perfect, and I didn't have to be.